THE STRIKE OF THE RED HORSEMAN

TALES OF THE FOUR HORSEMEN
BOOK TWO

JESS K. CHAVEZ

For the seekers,
May you learn how truly incredible it is that you are pursued
by the very source of love itself.

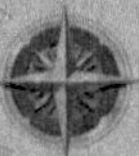

N
W
E
S

THE WASTES

The Ashram
Main FP Base
THE RANGE
Nash & Lottie's
Sidora's Farmstead
The Refuge
THE WORLD
OF THE
FOUR HORSEMEN

CONTENTS

GLOSSARY/PRONUNCIATION

Elohim {El-oh-heem} - God the Creator

Elohim Shomri {El-oh-heem Shaw-om-ree} - God my Protector

Feminea Potentia {Fem-in-E-ah Poh-TEN-C-ah} - Female Power/Strength

Dux {Duh-Ux} - Commander

Malkhut Shamayim {Mahl-KOOT Shah-MY-eem} - Kingdom of Heaven

Ruach {Roo-ahhk} - Breath or Spirit of God, the source of life

Elohe Tishuathi {El-Oh-Hee Tish-ew-wath-I} - God of my Salvation, or
    God who Saves

Lavo Veshuv {La-Voh Ve-Shoe-ve} - Come forth

Baim Lyy {Bay-Mm Lie} - Return to me

PROPHECY OF THE FOUR CORES

When the tipping point has been reached and darkness is unrestrained, four riders will be drawn forth out of necessity to lay waste to the world. Their destruction will be absolute. The only hope for mankind is in the gift of four living personifications of Elohim's heart, the essential Cores of His Pure Love. Each Core is created to bond with her Horseman, forever breaking the hold of darkness on them with the power of Elohim's love. The Horseman will then ride for Malkhut Shamayim, bringing about the destruction of all evil in the world. But if the heart of the Core is rejected or fails, the Riders will be leashed by hell, and all will be lost to darkness.

When a Core connects with her Horseman, an unbreakable bond will form. The Light to his

Dark, Woman to Man, the Cores will bring balance in every way to the Horsemen. The seal of each Horseman will be forever altered in outward appearance, as will the depth of their inner being. For once you are made weak, only then can you truly be made strong.

The Cores have been marked by Heaven, but the gift of Heaven will be unknown to them until activated. But just as they are touched by Heaven, they will also be pursued by evil. Evil must be overcome, dreams will guide, and love covers in multitude.

The only signs of the Cores' coming are this . . . born orphaned, alone, and unnamed, they will be brought to the world on a day made holy by its twin of seven. You will find them with three of sevens; a unique mark of Heaven they will bear.

PROLOGUE

Shakespeare

Letting her rage at what was taking place here flow over her like a rainstorm deluge, Sloane donned a mask of focused determination and let her training take over. Sweat dampened her skin as she shot forward with her sword, cutting a swath through a cluster of men twice her weight.

She dipped down and spun as one of them swung a pipe at her head. Lunging toward him, she swept her sword out in an arc that quickly removed his head from his body. She glanced over to see Mina rapidly fire arrow after arrow at any foe dumb enough to turn and face her. Sloane and her sister made fast work of this particular group of depraved monsters.

"Are there more?" Mina asked as she pulled one of her arrows from a body.

"I think Gemini found a group on the other side of the outpost. Let's head that way."

Mina nodded, her expression set in grim resolve. They had yet to find any survivors. Sloane hoped and prayed that the people had been able to flee when the fighting started. She was still nauseated about what had happened in the little farming community. They had received a tip that a group of drugged-up raiders had taken to tormenting the handful of families that lived here. Killing their livestock, torturing and crippling the men, and raping their women and young girls.

In retribution, the Feminea Potentia would leave none alive.

As she and Mina rounded a house, Sloane heard a baby's cry. Mina grabbed Sloane's hand, stopping her. Sloane sighed. She knew Mina in a way no one else ever would. In the Feminea Potentia, they were all sisters, brought together through their mission and bonded in battle. But Sloane understood Mina's heart with a depth that had been forged from their time growing in the same womb. Their heartbeats would be forever joined with a depth and understanding that couldn't be described with words.

"That's not our mission. We can come back," Sloane pleaded with her sister, knowing Gemini would not be pleased.

"I am not leaving without the baby, Sloane." Mina's face had taken on that stubborn expression Sloane had come to know so well.

Even though they were biological twins, they couldn't be more different. Sloane was the rule follower, focused and loyal. Mina was all heart, a dreamer and a lover of life. Honestly, she probably didn't belong with the Feminea Potentia, but Mina swore that wherever Sloane went, she would follow. So here they were.

There was no arguing with Mina when she was set on something, and if Sloane was being honest with herself, something in her rebelled at leaving the baby, too.

"Okay, but let's be quick about it," she murmured.

They silently made their way through the small house. The crying increased the deeper they went. Sloane opened the door to a bedroom, and Mina entered first with an arrow nocked to her bow. She stopped dead in her tracks, lowering her bow as she took in the sight. Sloane came around her sister to see what had her frozen. Her heart sank.

On the bed lay what she assumed was the young mother of the crying babe. From the looks of it, she was barely past puberty. She lay there, unmoving, open eyes staring at nothing, the life long gone from them.

The babe lay next to her mother. So small—maybe even too small—naked, a bit wet, and probably cold. Mina quickly picked her up, wrapping her in a blanket she found, but not before Sloane got a glimpse of a unique little birthmark between the girl's shoulder blades in the shape of a star. She couldn't help feeling that something monumental was happening as Mina began vigorously rubbing the little bundle.

"She's so cold," Mina said, her eyes wide and brows pinched. "I think she was just born, Sloane, this very night. This poor girl gave birth alone and died in the process, leaving this sweet baby all alone."

Rage flooded Sloane's veins at the thought of how the girl had ended up in this predicament in the first place.

"I want to kill those monsters all over again," she seethed.

"I know, but we have to focus," Mina insisted. "I will not leave this baby. She will be coming with us back to the base or I will be leaving the FP."

Gemini, the leader of the FP, required that orphans brought into the fold had to be well past infancy and toddlerhood. They needed to be old enough to dress, feed, and care for themselves. That way, the FP could focus on training and not being nursemaids. Gemini liked the girls to be young so they could be molded, but not that young.

Gemini aimed to squash any overtly feminine quality in the FP, which she made clear in her own appearance and mannerisms. Her head was shaved on both sides, and a long, braided mohawk lay across her scalp, snaking down her back. She was always seen with black war paint on her face, and her walk was stiff and predatory, with long, confident strides. She was intent on embodying everything that was far from feminine.

Mothering was about as feminine as it got.

This was going to be a challenge.

But as Mina looked at her with hopeful eyes, Sloane knew she would do anything to make this happen for her sister. After the sacrifice Mina made to join the FP with Sloane, it was the least she could do.

"You need to have another vision, Mina. That's the only way Gemini will say yes."

"You know that one was bogus, right?" Mina asked with a dry look. "It was a complete coincidence that saved our butts."

"Yeah, but Gemini doesn't know that. You'll need to be convincing," Sloane insisted, her brain flipping through scenarios like cards. Suddenly, the answer occurred to her.

"She has a mark between her shoulder blades that looks like a star," she provided. "Maybe you had a 'spell' where you blacked out and saw a vision of a star. You could tell Gemini that you felt with urgency this was symbolic of a future weapon that would be powerful in the hands of the FP."

Sloane saw the rejection all over Mina's face at those last words. But before Mina could speak and presumably say that she didn't want this baby to be forcefully trained by the FP, Sloane put her hand up.

"I know, Mina, I know. But we will be there to raise and train her, too," she encouraged her sister. "And as much as you want her to be able to choose her path, we don't live in the kind of world where choice is a luxury. If you don't want her ending up like her poor mother, she will need to be able to protect herself."

Sloane knew exactly what words would sway Mina. With a resigned look, Mina nodded. Mina fashioned a sling from a bedsheet to tie the baby to her chest, and they headed out to meet up with Gemini. Sloane didn't know why, but she said a quick prayer to whoever would listen that this would work.

"That's it, Ansel!" Sloane shouted over the repetitious *thunk* of the wooden swords. "Never give your opponent your back, no matter what."

Standing there watching the spirited little redhead spar with such fierce determination, Sloane couldn't believe it had been ten years since she and Mina had found the girl. Sloane couldn't even remember what life had been like before Ansel came into their lives. Life was good, despite the constant struggle for Sloane and her sister of trying to mask what they truly felt for the girl. For Sloane, it had been hard, but for Mina, it had been an almost impossible task.

Sloane often feared that Gemini was fully aware of Mina's affection for Ansel, how Mina thought of the girl as her child. Mina had even chosen Ansel's name based on her and Sloane's Celtic ancestry, but convinced Gemini it was because it meant "wise protector." Never mind that Ansel had similar red hair to Mina, only confirming in Mina's mind that the girl was hers.

Mina stepped up to the sparring ring with a wooden sword in hand and called off the other trainees. Sloane sighed. Mina thought she was being subtle, but she had a tendency to do this anytime she felt the other trainees were being too hard on Ansel, or Ansel was too immersed in the training. Mina's mothering side was coming out yet again and if she didn't learn to hide it better, Gemini would quickly lose patience with her.

And with how erratic Gemini's behavior had become lately, Sloane feared what decision could follow such a discovery.

Some of the FP believed that the tragedy of losing her twin brother years ago had broken something in Gemini, making her cold and unfeeling. Making it impossible for her to care about anything at all. But Sloane wasn't convinced. Though Gemini was heartbroken over the loss of her brother and she'd used it as motivation to destroy all evil, the shift in Gemini in recent years felt darker. She no longer resembled the Gemini that Sloane had first met.

When it was clear the other FP had moved on, Mina threw her arm around Ansel. The two laughed and giggled while Mina waved at Sloane and headed off to God-knows-where with the girl. Either to play a game, or take her swimming in the lake again, or play hide-and-seek. Anything to give her a proper childhood and keep her from being too influenced by the FP. Sloane hated to admit it, but it was time to have a chat with Mina. Gemini was bound to find out sooner or later, and she would not tolerate the situation.

Sloane turned to head to the compound, a collection of old brick buildings that had been repurposed to provide dorms, a mess hall, and an indoor training facility for the FP, all surrounded by densely populated forest. That was when she saw Gemini headed right for her.

"Where are Mina and Ansel?" Gemini demanded.

"I believe they just finished sword training and are planning to do some additional physical training."

"Playing is not physical training, Sloane. I heard rumors of laughter and giggles coming from the forest around the lake a few days ago. Hardly the sounds of training."

"You know Mina," Sloane said simply. "She tries to turn everything into a game, but Ansel is the best of her age group for a reason. The training challenges her physically and mentally. She thinks fast on her feet and she adapts easily. She's even surpassing some of the older girls already."

"I won't have Mina making a mockery of the FP. I am creating warriors here. Not silly, undisciplined playthings." Gemini practically spat out the words.

Sloane ignored Gemini's claim of *creating warriors*. As if she still did any real training with the girls.

"Well, it's a good thing that Mina is dedicated to Ansel being the best warrior in her class, then. One day, she might very well be the best warrior in the FP."

Gemini's cold stare felt heavy. She didn't speak, but she didn't have to. Gemini hated that Sloane was right.

As Gemini turned to walk away, a shiver tiptoed down

Sloane's spine; a warning. She worried that Gemini would soon not care about the results of Mina's training. More and more, she seemed to only care about her personal glory, instead of what the FP was supposed to stand for. She'd want the credit for Ansel's success, and that would only happen if Mina followed Gemini's training protocol.

Determined to talk with her sister before bed, Sloane made her way to the mess hall. She would get some food, then do some training, before this day was lost completely to the worries of her restless mind.

~

"Knock, knock," Sloane said. She entered their room expecting to find Mina and Ansel since she'd somehow missed them at dinner, but the room was dark and undisturbed. Exactly as they had left it this morning.

Closing the door, she headed toward the training hall. Maybe Gemini had found Mina and Ansel and forced them to get in some additional training. As Sloane rounded the corner, she saw Gemini at the end of the hall with what looked to be a satellite phone, heading toward the back stairwell door.

Since when did Gemini have access to a satellite phone?

The FP had always been firmly and proudly rooted in ancient warfare practices. Due to the world being what it was, any technology left was available only to the select wealthy who had sold their souls to get it. This couldn't possibly be a good omen.

A prickling in Sloane's gut urged her to follow the woman. Why would Gemini need to take a call in a dark hallway when she had an office?

Slipping into stealth mode, Sloane snuck up on the now-closed stairwell door and pressed her head against it. Hearing nothing, she gently grasped the handle, cracking the door just enough that Gemini's voice carried softly to her.

"She's headed your way. She believes it's a mission of reconnaissance on our behalf. I don't really care what you do, just make sure it finishes things. She's a complication I can't deal with anymore."

Sloane's stomach sank. She didn't know who Gemini was talking about, but her gut said her twin was in trouble. Abandoning the door, she headed to Gemini's office to see if she could discover the location of this so-called mission that Mina might be on at this very moment.

Gemini was known for documenting all her strategizing and conquests down to every last detail. Sloane shuffled through all the papers on Gemini's desk, but found nothing of importance. She moved to the woman's filing cabinet, skimming the files, looking for something that could potentially tell her what Gemini had planned.

"You won't find anything, Sloane," Gemini provided from the door.

Sloane straightened, mentally kicking herself for being so focused on her search that she didn't hear the woman's approach. She opted for directness instead of trying to defend herself—she wouldn't give Gemini the satisfaction.

"Where are Mina and Ansel?" Sloane demanded from the filing cabinet behind Gemini's desk.

"Well, Ansel is with the other younger trainees, doing some after-dinner workouts," Gemini said as she started making her way to her desk. Simultaneously, Sloane shifted in the opposite direction, not putting her back to her leader, which didn't go unnoticed by Gemini. "And Mina took a last-minute mission for me. Nothing dangerous, just carrying an important message."

Sloane's stomach turned sour. Gemini didn't know that Sloane had heard her call. But she'd seen Sloane digging through her desk, so she must know something was up. Sloane needed to play this smoothly so she could grab Ansel and get out of there.

"Where'd she head off to?" She forced a casual tone.

"Oh, nowhere of importance. Why don't you just head back to your room? I will notify you the moment she's back."

Sloane's pulse hammered in her ears. There was no way she was leaving without information on her sister's whereabouts. And by her smug expression, Gemini knew it, too.

So much for subtlety. Sloane was done playing coy.

"Look, let's quit with the games. I am not leaving here until you tell me where you sent Mina." She watched, her muscles tense, as Gemini turned to sift through the bookcase next to the wall.

"Well . . ." Gemini drew out the word, taking a big breath.

She turned quickly with what looked like a pen against her mouth, pointed right at Sloane. Sloane felt the sharp bite of pain in her throat. She reached up to feel some kind of dart sticking out of her neck. She yanked it out, ignoring the trickle of blood that followed. It appeared to be some sort of syringe dart.

"Then I guess you won't be leaving here," Gemini crooned, lifting her chin. "It pays to make friends in high places, Sloane, something you and Mina never seemed to understand. You both were always too idealistic. This handy little item was a recent gift from such friends. Quite an effortless way to dispatch obstacles, don't you think?"

Sloane's vision began to waver, her limbs growing heavy. She crumbled to the ground like a sack of potatoes.

"Don't worry, we'll take good care of Ansel. With more focused training, she'll become the best of us." Sloane watched helplessly as Gemini stepped over her, then left the room. As Sloane lay there, unable to lift her weighted limbs, she stared helplessly at the ceiling. Her eyes began to lose focus.

"I . . . I'm sorry, M . . . Mi . . . na." she whispered, breathing her last.

CHAPTER 1

9 YEARS LATER

ANSEL

"Okay, Nero, let's show her how it's done, huh?" I smile at the older bay stallion, patting his neck and rubbing his soft muzzle.

"I've watched you do it a thousand times, Ansel. That doesn't mean I am going to figure it out all of a sudden." Narrowed eyes peer at me from behind a collection of dark coily curls. Nayne sighs, crossing her arms over her chest.

This is why I like to work with Nayne—she's prone to whiny discouragement and Gemini has no patience for it. She would be all too happy to work it out of Nayne as she's done with other young ones, and that is often a punishment that borders on cruelty.

I would know.

When I was younger, Gemini made it her mission to help me overcome my fear of heights, but all her "cure" ended up doing was making it far worse. I would never admit it to anyone, but it's safe to say that fear has morphed into something completely unmanageable now. Lucky for me, I've become an expert at avoiding any situation that might put a spotlight on my issue with heights.

Years ago, when Nayne first arrived here, there was something about her that urged me to take her under my wing. Call it a case of like calling to like, but I recognized something in her spirit I couldn't turn my back on.

She is the youngest in training right now at ten, and she is small for her age, like I was as a child. But she has drive and passion. A fire in her that the world hasn't been able to smother. She has sometimes garnered nasty, jealous attention from the other girls, too, because she is striking with beautiful, chocolate doe eyes set in her gorgeous brown-skinned complexion.

I, too, feel like an outsider at times, so I instantly connected with her. In the four years she's been here, she's become a little sister to me.

"None of that, Nay Nay," I reassure her with the nickname I gave her years ago. I gather her mass of hair into a puff on top of her head and secure it with a tie. "If you think you can't, then you're already defeated. Now, this time we're going to take the course slowly. Nero has a steadier gait than most horses, and you are going to get used to stabilizing your upper body while your lower body is moving. Once you master that, then you'll have no problem hitting targets from your mount. You got this, yeah?"

Her eyes brighten at my confidence in her and she stands a little taller as she approaches Nero.

"Okay, let's do this," she says, determination in her eyes.

I hoist her up onto Nero, her ten-year-old frame smaller than most. She gets situated with her bow as I hop up behind her, grabbing the reins. A sudden pang of sorrow stabs at me at the familiarity of the position—this is how Mina taught me to shoot. A memory that I long ago suppressed because of the pain that always accompanies any thoughts of Mina and Sloane. I swallow past the lump in my throat and force a breath through my lungs to refocus on the task at hand.

"Part of your struggle is muscle control, and that will come with work and time, but if you find your balance now, you'll be unstoppable later."

I bring Nero to a slow, steady canter as we head into the training course, a narrow path through the trees lined with targets. Nayne is great with a bow when standing still, but this is the next step. During a fight, you're usually moving rather than standing still.

"Steady your breathing," I instruct her, "and imagine that your lower body sits on a ball joint, able to spin and move as needed without affecting the stability in your upper body."

I squeeze her at the hips with my legs, offering a bit more stability as we take the first turn. Part of why I picked Nero is because he knows this course so well, he doesn't need me directing him with the reins. The other reason is that he is the only horse in the FP's herd that closely resembles the red horse of my dreams. I don't remember when this majestic red horse started frequenting my dreams, but it's become a reliable source of comfort for me. And oddly enough, thoughts of the horse always leave me feeling hopeful.

Nayne takes aim and fires, narrowly missing the first target.

"Watch your mind frame, Nayne," I encourage her. "Stay focused—believe you can do it."

She takes another deep, steadying breath as we come around the next turn. She takes aim, fumbling a bit, fires, and clips the edge of the target. She continues to fire and miss as we go through the course until we come upon the last turn. She breathes deep, exhaling slowly as I taught her, and fires, hitting the outside ring of the target.

"I did it! I finally got one!" she exclaims, her excitement contagious.

I smile. "I knew you would. It was only a matter of time."

We dismount, and I lead Nero back to the barn. We give him a good rubdown and a treat, then head back to the compound to grab what's left of dinner before the mess hall closes.

As we reach the door, Athena and a small group of armored warriors are exiting. As usual, Athena looks like a dark angel. Tight black leather pants combined with combat boots and a too-small, skintight, zippered black leather vest complete her outfit. Unlike most FP, she exposes far too much skin for the purposes of camouflage and protection. The lack of protection is just another badge of her arrogance. But since her skin is a warm tan and not a beacon of pale white like mine, she can get away with the lack of camouflage. Not to mention, her dark hair helps her blend into the shadows, whereas my bright copper strands have the opposite effect. I need all the camouflage help I can get from my trusty khaki fatigues and well-worn leather jacket.

An exasperated breath leaves me as I prepare myself for her ridicule.

"Why, Ansel," she says with a saccharine grin, "what a surprise. I would've surely thought it past your bedtime?"

Tittering and jeering laughter rings through the air. Well, she's nothing if not predictable. Her jealousy has been a constant in my life since we were young and she over-heard Gemini say I was the best warrior in training. It's only gotten worse as the years go by.

"Hello to you too, Athena, and just where are you headed? Off to torture small, defenseless animals again?" I lean against the doorframe as they pass by. I wish I could say there was no truth to my insult, but she has a propensity for "honing" her skills on living things. Her eyes flash at my words, but she quickly composes herself.

"Why? Jealous? All you ever seem to do these days is babysit small, defenseless animals," Athena says with a cutting, mocking grin that also hides a threat as she glances at Nayne. I give Nayne a gentle nudge to continue on into the mess hall. Thankfully, after a scowl in Athena's direction, she obeys.

As usual, Athena can't resist the opportunity to brag. "Gemini requires the very best of the FP for a special mission to silence an enemy. It's only one man, sadly, so I plan to be back in time to get a good night's sleep." And, with a flip of her obnoxiously smooth and silky hair, she turns on her heels to head out, her cronies following in her wake. For a group that claims the bonds of sisterhood are thicker than blood, all I seem to find lately is evidence that disproves that motto.

Nayne is the only exception.

My mind wanders back to Athena's words. Silence an enemy? *Since when do the FP do mercenary work?* We've only ever undertaken missions to save innocents when they were under attack or being terrorized by the depraved humanity left in this world. Acting as a sort of savior for those in need of saving. Whatever mission Athena is on is something new. Either that, or I have been too focused on training to pay attention to what's been going on around here.

Which gets me wondering why I have not been sent on any missions since our return from the Amilign's ashram. Instead, I have been relegated to training. Not that I am complaining, seeing as I don't relish killing the way some of the others do. It's just curious.

My appetite disappeared with the train of my thoughts, but I find Nayne and force myself to eat something anyway. Then I head to my small room in a desperate search for some semblance of peace or purpose. Both are in short supply of late.

I lie on my cot, turning to the wall and running my fingers over the carved initials in the wood:

$$S+M+A$$

I carved the initials through a flood of tears after realizing that Mina and Sloane were not coming back. I was only ten at the time. And it was the only time I ever allowed myself to cry over them. Despite being surrounded by my *sisterhood*, I had never felt more alone than in that moment. Not much has changed in the years since, other than Nayne arriving, of course.

With the feel of the etched initials on my fingertips, I sink into a fitful sleep.

CHAPTER 2

ANSEL

I wake just before the sun, the graying of the sky announcing dawn is near. I can't continue tossing and turning; this restless energy in me demands release. I grab my weapons and head to the barn to saddle a horse, desperate for the distraction of the chilled morning wind biting into my face as I ride. Maybe I'll run through the obstacle course with my bow.

The smells of manure and hay assault my senses as I open the barn door. I head over to Xena's stall, as she's one of the faster horses and I need a challenge. I slide my hands along her legs and crouch down to check her hooves before I saddle her.

Suddenly, I hear Gemini's distinctive voice just outside the window. Something within me urges me to stay low and out of sight. She's talking, probably to one of the lieutenants who always follows her around.

"It's an easy decision, if you think about it. We can't

deny the benefit of aligning with the monks. The resources we'll have access to will be a game changer for the FP. And we will still have our autonomy if we give them Ansel."

I still. My heart and breath seem to stop simultaneously.

I wait to hear more, something that will make sense of what she's saying. Something that will offer a good explanation for what I just heard. I'm not surprised that she's working with the monks; it wasn't that long ago that we went to the mountain ashram and I met Lucia. Taken as a child from her beloved Aunt Sid and forced to live with the monks in preparation for some supposed honorary role, our friendship was instantaneous and I straightaway felt as if I had known her my whole life.

But the six weeks I stayed at the ashram with the FP left me with more concerns and questions than answers. Deep down, I knew those guys were bad news. Which was why I was glad to leave, even if it killed me to leave Lucia behind. I was only able to walk away because of the tracking bracelet I gifted her and the promise to myself that I would figure out how to free her from them.

That was almost two months ago. And the only thing that has prevented me from taking action is the annoyingly close watch I've been under since returning. At first, I thought that maybe our leadership had been shaken by our encounter with the monks and was being cautious and protective. Now I know the truth.

They've been guarding their bargaining chip.

The FP is supposed to be a sisterhood. We are not tools to be bartered. My fists are balled up and the air feels thick with anticipation.

"Ansel is one of our best. Will they not take someone else?" asks Gemini's short and stocky second-in-command.

Jay is otherwise known as Jane, as if the name Jane needs to be abbreviated further.

"They only want her. Something about a prophecy and a mark she has that confirms it in their minds. Apparently, one of the monks noticed it on the last day of our stay—when she was training—but we left before anything could be done about it. Honestly, it doesn't matter. She's good, but an easy sacrifice to make so we can get away from horses and swords, and acquire high-powered weaponry and more motorized vehicles. Not to mention the fuel to actually use them. I am sick of seeing the small number of all-terrains we do have spending more time collecting dust than being put to use.

"Plus, she reminds me far too much of Mina and Sloane. I should have gotten rid of them earlier. Maybe if I hadn't waited, Ansel wouldn't be as contaminated by their influence."

I am left rudderless in a sea of confusion. Anger begins to simmer in my hollowed-out chest at the implication of her words. They walk away, out of earshot. I want to scream and rage at what I've just discovered.

Mina and Sloane were my family, the only one I ever had. Mina was like a mother to me and Sloane was like a favorite aunt. And they were taken from me because of Gemini. Who is now selling me to the Amilign in return for some weapons and vehicles.

I was never given an explanation of what happened to Mina and Sloane, other than that they were sent on a mission and never returned. Gemini had implied they'd abandoned me, but I knew they would never do that. They would die before they willingly left me, which is how I always knew something had to have happened to them.

And that was when this seed of unsettled doubt first took root.

What made it worse was that I wasn't even given time to grieve. According to the FP, crying is weak and strength is all that matters—or Gemini's interpretation of strength. So after Mina and Sloane disappeared, I did what I've been doing ever since and shoved my grief down, burying it. I distracted myself and tried to never think about them again. And never allowed anyone close enough to cause the kind of pain that could break me.

It had been easy up until Nayne came into my life. And then Lucia, of course.

My heart cracks as I realize how unjustly I've treated the memory of Mina and Sloane, who sacrificed so much to raise me and love me. They deserve more than me trying to forget them. But I am like a frayed rope about to snap. Left too broken by the truth to do their memory justice.

Now that the chest of memories has been cracked open, I remember how Sloane had started to worry about the path the FP was on under Gemini's leadership. Something about a growing darkness in her. But Sloane was always the more serious one of the sisters, so I just took it as Sloane being Sloane.

After what I've just heard, I know her worries were justified.

I let the buried memories flood my mind as I sit in the musty, dank tack room, tears flowing down my face at what has been stolen from me. Finally allowing the grief a place in my heart. But like a release valve on a dam, it quickly becomes too much for me to handle. So I do what I always do and cut it off, burying everything once more.

Burying *them* once more.

I need a clear head for what comes next. I will not be

Gemini's puppet and I will not fall prey to her, as so many others have. She's clearly been up to something for some time, and I've wondered about it for a while now. Really, ever since she stopped bringing new girls into the fold. Nayne was the last, and that was four years ago. Many of the FP just assumed that our ranks were full, but Gemini isn't the type to be content with the power she's amassed. She's also not one to offer information or answers to questions. It's all led to me being increasingly uneasy about the FP's future.

This is just the final blow.

I choose another one of the faster horses, and get it saddled up along with Xena. I head to the barracks where most of the younger trainees are forced to sleep. Many are already stirring, getting ready to start a rigorous day of training. I'll need to put on a show for the others if this is to work. I muster a stern expression and find the cot where Nayne's prone form still lies. My swift kick to the cot frame rings through the barracks and causes Nayne to suddenly shoot upright in bed.

"You did not finish what you were tasked with yesterday, soldier."

Nayne's startled, sleepy eyes blink up at me.

"You will get dressed immediately and you will work until you finish in a manner that I deem sufficient."

Confusion is written all over her face, but she's well-versed in FP protocol and knows that talking back will only get her into more trouble. She also knows that when I call her "soldier," it's only ever for show.

"Yes, Dux," she says as she rises from the bed, rapidly throwing on her clothes and then following me like a dutiful trainee.

Dux is Latin for commander. The FP prides itself on

being rooted in Latin, even if it is just a handful of words and phrases, like our motto, "Non ducor, duco," which means "I am not led, I lead." I roll my eyes, now knowing what a farce this all is. It's just Gemini's play for power, and she will use and step on as many women as possible to get what she wants.

Nayne and I walk out of the barracks in silence. I lead her to the empty mess hall to grab some travel rations. I feel Nayne's eyes remain on me as I quickly load my pack and fill our canteens. She obediently follows me out into the crisp morning air. Once we are well out of sight and earshot, I feel Nayne's anticipatory gaze on me again.

"Not yet, wait until we get to the barn," I say quietly.

As we enter the dusty barn, I guide Nayne to the saddled horses. I quickly load the saddle bags with a few essentials—a knife, ropes, and a flint and steel fire starter. I don my weapons and make sure more weapons are strapped to both horses as well.

"Do you trust me?" I ask Nayne.

"Yes, always," she replies without hesitation, despite the furrow in her brow.

"We need to leave this place, and there's no time to waste. I can explain it to you if you need to know why, but the sooner we are gone, the better. I found out—"

"It's okay, Ansel. If you're leaving, I know it's for a good reason, and I am coming no matter what."

I'm a little surprised at her lack of resistance. At the very least, I expected some questions from her. I've always known that Nayne has never felt truly at home with the FP, but I never realized just how deeply that feeling went. Though I suppose, on some level, it's one of the things that has bonded us. We've both always felt a bit like outsiders. Not bloodthirsty enough to fit in with the other girls. The

FP is no place for compassion or empathy, or any emotion that isn't rage. But Nayne and I want more from life than just constant warring and grabs for power.

Now we have our chance.

I smile at her confidence and trust. I thought I no longer had a family, but how wrong I was. Despite my futile efforts to keep Nayne at a distance emotionally, afraid of becoming too attached and losing someone else I love, in the four years I've been training her and caring for her, she's become as much my little sister as if she were my blood.

As I finish loading up the horses with our meager rations and supplies, I resolve to do everything in my power to ensure Nayne's safety.

We quietly walk the horses out of the barn and into the trees, taking the narrow path that leads out of the compound. One of the perks of Gemini's arrogance is that there are no guards for me to contend with. Gemini always says the location of our compound is remote enough to be secure, and she's never met with outsiders here. And if anyone was brave or dumb enough to attack, it would provide an excellent surprise training opportunity for the FP. In their minds, those who didn't survive such an attack didn't deserve to be in the FP in the first place.

I'm not sure where to go, but I figure we can head toward The Wastes, an unnatural wasteland where life ceases to exist, and hide out there for a bit. I know how much Gemini despises The Wastes, it being where her brother died.

Once Nayne and I are safe, then I can make a plan to get Lucia away from the monks. If the Amilign are interested in buying girls, it is long past time for her to leave that place.

Despite all the uncertainty, I feel a sense of peace for

the first time in a long time. All the doubts and questions I've had about the FP have finally been lifted like a weight from my chest. I am leaving this place that's never really felt like home, and I am finally on the path to my true destiny.

CHAPTER 3

ANSEL

"Ahhhhhh!"

The bloodcurdling scream jolts me upright from my fitful sleep on the hard forest ground. Second nature to me at the first sound of danger, my bow is in my hands as my eyes search for the enemy. I mentally kick myself for falling asleep in the first place. But then the sounds of splashing and giggles draw my attention to the river just beyond our makeshift campsite.

There stands Nayne, calf deep in the water, kicking at something I can't see with a smile on her face. The morning sun behind her casts an ethereal glow on the quaint scene. Something about this feels different. And suddenly, it hits me—she looks like a child. I mean, of course she is a child, she's only ten, but I have been conditioned to see her as a warrior, to treat her as a warrior, to train her to be a warrior. And now, two full days' journey away from the reaches of the FP, with the morning sun preparing to take its position in the sky, it's like a veil has been lifted. I am seeing her for what she truly is . . . a carefree, joy-filled, ten-year-old girl.

I wonder when she last felt like a child. It's a moment I don't want to interrupt. But she must sense my attention because she looks my way and waves, then comes splashing out of the river toward me.

"You have to come see this, Ansel!" Delight shines in her eyes. "Hundreds of tiny fish. When you stand perfectly still, they come up to your legs and it tickles."

I smile at the joy that radiates from her. A light I have rarely witnessed in the girl in our years with the FP. I am loath to dampen it in any way, but it is my job to keep her safe, and to do that, we have to keep moving.

"It's time to go, Nayne. The FP are probably still after us."

"Aww, but I love this spot. It's so magical. Couldn't we just stay for one more day?" Her big doe eyes plead with me. I envy the naivety of her youth, something that left me long ago.

"Before, there wasn't time to tell you why we left," I explain, "but I think you need to understand the gravity of the situation. Gemini plans to trade me to the Amilign in exchange for advanced weaponry." I contemplate telling her of my other discovery, but that is a wound I am not ready to dig at. I need a level head right now, and thoughts of how Mina and Sloane were taken from me will not help me focus.

Nayne is young, but she's smart. She doesn't need me to state the obvious. Gemini is always after more power, and if I am her bargaining chip, she won't let me go easily.

I watch Nayne's face become a mask of determination, as if it is her job to keep me safe.

"Okay, no time to waste then."

I smile at her as we go to work packing up our measly supplies and readying the horses. I am checking the horses' tack when I feel it—like a chilled finger sliding down my spine. Goosebumps erupt on the back of my neck.

We are being watched.

Ever so subtly, I scan our surroundings, searching for the neutral and forest-colored hues of typical FP attire. A hodgepodge of dark browns, greens, tans, grays, and blacks are the go-to, each outfit as unique as the woman wearing it. The only similarities are flexible materials and colors that offer good camouflage. While pretending to check the horses, I scan for the telltale shine of Athena's black leather, knowing she wouldn't miss an opportunity to play a role in my capture.

I can see nothing concerning, but that only means that whoever is out there is no amateur. And for some reason, I don't think it is the FP that is hunting us. I highly doubt Gemini would hide—her arrogance would demand a direct approach.

Whoever or whatever this is, it feels different and deadly. As if an apex predator stands just beyond my sight, radiating aggression.

I bend down to where Nayne is finishing putting things in one of the packs. I place my hand on top of hers and tap out a code. It's a warning system developed by the FP, a silent way of communicating danger. She freezes but knows not to look at me. Instead, she gives a slight nod.

I stand by the horse, weighing my options. We could try to outrun whoever is after us, but if this hunter's been tracking us this whole time, which is most likely the case, then even if we manage to escape, we'll just be tracked down again. Whoever is out there is patient and astute. I need a solution that will confuse our trail completely. I get a feeling in my gut that the hunter is waiting in the direction we came from, across the field currently home to a herd of deer. The rushing river at our back hems us in.

And suddenly, I have an idea.

I walk farther into the copse of trees near our camp, making a clicking noise with my mouth for the horses to follow. Now that the horses are hidden from sight, I tie one of the thick blankets to the sides of the saddle. Then I pull a long stick that branches into a V at the end from the pile of firewood we collected earlier. I slip it into the blanket, laying it down across the saddle for now, placing the V where a rider's legs would be. I set up Nayne's horse in the same manner. I hate to leave the horses, but I can't see a better way to cover our escape. Plus, they won't survive in The Wastes anyway.

If we have any chance of losing whoever is hunting us, The Wastes is our best option.

Now hidden behind the trees, I pull Nayne close enough to whisper, "We're going to send the horses into the herd. When the chaos erupts, I want you to jump into the river with me and stay low. We're going to hold onto each other and ride the current as far as we can until it starts to veer away from The Wastes. Then we'll get out and make our way into The Wastes. Hopefully, the river will make it hard for our pursuer to track us. And if this hunter does figure out where we went, they may not be able to track us once we are in The Wastes."

I finish with the horses, propping up the stick under the blankets and securing it in an upright position with rope. It will not hold for long, but hopefully long enough to confuse the hunter until we are in the river and far away. It's a ridiculous idea, really, but hopefully it's crazy enough to work.

I am grateful for horses that are extensively trained by the FP. Not only are they bombproof, but they are trained to run at a full gallop with only a smack on the rump. We point the horses toward the field, each blanket secured around the large stick looking like a very pathetic and sickly version of a person. With a strong smack on one rump and then the other, both horses take off past the tree line and in the direction of the herd. As the wind whips around them, it fills up the blankets and causes them to billow out. It looks more like the hooded cape of a rider than I could've hoped for. Not too shabby after all.

We watch as the herd begins to scatter and the deer pounce away in a chaotic pattern, but the horses never falter. I wait, watching the distant tree line. I want to see some movement that indicates our trick worked before I take Nayne to the river where we might be vulnerable. A flash of red catches my eye, and then out of the trees bursts a behemoth of a horse, an unusual bright red color, with what's clearly a male rider on its back, his large size giving him away.

My fingers itch for my bow. One arrow, and I could put a stop to our pursuer right now. But something stays my hand. Maybe it's worry about missing, even though I never miss. But whatever the reason, my gut has never failed me before, so I turn and grab Nayne's hand, swinging my bow up over my other shoulder as we run to the river.

The cold mountain water bites into my flesh as we wade out to the deep part of the rushing water. I take hold of Nayne and the swift current surges around us, carrying us farther and farther away from the mysterious red rider.

CHAPTER 4

Ginger is a force of nature beneath me. She feeds off the fury consuming me like a fuel, and it ignites a fire in her veins.

I still can't believe that diversion actually worked on me. I wasn't distracted for long, but just enough for those two FP to escape into the river and leave me combing the banks for miles, looking for where they emerged. Even my enhanced senses were no help. More proof that I am too easily distracted lately.

I need to get a handle on my emotions. Watching my brothers, I've seen firsthand how high emotions can trigger the leashing. But the rage I feel over what happened to Lucia is a living and breathing thing.

That a piece of Amilign garbage would dare take one of our Cores—a sister to me. And hearing the brokenness in Nic's voice at what was done to her . . . it has consumed my thoughts, like a nasty splinter that's dug in too deep.

I always get teased for being the laid-back dreamer, but

I am fiercely loyal to those under my protection. And they seem to forget I am the Horseman of War, and nothing triggers the desire to war within me like an injustice done to someone who can't protect themselves.

Lucia has been through so much. When she first came to us, you didn't even have to talk with her to see it all over her face. The surprise she clearly felt at someone acknowledging her presence, like she was used to going unseen and ignored. Even worse was the emotion that overtook her when she experienced a simple act of kindness. It was so unexpected to her. And then my bonehead of a brother thought he was helping her by keeping his distance.

And yet, through it all, Lucia retained her wonder at the world Elohim created, at His goodness. Everything seems to be a gift to her. Her beautiful heart, her bravery, and her resilience won us all over almost instantly.

In a time when we had begun to wonder if the Cores were simply a myth, she has been a massive injection of hope.

Seeing Lucia and her connection to Nic solidified the rest of us. It placed an urgency within us to find our Cores. A blessing and a curse, in a way, because now the yearning pressing on each of us is impossible to ignore. I fear it will make the leashing that much more of a torment.

If I am being honest with myself, that yearning is partly responsible for my impulsive decision to go after the FP. I worry more for my brothers, especially Z. To know that your Core is out there somewhere, potentially harmed, and you can't get to them no matter how desperately you search. That's a special level of hell I wouldn't wish on anyone. I just pray to Elohim that we find her soon.

As for Azmaveth, or Mav as he's most frequently called by us, he's a hard one to read. He's naturally a bit of a loner despite our best efforts, and he keeps a tight leash on his emotions. I think that being the Horseman of Death, he believes his presence makes people uncomfortable. He occasionally checks in with us via the mind link, but I can't remember the last time he's been home. Elias believes that Mav's biggest struggle will be with his identity. That he may never feel worthy of a Core, that he will struggle to believe a Core will ever want to be connected to death.

But I don't have the mental capacity to focus on my concerns for my brothers right now like an old mother hen. If I am to single-handedly take down the FP, then I don't have the luxury of distractions.

Shortly after we found out that Nic got Lucia out of that hellhole, we received information that a small group of FP had separated from the base. At the time, Nic and Lucia had been closest to the base, so they went to scope out that location and I offered to pursue a second small group heading in the direction of The Wastes. Right before I left, we received information that the FP were forming an alliance with the monks and there were hints of dark plans in the works. So I was more than happy to have a little *chat* with them.

Truth be told, I could not stand idly by any longer, despite Elias's concern. The fact is that Z is in no shape to fight, and if he does, we might lose him forever. And Mav made it clear he can't leave his current location. So that leaves me, and honestly, I am more than up to the challenge, especially right now. This is just what I need to tamp down the restlessness I've been fighting lately.

Our sources tracked the location of the small contingent of FP, and Ginger and I left to catch them before they got to The Wastes, where my abilities would be rendered useless. Something about that place blocks the Horsemen's ability to mind link with each other and makes us incapable of distance jumping. Ginger and I distance jumped to the FP's last projected location, and then the hunt was on.

They may have slipped my grasp once, but it won't happen again. After I extract information out of this group and dispatch them if need be, I can head to the compound and finish the job, giving us one less enemy to contend with.

As I head into the sands of The Wastes, I slow Ginger down. The Wastes are unpredictable and alien with a general *otherness* to them. It's as though the footprint of darkness has irreparably altered the natural environment. Located directly to the west of The Range, a vast mountain range surrounded by forests that seem to abruptly end at an unspoken demarcation line, The Wastes are in direct contrast to their eastern neighbor. A history of bombings, destruction, and death, paired with unnatural storms and weather, give the area an eerie feel that makes the hair on the back of my neck stand at attention.

This place is devoid of any rhythm or purpose. In essence, it's chaos. Even most motorized vehicles fail to work here. Most people aren't even sure what lies on the other side of The Wastes, if anything does. A place where men and women fear to dwell, The Wastes is a well-earned moniker.

As the land starts to undulate, forming hills, the shifting sands beneath Ginger's feet make it difficult for her to progress. I dismount. "Baim Lyy," I say softly, and Ginger disappears in a flash of red, once again a part of me.

I stand there, the wind blowing erratically around me, and my heart begins to pound. I close my eyes and trust Elohim to give me direction. It's only a moment before I begin to move forward in the direction I feel pulled. The farther I trek, the more my restlessness increases until I am practically vibrating with tension. This is an unusual response for my body, but it must be a sign that I am close to a formidable enemy.

I see a partially dilapidated brick structure in the distance and pull the short sword from my back. I tilt my head side to side, working any kinks out of my neck. The armor of my true identity slides into place like a well-worn leather jacket. My senses sharpen, my breath steadies, and everything around me stills.

The Horsemen of War has arrived.

ANSEL

It's been a full day since we stumbled across the little brick building—if you can even call it that with one wall completely collapsed. But out here in The Wastes, beggars can't be choosers, and it allows me some cover to protect Nayne while giving us a good view of the surrounding area.

I am pretty sure we lucked out with our distraction because I haven't seen the red rider since, but I doubt our hunter will give up so easily. I just have to hope luck continues to be on our side. A day of rest is about all that we can afford before we need to move on.

I was able to bring some cooked fish and rabbit with us in one of the saddlebags, but that will only give us a few days, unless we miraculously find something edible out here. We will have to ration it to prolong our stay in The Wastes. The longer we can hide here, the higher our chances of losing our tail.

I have the workings of a plan in progress, but there are a lot of ifs involved. Lucia once mentioned the little homestead she grew up on, how it was situated in a valley between two mountains, near a large lake. After I was forced to leave the ashram without any warning, the first thing I did back at the compound was search our database for the place, based on the location of the mountain fortress of the Amilign and potential locations that fit her description and would be easily accessible by the helicopter they love to use. I found a few potential lakes that could be near her home, and one within range of where Nayne and I are currently located. So if we stay in The Wastes, heading south for about ten miles, then we can exit The Wastes into the Range, a vast stretch of mountains that extends for miles and marks the last true and untouched remnant of the old world. It would be another twenty miles or so to reach the lake.

I am taking a lot of chances, but I don't have anything else to go off. Fingers crossed, it will be her lake and we will find her farmstead. Even better if her Aunt Sid still lives there and we can hatch a plan to get Lucia away from the monks. I hate to delay, but I can't risk taking Nayne to the creepy ashram. I need her somewhere safe first. At the very least, there will be a body of water and I can hunt with my bow.

Nayne sleeps in the corner of the ruined building, curled up in the sand, still exhausted from the long journey on foot into The Wastes. After exiting the river, which we floated down for an entire day, we walked for another day before reaching the boundary of The Wastes. It was an additional day's journey into the depths of The Wastes before we stumbled across the ruins. By that point, Nayne was dead on her feet.

I watch her chest rise and fall steadily. I hope I can give her the future she deserves. My mind is a storm of emotions, mixed with memories that won't stay buried and what-ifs for the future. Sleep is not on the radar for me, especially now that the sun is parting from the horizon and beginning its ascent into the vast blue sky.

As I stare out into the imposing nothingness of The Wastes, a sense of unease causes the hair on my arms to rise. Ice coats my veins. I can't tell if it's my instincts warning me, or if it's just the nature of this place grating on me. Either way, I am on edge now, scanning my surroundings for movement.

It's been a while since I did a full perimeter search. I need to ease my mind that someone isn't sneaking up on us. With one last look at Nayne, I wrap a makeshift scarf around my head and face to protect myself from the strong winds and sand that inevitably rise to pebble any exposed skin. I grab my bow and quiver, then sling my short sword across my back. I check that I have my tactical knife, a blade with an intricately carved handle gifted to me by Sloane before she disappeared, in its sheath on my thigh. Then I head out of the shelter and around the other side.

The back of the building hides no surprises. I am scanning the surrounding area, paying close attention to anything potentially hiding in the sand dunes, when I see a dark spot appear, soon becoming a big male torso. The figure makes his way up the largest hill. He's still a good distance away, but far too close for comfort. My stomach sinks as I recognize the leathers and hood of the hunter.

I try to squash how shaken I am at how swiftly he found us. There's no time for emotions. I quickly nock an arrow and take aim, watching as he pulls a wide-bladed short sword from his back, twirling it skillfully.

The bold man doesn't stop walking toward me, despite my arrow aimed at his head. I pull back my elbow. I don't have the luxury of hesitation this time—there may be others hidden in the dunes. I let the arrow fly, my aim always true. He spins the blade in front of him, knocking the arrow to the side as if it were a mere fly annoying him.

I nock another arrow and let it loose, and he does the same. I pick up speed, shooting as quickly as I can while retaining accuracy, and he just keeps knocking them away. My increasing ire battles with awe at his skill.

He's closer now. I can make out a stubbled jaw, although most of his features are still hidden by the hood. Even so, I can see he's a brute, well over six and a half feet. I'll have to draw him away from the building. Nayne is my priority, and I can't fight him if my attention is divided. I sheath my bow on my back, pull the short sword from my back, and charge up the dune.

He stops walking, angling his sword toward the sand. As I get closer, I slip the tactical knife from my thigh sheath and throw it at him. The blade flips end over end, an expert throw aimed at his eye. I watch in awe or horror as he moves his head to the side and plucks the blade out of the air. It takes everything in me not to stop and let my jaw drop.

I've never been able to do that.

I ready myself, knowing the blade is headed back to me. He brings it forward and releases it, but I dive out of the way. I expected a headshot, but he aimed at my upper thigh, as if to maim me. As it is, he's nicked my favorite pair of fatigues.

"You arsehole!" I shout from my place on the ground, the scarf I wore for protection now lying loosely around my shoulders. "You ruined my favorite pants!"

He stares at me, his head tilting, as if he's taking my measure. I grip my blade and lunge to my feet, launching forward with the sword. But he meets me, strike for strike.

For some bizarre reason, he's not going on offense, only defense. Which only pisses me off more. Why is he toying with me? With dizzying speed, I lunge and slash with the sword, only succeeding in tiring myself out in this hot, unforgiving sun that took no time at all to begin blazing. I know better than to allow emotions into a fight, but I am tired from travel, lack of sleep, and little food, all a terrible combination for trying to win a fight.

Outmaneuvering me, he grabs the wrist of my hand that holds the blade, squeezing until I involuntarily let go. He twists my arm up behind my back, limiting any movement and pressing my body against his, all the while grabbing my other arm in his free hand.

At that moment, a gust of wind blows. My red hair stirs and billows around my head and the hood on the mystery man's face falls back, exposing bright hazel eyes that bore into mine.

Seconds turn into minutes as we stand frozen, staring at each other, our chests heaving from the fight. After the shock of his captivating eyes wears off, I notice that he's annoyingly, jaw-droppingly gorgeous. Dirty-blond, wind-blown hair, a bit shaggy on top but short on the sides, is complemented by a chiseled jaw. Any hostile words die on the tip of my tongue as I try to corral my traitorous thoughts. He looks as though he was carved out of stone by Heaven itself. Or maybe hell. After all, beauty is a great deceiver. Like the shiny red exterior of a perfectly formed apple, a beautiful mask can conceal rotten fruit beneath.

I feel like a bug under a microscope with his gaze burning into me. Chest to chest with him, the weight of his warm hand on my wrist is like a brand. But those eyes are like a tether that has grabbed hold of me.

Then something in his gaze shifts, a softening with a

dash of what looks like confusion. A wave of wariness sweeps through me. What is happening? This has to be a dream. The air feels charged, almost like this is something tangible. As if I could reach out and grasp this moment.

The emotion within me . . . it almost feels like hope.

A shuddering breath wracks my body, and to my horror, a tear rolls down my cheek.

CHAPTER 6

MORDECAI

A victim of her wiles, that's what I am. It's the only way to explain the lead weight of my tongue, unable to form words, and the fact that I am still gripping her wrist and staring at her like some mute doofus. But when the wind stirred up her hair right as the light cut through the haze, highlighting the dusting of freckles on her skin and those vibrant green eyes, my chest felt like it was in a vice, the air stolen from my lungs.

But it was more than that. Something unknown seemed to grab hold of me. Like her spirit was calling to me, recognizing a kindred spirit in my own, maybe. I can't put my finger on it and it's got me feeling off-kilter.

This fierce redhead just tried to kill me, and she is no unskilled warrior. She is a fighter to her core. The ferocity with which she fired those arrows was absolutely incredible, and, I might be ashamed to say, boiled my blood in the wrong kind of way considering I was fighting for my life. What is wrong with me?

When I threw that knife back at her, I was immediately filled with horror, and then relief that I missed.

And I don't miss. Ever.

Then the scarf fell away and those fiery words fell from her mouth and I was bewitched.

So here I stand, dumbstruck, her unreal green eyes like windows to her soul. They mesmerize me like the first sight of the sun after a lifetime lived in darkness. Her shuddering breath affects me more deeply than I care to admit. A lone tear treks down her cheek and my heart cracks into tiny pieces that crumble to dust in my chest.

Out of pure instinct, I lean forward to brush the tear away. Her warm breath caresses my fingertips, but then a loud crack splits the air, coming from beneath us. We both tense as numerous cracks tear through the silence. I look around us to try to discern what is happening. Her eyes grab mine again, wide with fear, and then we are falling.

It is impossible to tell up from down. Sand is pouring in all around us, and I sense a vast cavern beneath us. A yawning maw that opened up to swallow us whole. Luckily, I had the mental fortitude to hold on to her wrist when we started to fall.

I pull on her, trying to corral this wild thing into my arms so I can protect her. Telling myself it is purely so I can question her and learn more about the enemy, which I will be unable to do if she dies. But like biting into something rotten, the word enemy suddenly feels alien and wrong.

A sharp blade lashes out at me from the darkness, slicing my arm and surprising me into letting go. The resourceful girl must have grabbed her knife in the fall.

As much as I admire that, I will not be killed by this fall and she most likely will, since it feels like we've been falling forever. Again, I attempt to grab at her leg and get a kick to the jaw for my efforts.

Frustration rises and I do the only thing I can. I grab her jacket from behind her and manhandle her into my arms. I wrap my legs around her and effectively pin her arms to her side.

And not a moment too soon. I feel and hear the impact of my back against a hard surface. It knocks the wind out of my lungs. An agonizing fire shoots through my chest and my seal pulses with Ginger's desire to protect. The force of the impact sends the girl flying from my arms.

As my eyes begin to dim, the last image I see is of beautiful green eyes and red hair, disappearing over the edge of yet another gaping drop into darkness.

CHAPTER 7

Soft, hazy light dances through the darkness as I slowly blink my eyes open. The light is a welcome distraction to the throbbing pain in my back, head, and legs. In fact, finding an area that doesn't hurt at this point is difficult.

Taking a deep, rattling, and painful breath, I pull myself to sitting, muffling the yell that tries to force its way from my throat. The last thing I need is unwanted attention from any new threats.

My breathing feels labored—like I am breathing air through a straw. I press a hand to my side. The knifelike throbbing that steals what little breath I have suggests I probably have a broken rib that most likely punctured a lung. Great. Not a deadly injury for a Horseman with supernatural self-healing powers, but it's definitely an inconvenient kink in my plan to get out of here.

Where am I?

I look around the dimly lit cavernous space. Everything is coated in a thick layer of dirt and sand, but some of the unnatural shapes and surfaces suggest a man-made space. I move my hand through the dirt by my side, sweeping it away to reveal a smooth, hard surface, like a polished tile of some kind.

My mind is fuzzy on what happened to land me here. I try to sort through images. I remember gorgeous green eyes and copper hair, a loud crack, and the feeling of falling. I remember a frenzied urgency to save the girl and grabbing hold of her before slamming into something. Then the last image I have, of her continuing to drop downward, sends a chill through my veins.

Carefully, I hold my side and stagger upright. My vision threatens to plunge me into darkness again, but I stand still, breathing as deeply as my damaged lung will allow, and will myself to stay conscious. When I am convinced I won't return to dreamland, I make my way to the edge of the hole where the girl continued falling.

Looking down, there isn't much light to reach the depths, but it is enough to recognize fair skin, a leg twisted at an odd angle, and no movement.

My chest feels tight, and even more surprisingly, my seal is pulsing with Ginger's urgency to come to the rescue. Yet I sense it is not only me she is concerned about.

"Lavo Veshuv," I say softly.

Before I can blink, Ginger's soft muzzle is pressing up against me as she snorts and tosses her head.

"Whoa there, girl, I am not exactly in great shape right now," I wheeze. "Let me think for a minute. I need to figure out a way down to her."

As I look around, Ginger lies down to make it easier for me to mount her. We carefully make our way around the area until I see what appears to be some sort of ramp leading down. Definitely man-made—it has handrails—and as I take in more of the surroundings, I realize we must have fallen through the glass roof of an old shopping mall or office space, long ago buried by the constantly shifting sands of The Wastes.

It is a bit like being inside a time capsule.

Ginger reaches the bottom level, and I realize the center of the space is a tall, open atrium. I must have landed on one of the upper levels, and the girl wasn't so lucky.

We pick up the pace to get to her. Ignoring the pain, I slide off right as we reach her, lying too still on a pile of sand.

Seeing all the sand around her instead of hard ground gives me a spark of hope that her landing was soft enough to save her from serious injury. I ease myself down by her side and check for a pulse. The strong beat under my fingers forces a relieved exhale from me.

She's alive, but unconscious.

With her completely out, I figure now is as good a time as any to see what I can learn about her. She might not let me get so close once she's awake.

First, I check her hands. She bears the rough calluses and short nails of someone who's used to working hard, probably in training with weapons, given how skillfully she fought me earlier. Her red hair lies mostly in a fan around her head. I sweep away the few strands covering her face to take in the smattering of freckles across her nose and cheeks. My finger wantonly lingers against the soft, satin warmth of her skin.

Whoa, I need to get it together. This girl is the enemy, for crying out loud, and she repeatedly tried to kill me. I shake my head to clear the nonsense and try to focus on clinically inspecting her for more injuries.

I see a scar on her collarbone—it looks like it was caused

by a sword or knife. She also has small scars on the tops of her hands and a few on her arms. This fierce woman has not shied away from a fight. How did she end up in the FP? They have a reputation for "rescuing" young girls who have nothing and no one. But our sources discovered a nastier part to the story. The FP's corrupt leadership has been scouting strong prospects to join their ranks, and families that aren't on board with the forced adoptions frequently disappear or are killed in suspicious circumstances, leaving the FP to claim the girls.

Just another example of how power corrupts. Which only makes me wonder how deep this girl's allegiance to the FP goes.

Seeing her leg twisted the wrong way, I swiftly adjust its position, setting the bone in the correct alignment, something I learned long ago from the healers that live with the Prophets of The Way. The action elicits nothing but a swift inhale from her.

It is kinder to do it while she is out, even though I could use the injury to my advantage while questioning her. But at the thought, my stomach immediately threatens to rid itself of its contents.

A soft sigh escapes her mouth, and it does funny things to my insides. The way this girl affects me is far from normal. Is there more going on here?

I was restless and jittery before I left The Refuge, in a way I'd never experienced before. At the time, I chalked it up to simmering anger at what was done to Lucia, but now I wonder if it has more to do with the green-eyed beauty that lies before me.

Suddenly, a very relevant piece of the prophecy comes to mind . . . *the Cores have been marked by Heaven.*

Lucia once spoke about the mark on the back of her

neck that resembled the Holy Star. Well, no time like the present. Gently rolling the girl's lithe form onto her side, I shift her silky hair out of the way, trying to ignore how it feels in my hand. The glimmer of hope evaporates when I see nothing on her nape.

So, not a Core after all.

I gently roll her onto her back again, being mindful of her leg.

The range of my tumultuous emotions distracts me, but before I have time to lament this girl's lack of a mark, a sharp blade digs into my neck. A drop of blood trails slowly down my neck, while my eyes lock onto blazing green ones.

I put my hands up in surrender. She shifts onto her free elbow and glares at me with a ferocity that sucks the oxygen from the surrounding space and causes a surge of energy to roar through my veins.

CHAPTER 8

ANSEL

I hold my knife steady against his throat, shaken at having woken to his hands on my body. His face is a mixture of surprise, irritation, and curiosity. I don't know if he was checking me for injuries or if he had more disturbing motives. I attempt to calm the drumbeat of my heart, my fight-or-flight response urging me to take control of the situation. But there's a throbbing in my leg that suggests an injury and I am not sure what to do with that information as bright hazel eyes—a kaleidoscope of browns, golds, and soft greens—penetrate the haze of my thoughts.

A soft whinny pulls my gaze from his and I am completely dumbfounded to see a giant red horse standing behind the man. Even more surprising is how he is completely unconcerned by the animal's presence. Ironically, it bears an uncanny resemblance to the horse that likes to invade my dreams on occasion.

Am I hallucinating? What is happening? Where am I?

The last thing I remember is falling, and then warm,

solid arms pulling me against a firm chest before we slammed into a hard surface. Then I was falling again, and then nothing.

"Um, I hate to interrupt your murderous train of thought, but my hands are clearly up in surrender, so do you mind lowering your knife? I don't need any more injuries right now."

Anymore injuries? I wonder how this guy is even alive right now, let alone looking completely unharmed.

I ignore his request and keep my blade in place. My gaze firmly locks on him again. "Who are you? Why were you trying to kill me?"

The big man sighs, as if in resignation. "My name is Mordecai Cascus and I am the Red Horseman of War, but you can call me Cai. And technically, you attacked me first, remember? But despite that, I still saved your life."

My mind begins sifting through the memories, trying to sort fact from lie. Distracted, I'm slow to react to what comes next. Before I can think, he's got my wrist in a vice grip, and I watch helplessly as the blade drops to the sand. He's disarmed me again. He kicks the blade away from us.

I throw my fist at his temple in an attempt to free myself, but the movement causes me to shift forward, jerking my injured leg and sending a flare of pain through my body so intense, I completely miss. A sharp gasp bursts from my mouth, and I suck in ragged breaths as I try to get back into a position that doesn't hurt. I squeeze my eyes shut.

"Your leg is broken. I set it while you were out. You're welcome." He stands and dusts off his legs.

I open my eyes to glare at him. "If you are such a saint, why'd you follow me into The Wastes?" I seethe. "I am not naive enough to believe it was for altruistic reasons. I've seen enough of the world to know the true heart of men. You were hunting me."

At that comment, his eyes brighten impossibly and a flicker of indignation crosses his face. Then he schools his expression, once again stoic and emotionless.

"The heart of men, huh? You're one to talk. You're a part of the Feminea Potentia, for crying out loud." He crosses his arms, highlighting his bulky muscles as shadows appear to deepen around him. "The FP claim to be protectors of the weak, but it's no secret that you are murderers who steal young girls from their families and exploit the weak. The occasional good deed doesn't make up for the evil you've committed. I'd have done the world a favor if I let you die in that fall."

My blood boils. I know that the FP has plans to turn me over to the Amilign, to betray me, but the overall mission of the FP is supposed to be good and just. Could there have been more dark things going on that I just didn't see?

Confusion wars with shock in my mind. I flick through memories for evidence to support his claim. I think back to the day that Nayne was brought in. She was clearly stunned, and tears had left their mark on her cheeks. It took days for her to talk, and she woke up with nightmares for weeks following her arrival. Gemini never explained what had happened or how they'd found her. And she'd only allowed her top Lieutenants to accompany her on the retrieval mission, which was very unusual.

Shame spreads through me at the realization that if the FP were willing to exploit and kill their own, then of course they'd be willing to do the same to others. Their alliance with the monks only confirms it.

Could I really have been so unaware of what was going on that I didn't see the truth until it was too late? How could a total outsider know more about the FP than someone who's lived with them since infancy? But his last comment gives me pause.

"So why didn't you let me die, then?" I scowl at him through the veil of self-loathing.

His face is a conflicted mask as a muscle in his jaw clenches. "Because I am not like you. I don't exploit weakness. You would have died in that fall; I wouldn't. It seemed only right to help you. Plus, I have questions you're going to answer for me." His eyes narrow.

I laugh darkly. "Yeah, good luck with that, Mr. High-and-Mighty. You may think you're better than me as you sit on your seat of judgment knowing absolutely nothing about me, but I am in The Wastes because I fled the FP. I know nothing about what the leadership is planning. I only found out they planned to betray me right before we fled."

"We?" he asks.

I pause, breaking eye contact with him as I use my arms to shift my position in the sand, stalling for an answer. He had to have seen Nayne when he was hunting us, but if in the midst of all that's happened, he's forgotten, I don't want to jog his memory. I don't know what this guy is capable of.

"Yes, me and my horses. Both of which I was forced to leave behind, including all the supplies the second one was carrying, thanks to you tracking me. So good luck getting your questions answered. Sounds like you know more about the FP than I do." Not a single thing about his expression and body language says he believes me, but thankfully, he doesn't ask specifics about Nayne.

"And I am just supposed to believe that you had no clue what was going on around you? That you weren't part of plots to harm innocents and conspire with the Amilign, despite living with the FP? You may think you are brave for staying quiet, keeping your secrets safe." He crouches down and leans in closer, his breath on my cheek as he speaks in a low, steady voice. "But I am the Horseman of War. And I always win. I have ways of getting what I want."

I curse the shiver that crawls down my spine, mostly because it is not due to fear but his proximity. There is only a sliver of space between us, and I can feel the heat coming from his body. Tension pulls taut between us like a rope about to snap. His scent, a mix of sandalwood and citrus, settles around me, threatening to distract me. It takes everything in me to maintain my composure.

"Why wait?" I grit out. "I have nothing to hide from you, whether you believe me or not. So make your assumptions, torture me for information I don't have. You'll be just like them."

I sit there in the dirt, feeling more exposed and vulnerable than I can ever remember as he looks at me like something foreign he wishes to analyze. I want to rage, fight him with a sword again, or storm off; get away from his infuriating presence and the unwelcome sensations he elicits from me. But with a broken leg and no weapons, I am not going anywhere.

Since fleeing the FP, I haven't slowed down long enough to think about all that has transpired. After the initial shock, I protected myself by pushing it all behind a door in my heart and locking it tight. The FP have trained me to suppress distracting emotions during a battle. But now, I can't seem to focus on anything else.

Cai's face seems to soften as he takes in my expression.

"Look, I won't hurt you. I just want to get my questions answered and find the true enemy in this situation so I can rid the world of its influence. And despite my experiences with you thus far, I don't really believe that enemy is you."

I blink.

"Why?" My brows furrow.

"I am good at rooting out evil, and I don't sense that in you. Something in my spirit keeps telling me to protect you, and I believe it's Elohim Shomri guiding me. He is the One who protects."

Something pricks the back of my mind, reminding me of past conversations with Lucia. The sense of familiarity in his words unsettles me. But crowding that out is the indignation I feel that this man sees me as a fragile damsel in distress in need of his protection.

"Look, buster, I have been taking care of myself far longer than you can imagine. I do not want or need your help. And I definitely don't need your protection."

"Buster?" He smirks. "You can drop the prideful act. You're a fierce warrior capable of holding her own. But the fact is that you have a broken leg. So whether you like it or not, you do need my help. And you may have information that I can use. We can work together and help each other, or you can be a stubborn pain in the ass and I'll go my own way." He arches a brow in challenge.

Gah, this guy is infuriating! Even more so because he has a point. I will die before I admit that to him. Instead, I sit on my pile of sand and glare in his direction, chin lifted high.

"Fine," I spit out at him. I am annoyed by the situation I find myself in and, even more so, by my own childish behavior. I blame the pain in my leg and this frustrating man who excels at exasperating me.

"Look," he says, "I get it, the world is ugly and you don't trust me. That's fine. But you know I tried to save you when we fell and I've not tried to harm you since I found you wounded and vulnerable." A pointed glare at my less-than-ideal position on the ground.

I will myself to relax a bit—he's right. And I am in no position to fight him anyway. In fact, I am utterly exhausted from fighting. It feels as though my entire life has been one big battle, at least since losing Sloane and Mina.

The crack in my chest deepens.

With an agitated huff, he turns and walks away, one hand bracing what I assume is an injured side. The big red horse follows. Of all the things that could be going through my mind in this moment, I am dismayed by my brain's complete focus on the movement of his muscles underneath his shirt. The strong lines so clearly visible under a thin cotton layer reveal a statuesque male form that suggests a high level of physical discipline. Even his facial features are genetically blessed. A chiseled jaw with a light, stubbly growth surrounds full lips. And hair that reminds me of a wheat field during the golden hour of sunset, short on the sides and long on top, swept back from his face.

I shouldn't notice all these things. But I do.

How dare he have the audacity to look like that and be the enemy.

But as I recall his earlier words, I wonder if that's really the case. If he's hunting the FP and I am running from the FP, maybe we're not quite the enemies I initially thought we were.

Though I don't have the luxury of hopeful wishes and optimistic plans. I have met too many people who claim to be one thing but the truth is a far darker story. Words are often meaningless; it is real action that speaks volumes.

I suppose I am a bit jaded, but after the betrayal I've experienced at the hands of the FP, it is taking all of my efforts to not let it break me fully. And I am just so tired from having to hold myself together.

So I will let Cai help me, seeing as I don't have a choice. But I won't be reckless. I will keep my armor in place and be prepared for the moment of his betrayal. After all, there is someone whose protection and survival depends on me, and I will not let her down. I only hope I won't be too late to save her.

Even though I am not sure what I believe, but knowing it can't hurt, I say a quick prayer to Lucia's Elohim that He will take care of Nayne until I can be reunited with her again.

CHAPTER 9

ANSEL

It's unsettling. Being buried under the sand like this, in a place long forgotten to time. Like so much of the old world, I imagine. The choking scent of dusty, stale air saturates the space. It feels devoid of even the smallest bit of life. Not even the wind stirs here.

Like a monstrous, gaping jaw lined with jagged teeth, the vast hole looms above, allowing the bright sun to illuminate the space. I find myself fascinated by the way the light cuts through the darkness. Defiant, it pierces the vast, inky blackness.

I envy the light. To stand strong against such an overwhelming foe without dimming. To change the space around oneself.

I want that.

Maybe if I was like that, I wouldn't be running for my life from the only home I'd ever known. Maybe I'd still have Mina and Sloane. What I wouldn't give to be like light, persisting amidst the darkness.

The sound of shifting sand pulls me from the spiral of my thoughts. Cai is digging, presumably searching for any supplies that came in with us when we fell. I am surprised by how deeply he reaches his arms into the sand piles to search. There isn't much I fear, but the thought of the rest of the glass breaking and burying me alive or impaling me has definitely crossed my mind. I am eager to move away from the damaged glass that stands like the sharp teeth of a monster far above.

With that thought sliding tentacles of fear into my heart, I slowly begin the excruciating task of dragging my body away from the sand. It's a slow and tedious process; each pull of my arms strains my injured leg, sending white-hot pain radiating outward. Down my calf and into my foot; up my thigh and into my hip.

It's torture, but I manage to pull myself enough of a distance from the opening above that if another piece breaks off to dump in more sand and glass debris, I won't immediately be buried. I stop at the point the surrounding darkness begins to cradle me like a long-lost lover.

I'm breathless, and sweat beads on my forehead from the agonizing movement. I pause to collect myself.

"Where are you off to . . . I never caught your name?" A quizzical brow lifts at me over what couldn't possibly be a slightly concerned expression.

"It's Ansel. And I don't fancy being buried alive if more of that glass breaks. Or even worse, impaled. At least this way, I have a bit of a head start getting out of the way."

Cai considers me for a moment before returning to his work. He pulls my bow and quiver free from the sand. My heart leaps at the sight of it, intact. Cai's eyes meet mine. I wait to see what he'll do now that he has my weapon of choice.

Striding down the small mound of collected sand, he moves toward me, each step confident and purposeful. He stops at a pile of our stuff to grab a bundle of items and then continues toward me.

I try to ignore the fluttering deep in my belly. I school my features into a calm, collected countenance, attempting to hide the storm of emotions that seems to rise to my too-expressive face in his presence.

He stops before me and begins to remove his belt. Panic grips me as the truth of his intentions slams into me. I pull myself away from him in earnest, looking for something, anything I can use as a weapon.

He freezes, his face a mask of confusion. Then his expression switches to one of shock and horror. He holds up his hands again, his eyes softening almost imperceptibly.

"No, you don't have to fear me." He pauses, seeming suddenly unsure, rubbing the back of his neck. "It's not what it looks like." He kneels before me. "If you'll allow me, I would like to brace your leg. It will help with the pain and healing, and allow you easier movement. I was going to use my belt to secure it." His eyes plead with me to understand.

I blink.

He is so unexpected. I don't quite know what to say, so I just nod.

Still on his knees, he pulls his belt free, then extracts a piece of fabric from the bundle he grabbed, tearing strips from it and setting them next to me. He grabs two arrows from my quiver and quickly snaps the heads off them, causing a gasp to fly from my mouth. He lifts his eyes to mine, smirking as if he knows how attached I am to those arrows—one warrior to another.

Approaching me as if I am a wounded, wild animal, he gently grasps my leg behind the knee, lifting it carefully.

The sharp pain pulsing through my thigh is dimmed by the warmth of his hand.

I hold back a wince as he wraps my leg tight with the strips of cloak, the solid wood of the arrows holding my leg firmly. Knotting the fabric in two places to secure it, he takes his belt and sets to tightens it around the break in my leg. A sharp inhale escapes me and I squeeze my eyes shut against the flare of pain.

"All done." He stands and before I can protest, he gently scoops me up into his arms, clenching his teeth to hide his pain.

"Should you be doing this? You're injured, too, right? Honestly, I am surprised you're not more injured."

"It's minimal for a Horseman, more an inconvenience than anything."

I want to think more on this *Horseman* business, but I am overwhelmed by the sensations of him everywhere. His warm hands on my body, his breath across my cheek, his scent surrounding me. I feel like my brain is short-circuiting. What surprises me most is that panic doesn't grip me as it should. There is definitely a part of me that wants to push him away, but another, and, I fear, stronger part, wants to draw him closer. It feels traitorous and wholly concerning.

He carries me to a bench a little farther from the light, but very much out of the way of the broken ceiling.

"I hope you're not afraid of the dark?" he says.

A short, abrupt laugh erupts from me. I've spent so much of my life fighting the dark. And, in a way, it is the darkness that has shaped me into who I am today.

"Darkness and I are old friends. It may be known for breeding monsters, but sometimes it creates warriors like me instead." I freeze at my revelation, heat rising to my cheeks.

I definitely don't know this guy enough to be sharing pieces of my soul with him. I'm too easily disarmed around him, and it flusters me.

He looks at me quizzically, then leans my bow and quiver against the bench by my side, within arm's reach, only confusing me further.

The red horse that bears an eerie similarity to the horse of my dreams chooses that moment to approach, and a thousand questions flood my mind.

"So, this is your horse?" I ask. "How'd she get down here? Did you find a way out?" Hope fills me at the thought of an escape from this place, a way back to Nayne.

"Yes, she is mine," he says warmly, with a glance at the beautiful red horse. "She's a part of me, so she fell in with us. And no way out just yet."

My hope drifts away like the dandelion fluff I used to blow into the breeze as a child when Mina would take me away from training and let me be a kid. I quickly shake off the memory, not ready for the surge of emotions that is sure to accompany the image.

The horse walks over to me, her nose coming down to sniff my face. Her soft, fuzzy lips are like velvet and tickle my cheek, bringing a smile to my face. I've always loved animals, especially horses. She is a bright spot in this dark hole.

I bring my hand up to her soft nose and plant a kiss on her bright red hair. I suppress the desire to mention how similar she is to the horse of my dreams. Not sure what sort of omen that could represent, and I'm definitely not ready to explore that thought.

Surely, it is just a coincidence.

"What did you mean she's a *part* of you?" I lift my eyes

to Cai and the sheer longing and hunger in his gaze threatens to ignite me on the spot. He seems unmoored by my actions or my question, I can't quite discern. But he takes a deep, shuddering breath, his jaw clenching. A myriad of emotions flit across his face that look an awful lot like confusion.

There is a story there, I am sure.

He clears his throat. "I bear a seal on my back that holds my power as the Horseman of War. It's the location of my mount when I don't need her."

I stare at him, stunned, trying and failing to process his comment. Nothing makes sense. A headache starts to form behind my eyes. I close my eyes as I rub at my temples.

He lets out a laugh. "Don't think too hard. You don't want to hurt yourself again."

I open my eyes, doing my best to give him an annoyed, dead-eyed glare.

He laughs again and winks. "As I told you, I am a Horseman. Since she's a part of me, I can call on her when I need her, and she will physically manifest. Or I can send her back to me. Specifically, into the seal on my back."

I am sure my jaw is practically on the floor. No amount of schooling can get the shock off my features. I just had to end up trapped down here with a crazy person.

"How hard did you hit your head, Mordecai?"

"Call me Cai, and it's the truth; I can show you if you want. But something tells me you're not quite ready for that."

I hesitate. Something tells me he's probably right.

"Let's just table this conversation for now. Do you know where we are?"

"Not for sure, but we seem to have fallen into some sort of old mall or office space. I landed on an upper level, but the impact caused me to lose my grip on you." His eyes avoid mine and I am surprised to see a sheepish expression on his face, like he actually feels remorse for losing his grip on me.

Ignoring the conflicted feeling that observation stirs within me, I focus on the problem at hand. "Okay, so any thoughts on how we get out of here, or what our next move should be?" I quickly bypass any rumination on how easily the use of *we* and *our* flows from my mouth. And how a little kindness from him has begun to soften the ground around my barriers as if they were built on sinking sand.

"Well, Ginger and I are going to scope out the immediate area and see if there's an obvious way out we can't see from here. I should probably scrounge around for some food, too. Send up a prayer to Elohim that He has some provisions for us." He turns away as his horse follows in his steps.

Again, flashes of past conversations with Lucia rush to the forefront of my mind, easing the wariness and disquiet I've been struggling with. Lucia is one of the best people I know, and considering where she's spent much of her life, it is a real miracle. She's occasionally spoken of an Elohim, and I wonder if this is a sign.

But I don't really believe in that stuff. And yet, something about Cai and his words refuses to be ignored. Either way, I can't look too closely at him or any of this, not yet. I need no distractions from my goal. I have to get out of here so I can get Nayne to safety and find a way to get to Lucia. After all, they are all I have left in this world. I will not allow them to be taken from me, too.

"Thank you," I say to his back, "for helping me." He pauses, turning slightly to glance over his shoulder, and nods. Carefully, and with the ease of something practiced a thousand times, he vaults onto the red horse's back, leaving me with the turbulent storm of my thoughts.

This warrior has me captured in ways I am unfamiliar with and ill-equipped to handle. That worrisome thought festers as I watch the darkness swallow him.

CHAPTER 10

My exploration of our surroundings is not as fruitful as I hoped. There's no visible way out, and it's slim pickings around here when it comes to food. And with the sun starting to drop, light is fading fast in our already too-dim little underworld. I find a barely functioning water fountain that allows me to fill a canteen and some packages of nuts that I pilfer from an old vending machine. Everything else in there would be taking our life in our hands to consume it.

If I am honest, getting supplies and scoping out an exit was only an excuse. What I really needed was space from Ansel. Her encounter with Ginger has me completely rattled. Like my world has been thrown off its axis, and it is only made more confusing by her lack of a mark that would indicate she's a Core.

My heartbeats are like the pounding of Ginger's hooves against hard ground. What is happening to me? Am I so desperate for my Core that any beautiful girl will fill the need within me? Or is this just a distraction from the leashing? Am I getting so close to the edge that I can no longer trust my own starved heart?

It's not news to me that the leashing is getting harder and harder to resist. My brothers have always assumed that I'd have no problem because of my strong connection with Elohim. I feel drawn to know Him and be known by Him, and that relationship has always helped anchor me and give me strength.

But in the end, I am still a Horseman, fighting the leashing of darkness. And Elohim's way to save me is through my Core, same as my brothers. If anything, I have more reason to fear the leashing than my brothers *because* of my connection to Elohim.

Being leashed by hell would mean a permanent and eternal separation from Elohim and Malkhut Shamayim, the Kingdom of Heaven. Despite the fantastical stories, what truly defines hell is the complete absence of Elohim. Something this world has never experienced. And it is that thought that threatens to paralyze me.

Ginger and I head back to Ansel, and I try in vain to ignore the way my heart begins to beat a little faster at seeing her. I can't afford this distraction. I need to get my questions answered and get out of here. The sand in the hourglass of my control has begun to run out.

Although Ansel is technically an FP and doesn't bear the marking of a Core, something in me feels driven to protect her and bring her back to The Refuge. I don't understand it, but I am not one to question the guidance of Elohim.

I hop down from Ginger.

"Catch," I say, throwing a pack of nuts at Ansel. "It's

not much, I am afraid, but we are losing light fast. I'll do more searching tomorrow."

"Thanks." She looks at me with those bright green eyes that steal my breath. I glance away.

Sitting down on the bench across from her, I figure there is no time like the present to get some answers. I did bring her a peace offering, after all.

"So, what made you leave the FP for the glorious luxury of The Wastes?"

She fumbles with the packaging, heaving a heavy sigh as her hands pause in her lap. Her eyes lift to mine once again and the grief I see there is a war hammer to my chest. It is like the cresting of a massive wave that she has somehow kept from crashing, but that control will only last for so long.

"I lived with the FP far longer than most. I was a newborn, found in a village that had been decimated, and they took me in. Two of the FP—twin sisters—convinced the leader to keep me. I'll never know how they did it because the FP never takes girls below the age of five or six."

She pauses, and I can see the recollection of these memories is hard, like trudging through deep mud. Not hard because she can't remember, but because the pain of recalling them is acute. She looks down at her hands as she takes a deep breath and plows forward.

"These twin sisters raised me like I was their own family. Sloane was an aunt to me, and Mina was like my mother. So despite growing up in the FP, I had a good childhood because of them. Mina never truly belonged with the FP; her heart was too big and too bold for them."

I wait patiently, knowing the frequent use of *was* can only mean one thing.

"They disappeared without any explanation when I

was ten. I was told they never returned from a mission. Which I thought was odd, since they always told me when they were headed out. But I was young and Gemini explained it away, saying there hadn't been time for them to come by and fill me in on this mission, and they would probably return eventually. They never did.

"The day I left the FP, I overheard Gemini talking about how she *got rid of them* and how she should have done it earlier. She also admitted that she was planning on trading me to the Amilign for some weapons. So in a few moments, my whole world cracked wide open."

Any words of comfort I had planned to offer turn to ash in my mouth.

I had expected to have to argue with her to extract any valuable information. Instead, she's openly flayed herself before me, exposing her vulnerable heart. So unlike the warrior I know her to be, and it makes me think that this firecracker is tired of fighting. Of always warring and strategizing.

I can relate.

The thought that we have deeper things in common than us both being warriors catches me off my guard. She has a tough exterior, but there's a soft side hidden beneath. A side to her that she keeps buried, but like mining for rare gems, it's dazzling when it gets exposed to the light. Highlighting beautiful facets of the depth of her heart. Like the sweet tenderness she showed to Ginger. It's the last thing I expected, and the storm of confusion I've felt since meeting her spirals even more out of control.

"So you see," she continues, "I wasn't a part of their inner circle. I was just another tool for them to use and throw away. Other than trading me to the Amilign for advanced weapons, I don't know what their plans are. But I can promise you this: Once I get out of here and get my friend away from the Amilign, and get her and my little sister to safety, then Gemini will pay for her crimes. I'll make sure of it."

And just like that, the warrior is back, her green eyes brightening with rage. The boldness with which Ansel faces what life throws at her is inspiring. Her passionate spirit calls to me and it's just another confusing thing to sort through. Even now, the ferocity and protectiveness in her eyes are like a single match dropped into a tank of gasoline; only, my blood is the gasoline. But before my thoughts can head down a path they shouldn't, my attention is caught by one thing. A question I've been waiting to ask since falling in here with her.

"Are you referring to the child you were traveling with?"

She freezes and I watch, a bit in awe, as she carefully and expertly locks her shield into place, keeping me out in an admirable desire to guard and protect what she deems hers.

"It's nothing for you to worry about." She waves her hand, mustering up nonchalance as she avoids my eyes, but her face is so telling and I have already seen the depths of her heart. She can pretend all she wants. I know the truth.

"Why were you out in The Wastes, Cai?" She tries to steer the conversation in a different direction.

"Nice try." I smile. "I am happy to answer your questions when you answer mine. Who's this little sister? Is she in The Wastes? And you have a friend captured by the Amilign? I can't help you if I don't know the details."

She almost visibly enflames at my words, like a torch in the night. She holds herself as upright as her injured leg will allow. Her vibrant gaze pins me in place.

"I never asked for your help! And why would I trust you? You were hunting FP in The Wastes, Cai! And yet you want me to tell you all about my little sister who is FP. So you can *help*. Yeah, sure. Over my dead body will I ever put her at risk!" she seethes from her spot on the bench, her glare murderously protective.

"I would never hurt innocents, Ansel. I am not so single-minded to believe that even if the majority deserve punishment, that there wouldn't yet be those who were simply stuck in a bad situation. Never given the chance to choose a different path. And, being a Horseman, I am pretty good at seeing to the heart of a person. Believe what you will about me, but I was seeking the FP who plotted with the Amilign against my brother and his Core. So, from the sound of it, your enemies are mine as well. As for your friend, anyone stuck with the Amilign has my sympathy and sword. My brother's Core, now my sister, was forced to live with the Amilign for most of her life, and after discovering their plans for her, it would be my pleasure to unleash war upon them with you."

She relaxes a little bit at my words, as if sensing the conviction and truth behind them. "Well, I guess we have that in common then, because my friend was taken from her aunt as a child and forced to live with them as well. I met her when the FP visited the mountain ashram a few months ago. Even then, I wasn't privy to explanations as to why we were going to the Amilign. I was just supposed to focus on training, so that's what I did. But I almost sensed Lucia before I saw her, as if we were destined to be friends. In the few weeks the FP stayed there, we became fast friends. One of the hardest things I ever did was leave her behind."

I'm frozen, too shocked to offer any words of encouragement. Time ceases to move forward and I can barely hear myself think over the rush of blood in my ears. My mind rapidly combs through past conversations with Lucia, recalling her mention a friend who reminded her of Ginger because of the red hair.

It all starts clicking into place. The shock must be clear on my face because Ansel looks up at me with concern.

"What? What is it?" She looks around as if she can pinpoint what has me so shaken.

"Did you say Lucia?" I ask. She pauses, her brows furrowing, and nods slowly. "Long dark hair, striking golden eyes, and occasionally goes by Lu."

And now it is her turn to look shocked. Her jaw visibly drops and color leaches from her skin. If her leg wasn't broken, she'd probably be standing, or even pacing. "How do you know her? Where is she? Is she okay? Tell me every-thing." She leans forward, as if eager for news.

"I wasn't there; it was my brother Nicanor who found her. He's the White Horseman of Conquest. She fled the ashram and stumbled across him. He brought her to The Refuge of the Prophets of The Way, where she's been staying with us." I pause; I don't want to go into what she's been through. It's clear that Ansel has enough on her plate. Plus, it isn't my story to share.

I lean back against the bench, raking my hand through my hair. "This is wild. I remember her telling me about you. When I introduced her to Ginger, she got a little melan-choly and said my horse reminded her of her red-haired friend." I smile at the memory and comparison.

I glance at Ansel and watch as a bright smile lights up her face. It is the first time I have seen her smile, and it is as if a switch has been flipped. It's like she is gravity and I am suddenly the moon in orbit, willing or not.

My eyes take her in, but it's my soul that feels the

impact. A shudder racks me from head to toe as I grapple with the revelation. I don't understand what is happening, and based on what I have seen, this girl is not a Core. But my soul is telling me something different.

Who knew that in coming to The Wastes to find enemies, the real war I would battle would be within?

CHAPTER 11

ANSEL

It's been a few days since we fell into this bizarre space filled with mementos of a time long forgotten. Cai's done most of the exploring, seeing as he's actually mobile, and despite not finding a way out, he has come back with some very intriguing things, a few of which have been useful.

The clothing he picked out for me was helpful, and a surprisingly thoughtful gesture. More so because he got the sizes right and even picked out things I actually like. I try to shove down the memory of the butterflies that flit around in my belly following any encounter with him.

The most amusing discovery so far was when he broke into a space that reeked heavily of rotting flowers. I could smell him coming before I even laid eyes on him, a scowl on his too-handsome face. Apparently, he found an old bath store with products that had long since expired. That was the first time I had a genuine laugh since leaving the FP.

It's also been strange getting to know this guy who claims to be the Horseman of War, whatever that means. I hate to admit it, but my guard has lowered since I found out he knows Lucia. It is a huge weight off me, knowing she's no longer held captive by those creepy monks. But just because she is now with these Horsemen guys doesn't mean she is safe yet. I don't know enough about them, other than the fact that Cai might be delusional, which almost never equals safe.

I have to be cautious for both of our sakes.

Although he doesn't seem like a crazy person, I've been proven wrong about people before. But despite our first meeting over crossed swords, he's been nothing if not helpful, even weirdly protective at times, which has only added to the confusion and turmoil in me. I seem to be fighting an internal battle as to whether or not he can be trusted. Part of me wants to trust him, but then the other part urges caution toward a strange man whose true motives are unknown to me. It's all made even more challenging by the glaring fact that Cai is so damn likable.

I am a building whose foundation has been built on shifting sands.

It almost makes me miss when we were fighting above ground. At least then, all the cards were on the table. Now I feel like a detective on the hunt for signs of betrayal and sinister motives. Am I broken, incapable of believing there is any good left after everything that's happened?

A small voice tells me he's helpful and protective because he knows I am friends with Lucia, but it is quickly smothered by my deep desire for self-protection. Frankly, it's exhausting. Add the fact that I am terribly concerned about Nayne, and my mind has hardly let me have a moment's peace.

Thoughts of her wandering The Wastes looking for me, getting lost or worse, alternate with her thinking I abandoned her and heading back to the FP. I keep reminding myself she's smart and resourceful. She's a survivor—like me. But it's in my nature to protect and being stuck down here injured, vulnerable, and incapable is grating on me. And in reality, it doesn't matter how much I believe in her— the truth is there is no real food or water source in The Wastes and time was ticking away before I got myself stuck down here.

Before my thoughts can run away with more what-ifs, Cai is back from his latest exploration. He makes his way toward me, Ginger obediently following in his wake.

Sometimes he's riding her when he returns, but when I see her following him around like she is now, my lips twitch in amusement as I fail to stifle my smirk. The two of them together like this are an oddly comical sight. She looks like a big dog and makes him seem like a little boy with his pet. Which is far from the truth, but endearing nonetheless. As he gets closer, I notice he's carrying an awkward-looking contraption of some kind.

"You are going to want to kiss me when you see what I've found for you!" A rakish smile lights his face and blast that infernal man, he knows just what to say to make my face turn crimson. I swear he likes seeing me turn the color of a tomato. I give him a scowl in return that only makes him laugh.

One thing I've discovered about Cai since being stuck down here with him is he has a playful, easygoing side. At first, it surprised me, but it seems to be his true personality. The warrior is a mask he wears when needed. Like his armor, I suppose.

"I stumbled upon a store with contraptions for the body, which may come in handy, but specifically, I found this leg brace for you! Look, it has steel supports along the side and a knob at the knee, allowing you to turn it for movement or lock it for stability. Pretty cool, right?"

And damn it if he's not totally right. I could kiss him for bringing this back. The arrow shafts and fabric were nice, but this may actually allow me to move around easier and offer more security. The thoughtfulness of this big warrior is disarming and I don't know what to do with it.

As I take in the brace and look up into his warm hazel eyes, I am horrified to find myself overcome with emotion. I'm blaming exhaustion and pain because I am not a crier, I am a get-angry-and-punch-something kind of girl. And I am definitely not ready to accept the idea that my defenses may not be up to snuff, or worse, are not necessary in the first place. A tear slips down my cheek despite my best efforts, and I close my eyes and breathe deep to rein in my emotions.

A warm, rough-skinned hand cups my cheek, a thumb wiping away the tear, and it takes everything in me not to lean into his hand and deeply inhale his scent of sandalwood and citrus, which has far too quickly become a balm to my tattered nerves. I open my eyes and he's far closer than I expected.

He lowers his hand, eyes still locked on mine as silence stretches on. Then, without meaning to, I remember his strong, sure, and warm hands on my bare skin when he carried me. My thoughts shift to imagining those same hands moving up my back in a gentle caress. It's exciting and terrifying.

My face flushes at the heat now coursing through my blood. Yearning rolls down my spine as I inhale a shaky breath. Almost imperceptibly, Cai's eyes brighten and his nostrils flare as if he can smell my desire.

But he couldn't possibly, could he?

"Uh, I think it's time I show you the truth of what I told you before." His voice is husky and uneven, eyes blazing as if the sun is shining out from behind them.

"You mean the Horseman thing?" I question.

"Yeah." His hand rubs his nape and he looks sheepish. "I know you don't believe me, and this probably seems fantastical, but it's true. And you need to know that I am trustworthy."

All I can think at that is *I do, do I? And why would that be?* Searching again for a foul motive, always. But for the first time, I silence that voice. Instead, I nod.

"Okay, so the best way to do this is to just show you." And with that, he peels off his shirt.

It is times like this when I desperately wish my face wasn't so expressive. He is absolutely breathtaking, the physical embodiment of masculinity. Ruggedly sculpted, with a body that has been clearly forged through hours of training.

Although he says nothing at what I am sure is a wide-eyed, jaw-dropped, and potentially drooling expression on my face, a hint of amusement plays across his features. He turns his back to me and I take in the wide expanse of muscles on top of muscles that seem to cover him from his waistband to his neck. Most notable is a large tattoo of what looks like a horse hoof print and words from some unknown language, along with a green key in the center.

"What does your tattoo say?"

"It's actually the seal that holds Ginger, and when translated, the words mean 'I am he who wars.' Hence, the whole Horseman of War thing." He peeks over his shoulder and winks.

"Ooookaay," I draw out, struggling to form a proper

response. "I understand the horsehoof, but what about the green key?"

He visibly stiffens and then coughs or chokes, I can't quite tell, but a heavy silence now hangs in the air. He's trembling and I sense something raw and bright from deep within him.

But he says nothing. Ginger trots up and he runs a shaking hand through her mane. Concern suddenly grips me at this uncharacteristic unsettledness in him.

"Cai? Are you okay?"

His back to me, he nods. "Yeah," he says gruffly, pausing to clear his throat. "Let me just show you."

A few whispered words that sound like "Bame Lie," and a brilliant flash of red lights up the space. In the next blink, Ginger is gone.

I can barely hear myself think over the hammering of my pulse. He turns to face me and the intensity in his eyes makes me want to squirm.

"Now do you believe me?"

"I . . . Wha . . . How. . . Uh . . ." I stare at him stunned, my mind desperately trying to reconcile what I've just seen and running through my experiences with him over the past few days. He's the Horseman of War, apparently, which explains the exceptional fighter he is, the likes of which I've never come across. And maybe it explains how he was somehow not killed or seriously injured in the fall. And how his eyes seem to brighten in an almost otherworldly way at times of intense emotion.

He sits next to me, cautiously taking me in as if one wrong move will cause me to collapse like a stack of playing cards. I take a steadying breath, collecting myself.

"So, what does it mean to be the Horseman of War?" I look into his eyes, trying to assess the truth of what he's about to say and anchoring myself in this moment that I sense will be a monumental shift in my reality.

"There is an ancient prophecy that speaks of the end-time of this world. It says that when evil is unrestrained, four riders will be pulled forth out of necessity, created to lay waste to the world. Elohim created a loophole, if you will, in the form of a physical manifestation of His pure love, called the Four Cores. These Cores were created to be a sort of redemption of the purpose of the Horsemen, and instead of being leashed by hell for the destruction of every-thing, we would each be bonded to our Core and ride for the destruction of all evil and the redemption of the world, ushering in a time of Malkhut Shamayim, or the Kingdom of Heaven."

A heaviness seems to press on his shoulders as he lets out a sigh, rubbing the back of his neck, which I've come to realize is a sign of nervousness in him. "My brothers and I have been on earth for about a hundred years now, waiting for the prophecy to come to fruition. Every day, the internal battle that wages inside of us against the leashing of hell gets fiercer. Like the rattling of a beast inside a cage, demanding its freedom."

It doesn't escape me that he mentioned Elohim again. But my mind is abuzz with a million questions. I should be stunned by him having been on this world for a hundred years, but in light of his disappearing horse, it hardly seems that shocking. The most pressing matter seems to be this issue of the Cores. Whatever they are, it seems urgent that they are found and brought to the Horsemen.

"Okay, so if these Cores are so essential to keep you from being leashed by hell, then shouldn't this be your number one priority? Why were you in The Wastes fighting me if you should be out there finding this Core thing?"

"It's not as easy as it sounds. The Cores are not things." He pauses as his eyes seem to peer into my soul, and I get a keen sense of something deeper going on here, almost as if he's willing my spirit to see things unseen. "They are women. Hence, the *love* aspect of the prophecy. They are our balance in every way, bringing light to our darkness. And we won't know who they are until we meet them. Trust me, we have been looking for a long time." A note of reverence tinges his voice.

A spike of jealousy flares in me, and I hate to admit that a part of me is disappointed Cai is destined for another woman. But maybe it is for the best. I am far too drawn to this Horseman of War and can only imagine how badly this will end for me and for Nayne.

If there's one thing my years with the FP taught me, it's that men can rarely be trusted.

For every rumor of destruction that led us to save a town or village from some horror, it was always some power-hungry, corrupt man leading his followers to commit atrocities I wish I could banish from my mind. Cai may seem kind and so far he's been honest, but he's the Horseman of War for a reason. It's safe to assume I am only skimming the surface of all that he really is.

And I bet that when the time comes to bring the horrors of war to the few innocents left in this world, his nature will demand he be the champion of all destruction.

CHAPTER 12

Nothing has gone as I expected. Ansel's face and body language betray her—my revelation has only made her more cautious with me. I am baffled as to why. It's like I can see the progress we've made being blocked, and her armor falling into place once again. I am at a loss for how to proceed. And despite her not bearing the mark, the existence of the green key in my seal seems to confirm the truth my heart has been pounding away.

She has to be my Core.

Do I keep spilling the details and tell her my theory, or will that push her over the edge? Do I wait for more proof, ever the patient hunter? Giving her time to come to terms with everything and trust me? Or will time only firm up the barriers between us? I need Ruach, the breath and spirit of Elohim, to guide me in this. Saying a silent prayer, I feel a sense of peace wash over me and decide to plow forward.

"I know this is a lot to take in, Ansel, but I've never been worried about the prophecy. I trust Elohim's hand in everything. He guided me to The Wastes through the restlessness in my blood. He led me to you, even if I was confused by the reason at first, and even helped me to save you from death when we fell. I sense His leading even to this very moment."

Her brows furrow, confusion highlighting every feature of her lovely face.

"What are you saying?"

I take a deep breath—here goes nothing. "I believe you are my Core, Ansel. When you said that I had a green key in my seal, that only confirmed it. I did not have that key in my seal before I met you. Our seals change when we connect to our Core."

I watch as her wide-eyed expression shifts from shock to disbelief, finally landing on fury.

"I knew it! I knew you couldn't be trusted. How dare you try to manipulate me! You probably orchestrated the fall, didn't you? You wanted me trapped in here with you. To what end, Cai? What role am I to play in your wicked plans?"

My hands are up again in the old familiar position of surrender. It's not lost on me how for someone who's never surrendered, I've surrendered to her more times than I care to count.

"I don't know what you expect me to say. I've been honest with you. If I orchestrated this whole thing, don't you think I would have planned a way out of here? And why would I arm you if I have *wicked plans* for you? Have you forgotten that I retrieved your bow for you?"

Breathing out a weary sigh, I rake my hands through my hair. "Look, I am sorry if I scared you. I don't expect anything from you. I am not the kind of man to take anything from someone who is unwilling."

"What about this Core business and you fighting some leashing of hell thing?" Skepticism coats her every word.

"I will not lie to you, not ever; that is not who I am. I believe you are my Core, no matter what you may believe. The key in my seal is green because your eyes are green . . ."

But before I can finish, her face flushes crimson. "I don't belong to anyone or anything, not even some prophecy, you got it? I will not be some flower picked and left to die! I am my own person! I will never be controlled again." She is seething; her chin lifts in challenge. Even with an injury and from her seated position, she is a ferocious thing to behold. But it is the last word she spoke that steals my focus. *Again.*

Her reaction is about more than this moment, a lingering fear or trauma from her betrayal at the hands of the FP. It's clearly a wound that goes far deeper than she realizes. My chest aches over the pain that holds her captive. And I will do whatever it takes to make her feel safe and help her heal.

Kneeling in front of her and placing my hand on my heart, I look into her blazing green eyes and will her to feel the truth of my words.

"I will die before I force you into anything you don't choose of your own free will. And that is something the love of Elohim has taught me. Above all, I think I've shown I will protect you and help you however I am able. As for the leashing, I have not battled with it the way some of my brothers have. I believe my walk with Elohim has kept me more protected. I trust that He will guide me with His Ruach even now."

She stares at me for a long time. Her feverish eyes dart across my face, as if seeking a crack in the facade. Finally, as if she sees something that satisfies her, she gives me a quick nod. Desperate to see the tension leave her, I decide to call in the big guns.

"Lavo Veshuv," I whisper softly, and in a flash of light, Ginger stands before me. She knows my thoughts and feelings without a word, so she knows what's needed in this moment.

She slowly makes her way to Ansel, her soft nose lowering to Ansel's cheek as she gently nuzzles the girl. Ansel's hard exterior cracks, though I pretend not to watch; instead, I get the brace ready to put on her injured leg. When I glance up again, she has a hand under Ginger's big head and is gently stroking the horse, her forehead leaning against Ginger's muzzle, the red of her hair blending with Ginger's red mane. My heart squeezes at the sight of them together and I have to will myself to chill out.

The last thing I need to do is scare her away more.

"You'll see in time," she says. "I couldn't possibly be this Core you're looking for. I am not gentle. I am not warm and soft. I am nothing like Lucia; I am mostly jagged, broken pieces."

I don't tell her that I see the real her that she tries to hide. I don't confess that she is lightning, and I've been fighting darkness my whole life without her.

"Let's get your leg squared away so you can feel a bit more comfortable, if it's alright with you?"

"Okay," she says, so softly I almost miss it. It's a knife in my heart to know she was betrayed by those she trusted and that trauma is now the lens through which she sees everything. It makes me want to unleash war on what's left of that wretched group. For now, I'll have to be satisfied with taking care of Ansel.

Ever so gently, I unwrap the fabric binding her leg and unbuckle the belt. Her hand reaches down, rubbing the spots where the arrows were pressing against her leg. Her pants are covered in sand, which can't possibly feel good against her skin, but after what just transpired, there's no way I can suggest she change.

Instead, I bring the bag of clothes over to where she's sitting, her eyes ever watchful of what I am doing. I begin pulling items of clothing from the bag, setting them next to her, and continue sifting through the bag as though I am looking for something. At least now she can see the various pants that I brought from one of the abandoned stores. That'll have to be enough. As I get the brace fully opened and prepare to put it in place, she grabs my wrist.

"I need your help with my pants first," she says matter-of-factly. "There's sand in them from the fall and it's rubbing me raw in some spots. I don't want the same thing happening with this brace."

Secretly pleased that she's willing to trust me this much, I nod. "Okay, what do you need me to do?"

"Can you help me get these off? Then I'll put on one of the new pairs that you brought."

Nodding again, I watch as she undoes the buttons at her waist and begins to shimmy the worn, canvas-like material down her hips as she shifts side to side. My mouth goes dry and I quickly bring my eyes to the ceiling, looking anywhere but at her removing her clothes. Trying in vain to think of anything other than the sound of the fabric sliding against her satin skin.

"Cai, you need to look at me if you're going to help."

Swallowing the lump in my throat, I bring my eyes to her. She's gotten the pants down to her knees. Pulling my shoulders back with a determination to be purely clinical, I gently grasp the fabric and begin pulling it down to her ankles. Kneeling before her, I untie the laces of her boots and stretch them out so I can remove them without pulling on her leg. My fingertips slide around each foot, taking off the socks next and softly skimming her ankles.

My fingers graze the skin of her legs as I finish removing the pants. I am quickly becoming addicted to the feel of her skin. The quick intake of her breath tells me everything I need to know about how she feels about me, even if she isn't ready to admit it.

She coughs. "Let me just brush this sand off." I grab the new pair of pants and wait as she tries and fails to get the sand from her backside in a seated position. She seems to come to the same realization as her eyes meet mine.

"Uh, maybe you could help me stand on my good leg so I can reach the backs of my thighs?"

Not trusting my voice, I nod again. I hold out my arms and she grasps my biceps as my hands grab her sides, well above the wispy-thin undergarment hiding her lower half. I grit my teeth at the feel of her skin under my hands and her soft fingers gripping me. She releases her hold with one hand while the other clings to me. She twists at the waist, using her freehand to sweep off her backside.

It's not lost on me that even this requires a great deal of trust. Right now, I will take my wins where I can get them.

"Here, put your hands on my shoulders to steady your-self. It might be easier if I hold out the pants for you and slide them up, rather than you sitting in the dirt and dust again."

This time, she visibly swallows and nods while I lower myself in front of her, careful to keep my eyes on her feet. Opening the pants and helping her to position the injured leg, I begin to slide it up, almost reaching her knee when I realize we're kind of stuck. She can't put weight on her bad leg, and she needs to if I'm going to get the pants in position.

I look up into her eyes. "I know you don't completely trust me right now, but for this moment, will you trust me to at least help you get your pants on without hurting you?"

A look of exasperation wrinkles her brow and she rolls her eyes. "I may not understand your motives or trust your story fully, but I think I've already shown that I trust you with this, Cai. I am standing in front of you in my underwear, for goodness' sake."

Moving fast enough to avoid her protests, I press my shoulder into her stomach and stand, swinging her up onto my shoulder so her legs are both dangling in front of me, her hands on my back bracing herself. Before she has a chance to do anything but scoff, I bring the other pant leg up onto her good leg and then bend back down to gently place her on her good foot again.

I smoothly slide the pants up her strong, trim legs and take a step back with my arms out, offering her stability.

"Ta-da!" I smile at her.

Her lips twitch as she struggles to stifle a grin. Just as adeptly, I secure the brace to her leg. Even though she can't yet walk, the smile and hope that radiates from her at being able to move her leg more comfortably steals my breath and makes me want to do whatever it takes to see that expression on her face again.

And a spark of hope lights in me as well.

This will not be an easy journey, but my soul recognizes its partner in her, and I have faith in Elohim's design, that soon she will be unable to deny what is so clearly between us. And despite wanting to find a way out of here, I get the feeling that I shouldn't be in too much of a hurry.

So, in the meantime, I will be the patient hunter. After all, the most powerful weapon a warrior carries within is patience, and a mind and heart that are surrendered to it.

CHAPTER 13

MORDECAI

I have my work cut out for me with Ansel. There are moments when I think I am breaking through, only for the shield to fall back in place—which seems second nature for her. At least she's not trying to physically harm me anymore.

As Ginger and I wander through this mausoleum of the past, we have to pause every few feet to clear the dust from the glass walls and see what manner of goods each little nook offers while simultaneously searching for a potential exit. With my Horseman abilities rendered worthless, I'm stuck seeking ordinary methods of escape. So far, we've seen jewelry, a shop that once sold children's toys, and a few clothing stores.

No exits.

We continue to meander in hopes of finding something edible and more substantial than the dried fruit and nuts we are quickly getting sick of, but seeing how long ago this time capsule was buried, I am not expecting much.

Lucky for me, the next store I check is a jackpot. It seems to have once offered spices and seasonings, but along the back wall sits a variety of dried beans and pasta. There's not much, but it is something, and I am in no position to complain. I find a small metal bowl that I might be able to make into a pot. Now I just need to refill our canteens and we'll be set for a while. I've just finished loading the goods into a pack I pilfered earlier when a scream rends the air, turning my blood cold.

I throw myself back up onto Ginger—my lung and rib give only a twinge of pain with my body's quick healing at work—and she wastes no time getting back to Ansel. As Ginger pulls up, I see Ansel in a panic, dragging herself away from the benches we've been camped out on. She's removed her jacket and her shirt and now wears only a sports bra. I choke out a dry, humorless laugh, attempting to corral the wayward path of my thoughts while trying in vain to figure out what exactly I'm witnessing.

"Don't just stand there, help me!" she says in a frenzy, not making much movement on the dusty, sandy floors.

I head her way and dismount, not sure what she expects from me. "Help you do what, exactly?"

"There's some sort of bug in here; it was crawling on my back. It was black and huge and had a long, curled tail with some sort of stinger and pincers."

I bite my lips, attempting to squash the laughter that wants to break free. When I gain some semblance of control —and with a valiant effort to keep the amusement from my voice—I say, "Do you mean to tell me the fierce warrior is afraid of a bug?"

She bristles at my words and her glare turns deadly. If looks could kill, I'd be a goner for sure. And at that, my resolve dissipates and I burst out laughing, doubling over and holding my sides. That is, until I open my eyes and see said creature making its way toward me.

"Holy mutated harbinger monster!" I yell as I run to Ansel, scooping her up off the ground and hightailing it far away from the assumed area of origin that could be hiding more dark and disturbing secrets.

"Told you," she says smugly, her arms tightly wound around my neck as if she can prevent me from putting her back down on the ground. Little does she know, I am fighting the desire to keep her in my arms for the foreseeable future. Not just because holding her is a slice of Heaven, but I am unsettled by whatever that thing is. We've always known The Wastes to be a dark, twisted place, but I wonder when it started becoming home to monsters not of this world.

"That is not a bug! That sucker is the size of a rodent. It's like a scorpion mated with a crocodile or something."

Amusement and a bit of mischief play across her features. It is such a refreshing change from the cold, locked-down version of her I've become so familiar with. That is, until she opens her mouth.

"Awww, is the big, bad Horseman of War afraid of a whittle monster? It's okay, Ansel will keep you safe." She pats my cheek in playful mockery, but it doesn't have the intended effect.

Instead, I instantly become aware of all the places my arms and hands rest against her bare skin. Suddenly, the only thing I can smell is her vanilla-and-jasmine scent. I inhale deeply; her hand is frozen on my jaw. Her eyes are sultry and that beautiful crimson blooms on her neck and cheeks. Her chest heaves as her breathing becomes erratic. There is a charge in the air between us, like lightning about to strike.

With a willpower I don't possess, she lowers her hand, and my jaw immediately misses the warmth of her touch. She clears her throat and looks back over her shoulder.

"Uh, we should probably take care of that thing or we'll never have a moment's peace," she suggests. "As it is, I doubt I'll ever sleep again knowing we were probably lying near that thing last night."

"Right." Without relaxing my grip on her, I turn us to face that grotesque monstrosity and let out a sharp whistle. Ginger stomps up to the creature, nostrils flaring, ears pinned back, and mercilessly stomps that creature into a gooey mess. Ansel stares, slack-jawed.

"Okay, then, good to know Ginger's around to keep us both safe." Her eyes twinkle.

I am enjoying our easy banter far too much. Regrettably, I know I need to set her down or this is going to get awkward. A mischievous part of me wants to hold onto her and see what happens. But I remind myself that I am trying to earn trust, not push her boundaries.

I notice what appears to be an old, dried-up fountain with a ledge. It is far from the sand and benches but still cast in light from the gaping hole we fell through. We can hideaway inside it for now and have a meager barrier between us and any more creepy-crawlies.

"That looks like a safe spot," I say. "I am going to set you down over there and then I'll show you what I found."

She avoids my eyes, but gives me a short breathy *okay*. Her reddened cheeks betray the intensity of her emotions again. I am quickly coming to love her expressive face. And every time that flush graces her creamy skin and I am the cause, my stupid male pride has me wanting to stand a little taller.

If I were a peacock, I'd be flaunting feathers right about now.

I carefully place her down on the ledge. I shift her injured leg so it is spread out in front of her, a bit elevated. It's then that I notice her too-bright eyes darting around. She seems nervous. I suppose the monster bug bothered her more than she let on. She is a warrior, strong and brave—skilled at presenting a fierce front. But she is also young and injured. Vulnerable to whatever threat this place presents. Any platitudes I offer will not be welcome, implying she is scared or unable to handle herself.

As a warrior myself, I know what will give her peace.

Pulling a carved blade I found in the sand from a sheath at my leg, I flip it in the air and grab the steel blade, pointing the handle at her.

"Here," I offer. "Keep this on you so you have some protection. I'll go grab our stuff."

She nods, rendered speechless by the gesture, and a glimmer in her eyes suggests this is no ordinary blade to her. I turn to walk away.

"Thank you, Cai," her words softly drift to me, and the way she says my name does funny things to me.

It doesn't take long to grab my pack and her bow and quiver, then retrieve the food I've found. I search the area, now knowing what could be lurking in the depths. Hopefully, that was the only creature that fell into the cavern with us, but I can't be certain it fell in with us at all.

When I return to Ansel, her back is to me, and suddenly I am rooted to the spot. Her hair is pulled over her shoulder, so other than the sports bra, the bare skin of her back is on full display. And there, just between her shoulder blades, is the mark of what looks like the Holy Star.

I knew it in my soul. But seeing the visible confirmation

that she is my Core after all is completely arresting. Like the pieces of an elaborate lock, everything has just clicked and opened to reveal the truth I prize above all else.

When she glances over her shoulder at me, those green eyes reflecting the light, my heart clenches. The awe and gratitude I feel toward Elohim for such a gift is astounding.

"You okay? You look like you've seen a ghost."

Swallowing past the lump in my throat, I school my features and give her a reassuring wink and a smile, despite the steady thundering of my heart in my chest. The truth is that I am heading into a battle, the likes of which I've never before experienced, with a potential outcome that could destroy me and this world. I mean, how do you even begin to convince someone you've just met, who's been betrayed so severely by those who claimed to care for her, that they hold the key to your salvation and to the redemption of the world?

No pressure.

I send up a quick prayer to Elohim that He will help me to show her what she is to me and help her to believe the sincerity of my heart. I suppose it is a good thing I am the Horseman of War. The time to strategize is at hand and the battle to win a heart is nigh.

CHAPTER 14

ANSEL

It's been seven days already and the restlessness I feel, coupled with my inability to do anything helpful, is grating on my nerves. I've never been this useless. And Cai's patience toward my ever-worsening attitude is only making me feel more miserable.

I don't want to admit it, not even to myself, but Cai's steadfast calm is a refreshing change to the energy I had become accustomed to. Of late, most of the FP have been on edge and tense, operating with an almost anxious energy at all times. But Cai is the opposite. He's like a lighthouse on a hill, and I find I can't look away.

I don't know what to think about our conversation where he claimed I am his Core. Initially, it sparked a rage in me that brought up feelings of being used as leverage by Gemini. It poured salt in the wound that betrayal has carved deeper in me than I realized. And unfortunately, however misplaced, Cai bore the brunt of that pain.

Yet, he's stood by his word and not pushed me toward anything involving him. Even more surprising, he's not brought up the topic again. If it weren't for the unabashed way I sometimes catch him looking at me, I would've thought he'd forgotten all about it.

We've fallen into an easy rhythm and, I dare say, I am becoming used to having him around. Not just because he is helpful, but his presence puts me at ease, which is unusual for me.

He is quickly becoming my source of equilibrium and I don't know how to process that.

I purposefully don't ask him the hundreds of questions that keep forcing their way to the forefront of my mind regarding this Core and Horseman business. Nor do I dwell on the emotions such a possibility, if true, elicits from me, the most surprising of which is hope.

Part of me is afraid to encourage him. Scared of what could come from exploring this thing between us. The thought of allowing a deeper attachment to form sends cold terror racing through me. I don't think my heart can take that level of vulnerability, like one more hit will break me irreparably. So I ignore the small seed of something bright that tries to take root whenever my thoughts head down the path of what-ifs. As it is, allowing Nayne the small space in my heart already has my nerves frayed and I feel like I am teetering on thin ice. It's that feeling of being out of control that I despise—it makes me edgy and crabby.

The good news is that my leg itches like the devil and movement is getting a bit easier, so that must mean it's healing, but I am still a long way off from putting weight on it. Cai offers to have me ride Ginger long enough for us to head deeper into this catacomb and look for a way out of here, which is just what I need. The idea of doing some-thing—anything—is a bright spot in the otherwise monotonous days. It is uncanny, the way he seems to know what I need without me saying anything. And it has me wondering again if it has something to do with this Core/Horseman connection.

As we wander through the peculiar space that has weathered the passage of time, I'm disturbed by how it feels void of even the smallest bit of life. The atmosphere is unusually oppressive. Nothing but the clacking of Ginger's hooves on the hard, dusty floor breaks the muted silence. Cai walks out in front like a point man, and the caution with which he leads us deeper and deeper into this uninten-tional catacomb chips away at the armor around my heart. He is the warrior I first met, only this time, it is me he is protecting.

After walking for at least an hour, we reach an area that has seen some of the destruction from the past wars, with collapsed walls and debris.

"Stay here with Ginger," he states. "I am going to see if there's a way through this debris. Maybe we'll luck out and there will be a way out of here, too."

As he heads farther from view, picking his way through the wreckage, a wave of wariness washes over me. I am uneasy at having him out of sight. The thought is like a rock sitting in my gut.

What is happening to me? Good grief, when did I become this starved for positive human contact? I have to get it together. Though something in the back of my mind whispers that it is not just any human contact I crave.

We're quite a ways from the light of the giant hole in the ceiling, but the shifting sands of The Wastes have mercifully left sections of the glass ceiling exposed for the sun to break through. It's not an abundance of light, but these makeshift skylights are just enough. Though it appears to be dusk now, the light having dimmed more than usual, it's quickly reaching a new level of dark.

I am grateful to be sitting on Ginger instead of vulnerable on the ground—she's easy to trust and I sense she would do anything to protect me. After a while, I finally see Cai making his way back.

"It's far too dark here and only getting darker." He sighs as he fiddles with a small and dim LED flashlight he found. "I'd kill for some real light or another set of matches."

We burned through the few matches Cai found cooking the dried beans and pasta. Despite our attempts to keep a fire going, there isn't much to burn down here and something about the environment isn't conducive to keeping flames alive. Now we are back to eating nuts and freeze-dried fruit.

"I vote we find a good spot to camp, eat, and start looking again tomorrow. What do you say?"

His use of *we* when I am not doing anything to help, and the fact that he cares enough to ask what I think, hacks further at the already failing armor around my heart.

"Sounds good." I look anywhere but into his eyes. I'm afraid of what I'll see there and how I'll ever look away once I do.

Cai finds an area where the debris acts as a kind of cave, protected on all sides except one. He places the sleeping bags he found earlier on the ground. Without a word from him, Ginger makes her way to that area, with me along for the ride. Again, it's uncanny how she seems to be an extension of him, which gets my inquisitive mind going.

"Does Ginger need to eat?" I ask. "I don't recall her eating or drinking this whole time."

"She can, and she definitely loves food." Cai smiles, looking up from his task. "But she doesn't need to. When I call her back into my seal, she can get everything she needs from our connection. Kind of like recharging a battery, only it doesn't drain either of us. It only strengthens us."

"Do you speak to her in your thoughts?"

"No, it's not like that," he says, looking up contemplatively. "It's more like she just knows what I need or want. She feels all my emotions and responds. Our connection will come in handy during any future battle."

"Have you not fought alongside her yet? I thought you'd been here for a hundred years."

"We have been here that long, my brothers and I, but no, other than training, we've not seen much battle. Our time has not yet come, although we are fast approaching it. We have spent these long years seeking . . ." He hesitates, a hand on the back of his neck, his telltale sign of reluctance. The quiet seems to grow heavy, thickening with all the words unspoken.

"Seeking your Cores?" I boldly fill in for him. At that, his eyes lock onto mine and he stands before me as I sit atop Ginger. Such raw hope fills his eyes that it is almost painful to look at him. My heart careens in my chest as his hands reach for me. I am sitting sideways on Ginger to dismount, but she is no small pony. It's going to be a feat to get me off her back without further injury. Cai slides one hand under my knees and the other comes up to Ginger's back, one brow raised in question.

With a quick nod, I push off Ginger, effectively falling into Cai's waiting arms. The action has me throwing my arms around his neck for stability. Cai has carried me many times before, but somehow this feels different.

He stands unmoving, and time itself ceases to exist as he holds me. Sparks dance across my skin everywhere Cai's body touches mine. He holds me so gently, yet with a predatory protectiveness. As though I am the most precious thing he's ever held.

His gaze memorizes every inch of my face as though I might disappear. So close, our breath intermingles and the scent of him surrounds me. Only an inch or two and my lips would touch his. At those thoughts, his eyes become hooded and his gaze moves to my mouth. And the look in his eyes is like kindling on the smoldering embers of my heart.

I shouldn't want him. All the ways I will come to regret it circle the raging tempest of my mind. But those regrets and fears are suddenly different from what they started out as, and that catches me off guard. Instead of fearing him as an enemy, what I now fear most is what would happen to me if I lost him.

Every person I have ever let myself love has been taken from me. Those that were supposed to care for me instead betrayed me. Even Nayne I try to hold at arm's length, caring for her and loving her, but keeping pieces of myself locked away.

Protection is my defense mechanism, and yet, somehow, this infuriating man has strolled right past it and taken up residence in my heart. Which only means I am vulnerable in ways I won't be able to protect against and there will be no recovery for me. Not this time.

A knot of emotion forms in my chest, pushing its way up my throat. I'm inhaling a ragged breath when, to my complete horror, a tear slips down my cheek. Then another, and another.

It's as if all the pain of loss, betrayal, and fear that I have been suppressing has finally found its release valve in the Horseman of War's arms. Tears flow in earnest down my cheeks and I close my eyes, desperate to stop the display of weakness.

I feel myself moving downward, still held by Cai, but resting now in his lap as he sits down. My eyes open and take in a hazel gaze that is almost glowing, fixed solely on me. It is tender, yet intensely possessive. That charge in the air is back as his hand comes up, his knuckles wiping the tears from my face. I feel Ginger's soft nose in my hair, as if she too senses my pain and wants to offer her solidarity.

Cai holds me as if he can protect me from the onslaught of previously suppressed pain. My head rests in the crook of his neck and shoulder, and he rubs a thumb in comforting circles on the small of my back.

Soon, the feel of his soothing circles pulls me from the pain of the past and the tears cease flowing. I lift my head to look into his eyes, seeking the anchor he has quickly become to me.

His hand brushes my face, moving a few loose strands of hair from my eyes and tucking them behind my ear. His face is so close, I can see the stubble on his jaw, the earthy hue of specks in eyes that have become a familiar map written on my mind. And, I dare say, my heart.

"Tears are words your heart can't speak, and they are precious to Elohim, like a prayer all their own." He leans even closer and my breath catches.

"Do not be ashamed of them," he whispers, his lips so close, they almost touch mine. Something hard breaks free in my chest. He moves his mouth to my forehead and places the sweetest chaste kiss there, and just like that, the armor around my heart crumbles until there is nothing left.

"I don't know your Elohim, Cai," I confess. "Lucia liked to speak of Elohim too, but I've always been on the outside of understanding when it comes to Him. I have no experiences to go off of."

"Oh, but you do, Ans, even if you don't realize it. Elohim's presence is like oxygen. You may not understand it fully or even be aware of it, but that doesn't change the truth that it is all around you. And you would definitely notice if it was missing. He's been near your whole life. You need only seek and you will find." His warm smile is a balm.

He leans back and I take in the damage my deluge did to his shirt. My cheeks heat. He looks down, holding his shirt out. I don't know how to tell him that I am not really a crier—at least, I wasn't before I met him—but there is something about him that totally disarms me.

"This is nothing, I was in need of a bath anyway," he says with a wink and that charming half grin. He shifts me off him and onto the sleeping bags so he can stand. "I don't know about you, but I am starved. Let's see what's left in this pack, huh?"

And just like that, it's forgotten. No prying questions, no guilt or shame, just quiet acceptance. I watch him, amazed. He's like nothing I expected, and somehow, he's everything I am missing in my life.

"Well, it's not a feast. The pickings were slim a few days ago." He hands me a pack of nuts. "I can try to scrounge up some more food, but seeing how dark it is, I might not find much."

I fail to stifle a yawn. All these new revelations, coupled with the emotional storm I just survived, have left me completely wiped out.

"Let's wait; I am exhausted anyway. Sleep sounds better than food."

Soon, I am drifting off to sleep. Before I am fully out, I feel a blanket cover my body and sense Cai lying down next to me. His hand strokes the hair from my face again. The last thing I hear is Cai's soft voice while he assumes I am fast asleep.

"Like a spark that ignites a raging wildfire, I could burn the world down with what I feel for you."

CHAPTER 15

Cai's words stay with me in my dreams. They are a warm, gentle breeze across my battered, aching soul. I dream of glowing hazel eyes, a stubble-covered jaw, and the tough yet warm feel of his skin beneath my hand. I dream of my hands sliding up his neck and into his soft, thick hair. My body learning the feel of his body against me. I dream of his lips taking mine, his hands in my hair holding me to him.

My body is alight when I sit up suddenly, my breath ragged, trying to calm the inferno in my blood. Glancing to the left, I can barely see Cai's form in the dark, but the light of a full moon casts just enough of a glow through the exposed glass in the ceiling that I can see his chest rising and falling gently. He is still asleep. A blanket pooled low around his waist, he has one arm behind his head, the other slung across his shirtless stomach. I quickly pull my gaze away, the sight of him doing nothing to help me cool off.

If I could walk, I'd be pacing right now.

A noise quickly shifts my focus as I look around, but it's

hard to tell where it is coming from. The depth of darkness in the cavern beyond where we are camped is unsettling and disorienting. The thought chills my blood. I am very awake now, remembering what fell into the cavern with us and wondering what other mysteries lie hidden in this makeshift tomb. Ginger is back with Cai, so not even she is around to offer protection while we sleep.

I am loath to admit it, but lying here immobile, a sitting duck for whatever lurks in the darkness, definitely heightens my fear. I rise onto my elbow and lean over Cai to try and wake him. Closer to him now, I am instantly captivated by the sight of him asleep. His mouth is slightly parted, and my thoughts go unbidden to the feel of those full lips pressed to mine in my dream.

I shake my head to clear the dazed, delirious, and what have to be exhaustion- and hunger-addled thoughts from my head. Attempting to stay focused, I gently grab his shoulder.

"Cai" I whisper, trying to softly shake him awake.

All of a sudden, his arm reaches around my waist, gripping me, and dragging me on top of him. I am shocked by the strength of his half-asleep arms. His other hand comes up to twist into my hair, tugging me closer, his eyes still closed. As if instinct guides him, his mouth finds mine in the dark.

The press of his lips is a dream brought to life.

Before I have time to overthink, I am kissing him back. The taste of him sends my senses into overload. His kiss is like the hunger of a starving man and I am the platter of delicacies.

And all at once, I catch fire again.

Just as quickly, the fervent kiss is replaced with something tender and precious. Almost worshipful. It is unhurried, like a flower blooming. The beauty of it steals my breath and creates a need in me that I don't know what to do with. The heat smoldering inside me becomes a soft, gentle warmth, melting what remains of my barriers and softening the broken edges within me.

He rolls with me until I am under him, but his eyes remain closed. Is he even aware of what is happening between us? At that thought, an icy wave washes over me. I put my hands on his chest, preparing to push him off, but then one of his hands begins to move. Down my face to my neck, across my collarbone and down my arm to my side. I fight back a shiver as his hand slides to my waist and eventually grips my hip before sliding around to the back of my thigh, as if he is trying to commit every inch of me to memory.

I lie there, frozen, my body rendered immobile at the warm brand of his hand. My breathing comes in short bursts as I try and fail to come to my senses, but then an even louder noise makes me jump. My hands grip Cai tightly.

Apparently, that is enough to wake him, because his eyes are open and confusion coats his expression.

"Wha . . . why? Uh . . ." Cai stares at me. His throat bobs as he swallows and then coughs to clear it, clearly just as unsettled as I am. "Why do you look like you've been thoroughly kissed?"

At that, my whole face heats with a blush that I am sure turns my cheeks the brightest red, and my body's response annoys me as much as his question. As if he doesn't know.

"Why do you think, big guy? If this is how you respond to every person who attempts to wake you up, you should come with a warning label."

With a final shove, he sits back, shifting his weight off me. I sit up and scoot back, putting some much-needed distance between us to calm the inferno raging inside me. Then I remember my dreams and I wonder about this link between us. Maybe I did somehow play a part in what just happened?

Confusion wars with shame on his features. A flash of misery sweeps through his expression, acute and searing. His face is ashen and my heart constricts as I watch him process what transpired between us.

"Cai?" I reach for him, attempting to reassure him, but he almost jumps out of his skin. He quickly stands before me, his chest rising and falling rapidly.

"Did I hurt you?" The cool, deadened voice with which he speaks is so unlike Cai that it startles me. His eyes are trained on the ground.

"Look at me," I firmly command him. Ever so slowly, he lifts simmering obsidian eyes to mine.

I gasp.

I don't know what is happening here, but I sense a very real internal battle is waging. And seeing how Cai has been there for me, I will do nothing less for him.

"I am not injured, Cai, and whatever happened when you were half asleep is not your fault. You were unaware."

"That's no excuse!" he bellows. Fists clenching at his sides, he shakes his head. "I am supposed to be protecting you, not taking advantage of you. I told you I would never force anything on you. And I broke that promise." His chest heaves.

"Listen to me, Cai, I am fine." I know what will reassure him, but it requires me to be vulnerable and admit the truth in my heart to him. I owe him that much. I look into his eyes, wrapping my arms around myself to steady my nerves. "And I am equally guilty. I could've stopped you, but I didn't." Taking a deep breath, I sigh. "You may have initiated it, but the truth is that I was kissing you back."

My words don't have the effect I was hoping for. His eyes are still black and his fists are still clenched. "Did you hear what I said?"

"It doesn't matter—I took advantage of you. I failed in my promise." Then, so quietly I almost miss it, he says, "I am undeserving." He shakes his head again as if he's trying to clear something out of his mind. His eyes are still black but are now flickering.

This whole situation feels off.

"What's going on with you? Why are your eyes black?"

It takes him a while to respond, as if he's fighting to speak.

"Leashing," he finally gets out through gritted teeth. "Need a minute."

But as I watch him struggle, something in my spirit calls me to go to him. Something tells me he needs more than just a moment. Slowly standing on my good leg, I awkwardly hop the short distance to him.

I stand before him, my hands holding his arms to steady me. His fists are still clenched at his sides. I pull his arms toward me, forcing him to take a step forward, then I wrap his arms around me and press my head against his chest. His heart pounds like a war drum about to beat right through his chest. Standing in that embrace, I feel the tension in him begin to release as his heartbeat slowly returns to normal.

One of his hands slides up my neck and into my hair, gripping the back of my head—clinging to me like a lifeline. He pulls my head back in his hand, tilting my eyes to meet his. "How did you know to do that?" he says reverently.

"I can't really explain it; I just felt that I should go to you."

His eyes bore into mine, but he doesn't speak.

I sense he's hesitant to say what he's thinking. But somehow, I don't need him to say it. I know. It's the bond. It's because I am his Core. I am his anchor as much as he has become mine. Against all odds, this wild, funny, gentle, and yet dangerous warrior is mine. And miraculously, somehow, I am his.

He seems to see my realization on my face as something akin to hope starts to shine in his eyes. But then the distant *clack* of something crawling on the floor draws our attention.

The back of my neck prickles as I strain to listen. It is almost dawn, so light is beginning to illuminate the vast space, but not enough to see clearly. More *clacks* begin to reverberate off the walls, sounding like thunder as whatever it is draws near.

"Lavo Veshuv," Cai says, and Ginger appears before him in a flash of brilliant red light. She tosses her head and stomps at the ground in clear agitation. Cai quickly swoops me into his arms and places me back on the ground where we were sleeping. Ginger moves in front of me like a protective blockade.

Cai pulls his short sword from the sheath by his bed and quickly straps a tactical blade to his thigh. He puts my bow and quiver next to me, and with one last mournful, longing look at me, he heads into the darkness.

"Cai!" I yell. Fear coats my skin at the thought of him facing whatever horde of monstrosities are bearing down on us. I can't let him face this alone. If anything happens to him, I will not be able to live with myself.

Bracing myself against the debris, I carefully stand on

my good leg. I strap my bow and quiver to my back and hop up to Ginger.

"Help me, girl."

She goes down on her knees for me, and I am easily able to climb up onto her back. She quickly stands facing the darkness. I make out Cai's form. He stands like he did the first time I met him. Blade held low, out at an angle from his body. It isn't lost on me how much has changed in that time.

This time, I stand at his back, ready to war with him, instead of against him.

I nock an arrow and calm my breathing, waiting. Finally feeling like myself for the first time in a long while.

It isn't long before a horde of the same black, bug-like monsters appears. The one we first encountered must have been a baby based on the size of these. They are unholy and unnatural, a product of The Wastes but somehow more.

It's like glimpsing hell.

And, like an explosion, Cai attacks. He is breathtaking to watch. Like a dance, his lethal movements flow with power around whatever dares to cross his path. Limbs, stingers, and pincers litter the ground around him, and he shows no signs of slowing. He fights like a man possessed. He seems unstoppable, but then I notice the creatures beginning to surround him.

Arrow already nocked, I draw it back, taking a steadying breath, and release the string. The arrow strikes deep with a *thud*, felling a monster instantly. Grabbing another arrow, I quickly switch my aim to the other side of Cai, drawback, and let it fly. This one hits the creature right in the eye. Cai instantly turns to look at me, too far away for me to read his expression.

All is still around him.

He starts to make his way to me, but then he suddenly

stands erect, back bowing and neck straining. Ginger makes a heart-wrenching screaming sound and takes off toward him.

As we get closer, I can see he's been attacked from behind. A stinger to his back, attached to one of the monsters that is missing a claw and leaking blood, quickly weakening. This is a vengeance strike. The creature will be dead soon, but I will make it sooner.

Clenching Ginger with my thighs as she gallops, my injured leg protests but I ignore it. In a single, fluid movement, I pull an arrow from my quiver, nock it, draw it back, and release. The stinger of the beast, as long as a small blade, rips free from Cai's back with the force with which my arrow strikes the creature. I watch in dread as Cai drops to the ground with a *thud*.

CHAPTER 16

MORDECAI

Damn, that hurt.

And what an amateur move, to turn my back on the enemy, even if I was sure they were all dead. But when I saw Ansel sitting astride Ginger, her bow in position, a wild and murderously protective look on her face, I was undone. My heart took flight and I had eyes for nothing else.

After what happened between us, and what I believe she saw in my eyes earlier, I expected her to want nothing to do with me.

Miraculously, that doesn't seem to be the case.

As I lie on the ground, a liquid burning sensation radiates outward from the wound, limiting my ability to focus on any line of thought. I roll onto my side, attempting to stand right as Ginger and Ansel arrive.

"Cai, are you okay? How are you even moving after that?" Concern etches her brow, her wild, windblown hair adding a frenzied air to her expression. Even through the pain of this sting, the sight of her is like the sun breaking through the clouds on a blustery, overcast day.

A cough rattles through my chest, and I bring my hand up to Ginger to brace myself. When I pull my other hand away from my mouth, it's coated in blood. Ansel must see it, too, because she suddenly sucks in a breath.

"Can you get up here?"

The thought of mounting Ginger in this state makes me want to lie down and never get up. But the color rapidly draining from Ansel's face has me nodding at her. I will do anything to ease her fear.

Heaving myself up with my arms, I grunt, grinding my teeth to keep from yelling as my back protests at the agonizing movement. I feel Ansel's arms pulling me, too, and somehow, I miraculously get a leg over Ginger and end up seated behind Ansel.

"Put your arms around me; I don't want you to fall off." Her voice trembles.

I obey, my head coming to rest on the back of her shoulder as my leaden arms painstakingly ease around her. Her hand slides over the top of mine, gripping me tightly as we start back to our makeshift camp.

"I'll be fine, Ans . . . I'm kind of immortal," I slur into her ear as the poison continues to work through my body.

"Yeah, well, pardon my lack of faith, but you're not exactly the picture of immortal health right now."

As if to prove that statement true, I involuntarily slide off Ginger's back, landing on my side with a *thud* and a groan as pain reverberates through my body.

"Cai!" My heart beats painfully and erratically as Ginger prances around in a panic. Suddenly, Ansel is on the ground with me. My breathing is labored—too labored.

Something is very wrong.

Suddenly, it dawns on me with excruciating clarity. My marking changed and I fully accepted the bond with Ansel —almost immediately actually—which, based on what Nic believes about the prophecy, means that my immortality is gone.

Well, damn.

I reach out to touch her face, her satin skin like a healing balm. "It wasn't supposed to be this way. I . . . I'm sorry."

Ansel grabs my hand between hers, holding it to her chest. "Don't you dare start saying goodbye. Tell me what to do. You're the Horseman of War, for crying out loud; there's gotta be something I can do."

And there is, but I promised her I would never push her into anything, and even though I failed once, I will not do it again.

Her panicked gaze wills me to speak, to give some solution to my present predicament. As the poison reaches my mind, it's as if I've finished off a barrel of bootleg whiskey. I welcome the numbness in every limb.

"It's okay—you are worth it. Always and forever worth it."

"What are you saying?" A frenzied dread lights her eyes.

"I'd give up much more than my immortality to love you. And it doesn't even matter that it's one-sided. Because I have enough love for both of us." I smile, letting my love for her wrap around me like a blanket as I feel myself drift. "S-s-s . . . sorry if that scares you."

Terror flashes across her features. Her eyes widen and her chin trembles. "You can't say that, Cai. It's not the truth. Not anymore. I was going to talk with you, before the fight. I was going to set you straight."

Tears flow in earnest down her beautiful face, dropping

onto my hand that she has cradled against her chest, as if she can hold me here with her and wash away the pain.

"I had my barriers up with you. I was afraid. I lost the only people I ever truly loved and those I devoted my life to betrayed me. But somehow, you demolished the armor I had around my heart and walked in like you always belonged there." Her voice shakes at the declaration, but she plows forward, determined, taking a shaky breath. "I think I've known for a while now, but I've been too scared to speak it. You are a dream I didn't dare give life to."

Her soft lips caress my knuckles. I crack open my heavy-lidded eyes. A weighty grief presses down on her as the tears flow. She leans forward, cupping my jaw as she gazes into my hazy eyes, like she's willing me to stay with her.

"I love you, Cai. Please don't leave me." And then her lips press against mine; the taste of her salty tears mixes with the amazing taste that is her. And all at once, I am enraptured by the undeserving gift that she is to me. She has pierced through the darkest pieces of my world-weary soul. Elohim's whisper on the wind assures me that the darkness will not overcome the light.

An anticipatory urgency fills the air around us, almost like the calm before a storm, and then suddenly, a healing warmth spreads through my body. Everywhere she touches me, with either her hands or her lips, this warmth spreads, eliminating the poison and knitting my flesh together. I marvel at the fact that she's the source of it all. But above everything is overwhelming joy. This can only mean one thing.

She's accepted the bond as my Core.

As I slide my hands through her hair and cup her head, the kiss morphs into something deeper. And I am in absolute awe of her. She doesn't know what it means to be a Core, she knows nothing of my world, and she fights an internal battle as a result of past betrayals, but despite everything, she took a leap of faith and chose me.

She sits back, her hands on my chest, her bright, wide eyes absorbing me like a sponge. I sit up and pull her onto my lap.

"You healed me," I whisper.

She stares at me as her mouth drops open.

"You know how?" I gently move her loose copper strands of hair behind her ears. She shakes her head. I lean forward, my lips a hairbreadth from hers. "With your love for me. You accepted the bond between us, and this is one of Elohim's gifts for us. We can heal each other."

Unshed tears shine in her eyes.

"You know what this means don't you?" I pause. "I get to repay the favor."

And with that, I wrap one arm around her waist. The other snakes its way into her silky hair and my lips crash into hers. Lowering her down onto her back, I let all the desire, love, and passion I have been restraining explode out of me, crashing over her like a wave. Her back arches when the force of what I feel slams into her, and she clings to me. I will her to be healed and whole and let my kiss express every piece of what I have hidden away in my heart.

I slow the kiss down, tenderly moving to her jaw, her cheeks, her eyes, and finally the tip of her perfect nose, before begrudgingly pulling back completely. She lies there before me, hair mussed, cheeks tinged pink, and her lips glistening and swollen. It takes all of my restraint not to continue, but I need her to see the power of Elohim's love at work in us.

Holding my hand out, I clasp hers and pull her to a

sitting position, then I work to remove the brace on her leg. She looks at me with a question in her eyes.

"Let's test it out, shall we?" I stand, pulling her up with me, but out of habit, she still balances on her good leg.

"Do you trust me?" I ask.

Her gaze shoots to mine. "Yes," she says firmly, then she puts her weight on the once-broken leg. Her expression shifts from shock to awe, and then pure joy radiates out of her. She throws herself into my arms, wrapping her legs around my waist. She squeezes me tightly as I hold her to me. And when she pulls back to look at me, the tenderness and love I see shining back at me sets my heart soaring.

"Thank you, Elohim." I heave a grateful sigh. She smiles at me and then gently presses her lips to mine.

With her in my arms, I am happy to stay in this place and relish the feel and taste of her. Now that she's accepted the bond, the connection between us has solidified and I have an even deeper sense of her, as if our souls have become intertwined. Melded together forever. The knowledge of her love and acceptance is like a shield around us.

But as much as I wish to shut out the world, a quiet foreboding reminds me that we aren't safe yet. Despite Ansel's joy, there is an undercurrent of concern and worry in her which I am determined to figure out. From now on, she will never face anything alone.

She doesn't need a knight in shining armor, but I am happy to forever be the sword she wields.

CHAPTER 17

A faint, steady tapping draws my attention. Nothing like the clacking of monster pincers we just heard, this noise is a steady, rhythmic tap reminiscent of an old song. Definitely human created. I gently place Ansel's feet back on the ground and she grabs my hand, interlacing our fingers. The gesture is as natural as breathing, and a thrill shoots through me.

I look down at her face as she tries to pinpoint the direction of the tapping, her brow furrowed in concentration. I am struggling to focus on anything but the awe I feel in her presence. Everything feels surreal. Like a dream I will wake from at any moment.

Sensing my attention, she meets my gaze. Her eyes widen ever so slightly at the intensity she surely must see there, and she smiles.

With a mind of its own, my hand reaches up to caress her face. Her soft skin is fast becoming a medicine I desperately crave.

"You once said that I should be glad not to have you as a Core," I begin, "because you weren't soft and gentle, and you were mostly broken pieces. At the time, I knew any response from me wouldn't be well received. But now, what I would have you understand is that Elohim knows you are exactly what I need. I never wanted or needed a Lucia. I need a firecracker that won't take my crap, who will dish it back out to me, who will fight for me and fight beside me, and light up the darkness inside me. You may think you're just broken, jagged pieces, but so are shooting stars. And your light blazes so brightly that it eviscerates the darkness."

She stands still. Then she lets go of my hand and brings hers up to my nape. She boldly pushes up onto her tiptoes and presses her lips to mine. The heady scent of vanilla and jasmine is everywhere. All too soon, she pulls away.

"You found the pieces of my soul that I thought had been lost, and in you, I found a dream I never believed could come true. I love you, Cai." Her smile captivates me, and suddenly the air is heavy with something weighty and anticipatory.

"As much as I love the way you are looking at me right now," I say, "we need to figure out where this tapping is coming from."

Breaking away from each other, we both start scouring the ceiling-high mountain of debris we spent the night near. I can almost feel the deeper vibrations, so I begin climbing the debris. I move some of the more manageable chunks and throw them off to the side, out of the way of where I think the sound is coming from. The tapping stops and eventually, I clear enough away that a man-sized hole appears before me. Ansel stands a few paces away, but she must feel my gaze on her because she looks up. I pull my knife from its sheath and wink at her before I drop into the hole.

Once inside, my eyes begin to adjust to the darkness and I notice a dim, LED-type lantern in the corner. A pale girl with almost white hair sits on a blanket on the floor. Her back is to me, as if she's completely unconcerned by the presence of a strange man in her hidey-hole.

The hole appears to be a makeshift home or den, complete with a sleeping area and even a stack of books—it looks like she's been here for a while. On one side, a narrow pathway seems to lead out of the small cavern. I take a step toward the girl, but a sharp blade cuts into my throat and I feel another blade near my left kidney. I freeze, raising my arms.

"Drop the knife," a scratchy yet soft voice orders.

I do as she says. An anger that is not mine surges through me, and I know Ansel is near. Then my fiery redhead drops through the hole with an arrow aimed at the hand holding the blade to my throat. Fury burns white-hot in her eyes.

I am astonished at her fierce determination, all in defense of me. It's weird, being on the other side of a conflict like this.

"Back away from him," she says with an eerie calm. "Or this arrow will force your arm away."

"Sida, it's okay. Something in me senses this girl is not an enemy." A new voice speaks softly from the floor. At her words, the blade at my throat disappears. Ansel slightly lowers her bow but still remains at the ready.

"I don't like this," the first voice speaks from behind me, and there's something about it that knocks on the door of my memories, demanding entry. I turn and take in the familiar, spiraling white hair and skin the color of warm tanned leather.

"Sidora!" I stare, dumbfounded.

A gasp flies from her lips as she sees me face-to-face. She throws her willowy arms around me. "Oh, thank Elohim, His timing couldn't be more perfect." She pulls back, grasping my face in her hands. "You are an oasis in a parched desert, Mordecai Cascus." She smiles warmly at me and memories come flooding in.

She first came to The Refuge as a young, rebellious, and abandoned teen. My brothers and I saw her potential and helped train her to work with the Prophets. She has been like a sister to us, even though she now looks like she could be our mother. One of the curses of being here so long and living ageless is that we have to watch those we come to care for age and pass on without us. We only have each other and Elias, who's been here far longer than us.

"We were trapped down here after a cave-in when we were fleeing some Amilign," Sidora explains. "We wandered as far as we could before finding this wall of debris. We found a small path that led into the debris for a short distance, but it ends here in this little cave. Our water sources are down to a faint trickle and we are running out of food. I've been praying for a miracle, and boy does Elohe Tishuathi know how to deliver."

I smile at her familiar humor.

Man, I've missed her. It's been years since I last laid eyes on her.

"I'm sorry, what is Elohe Tishuathi? Who are you?" Ansel huffs from beside me. I sense the warrior in her attempting to strategize. I grab her hand, forcing her to fully lower her bow, and pull her forward.

"Sida, this is Ansel, my Core." I beam at her.

Her face lights up and tears fill her eyes. "Oh, Cai," she says, smiling up at me warmly. She turns to face Ansel, grabbing her hand from mine. "And Ansel, what an honor it is to meet you, my girl, a representation of Elohim's pure love in physical form. I am truly blessed to know you."

Ansel stands frozen. I put my hand to her lower back to reassure her; this has to be overwhelming for her.

"My name is Sidora, or Sida, and to answer your question, Elohe Tishuathi is one of the many names of Elohim. It means 'my salvation,' which He has been for us these many months we've spent trapped."

"Nice to meet you," Ansel says, her brows pinched as if she's still trying to puzzle everything out. "But how do you two know each other?"

"She works with the Prophets of The Way," I explain, "as do my brothers and I. And I am not sure how much you know about Lucia, but Sida here raised her from infancy until she was taken."

At my words, a shadow passes over Sida's eyes. "Do you have any word of her, Cai?" she says softly, as if afraid to hope.

"I do. She escaped the Amilign, and Nicanor was there to help her and bring her home. She's now at The Refuge and bonded with Nicanor. She's safe."

Tears roll down her cheeks and a myriad of emotions flit across her face—surprise, relief, and joy tinged with sadness. She reins in her emotions and dries her eyes.

"There are things you aren't telling me."

I grab her hand. "None of it matters now. All you need to know is that she is home, safe, loved, and happy. Now we just need to get you home so you can see her for yourself."

"Wait, you're Aunt Sid?" Ansel squeaks from beside me. Sida nods. "Lucia spoke of you when I met her at the ashram. She was so alone in that place. I'm sorry, but I don't understand why you would let them take her. Working for these Prophets, you had to know the monks were bad news." Ansel seems to simmer with righteous indignation, but I place a hand on her shoulder. I understand her response, but Sida doesn't deserve her ire.

I lean down to her. "Trust me, there's much you don't know about this."

Sida heaves a burdened sigh. "It nearly killed me to let her go. I raised her as if she were my own daughter. So when Elias came to me with the message that all the Prophets had seen the same vision, that the Amilign would come to collect Lucia, and that I was to let them take her, it nearly broke me. I trust Elohim and I know His ways are good, but I also knew it wouldn't be an easy path for her and I so wanted to spare her hardship. As any mother would, I suppose. So we stayed at the farmstead, and every day I prayed that they were wrong, that it would never come to pass. But it did.

"You see, the Prophets saw that any attempt to avoid this path would lead to catastrophic results, not just for us but for Lucia and the world. For Lucia to become who she was meant to be, she had to come face-to-face with the darkness that she would be expected to one day battle. Light shines brightest in the deepest darkness. So she had to walk this path. And because I didn't fight them when they came for her, she was accepted under the guise of being a willing pupil. So she learned about them, and it sounds like Elohim guided her to leave at the right time and made a way to bring her safely home through Nicanor."

Ansel releases a loud exhale and gives Sida a slow nod, begrudgingly seeing the truth of her words.

"I am not so naive as to believe it wasn't hard and even

heartbreaking for her, and I am sure Cai is trying to spare me the details. But they took a piece of my heart when they took her from me. I tried to go back to The Refuge for a while, but I was fading away, as Elias would say. He thought it would be best if I kept busy by searching for more Cores. And that's how I ended up here, actually." Sida looks fondly at the girl on the floor.

I glance at the almost pale-haired girl. Her crystal-blue eyes are penetrating even in the darkness. The next thing I notice is that she is missing the lower half of her right leg below the knee. She reaches a hand out to me.

"Give a girl a hand, will ya?" she says with a soft smile. I extend my hand to her and she grips it to pull herself to a standing position, leaning a hand against the debris for support.

"Let me introduce you to Vale." Sida's voice pulls me out of my thoughts. But before she can continue, the answer is suddenly staring me in the face.

"You're Z's Core!" I gape at her, speechless. No wonder he couldn't find her; she's been buried under The Wastes. I turn back to Sida, grabbing her shoulder. "How long have you two been down here?"

"Well, I don't know whose Core she is, but I found Vale injured a few years back." Sida's eyes dart to Vale's and an unspoken message seems to pass between them.

"Sida helped me recover," Vale says, "and we've been on the run ever since. That's how we ended up here."

I look between Sida and Vale, my eyes settling on Vale. "Zion is definitely your Horseman. He felt whatever happened to you with your leg. It has tormented him these past years and he has searched for you obsessively. Only recently was he forced back to The Refuge because he's losing the battle with the leashing. We have got to get you to Z, Vale. He's not doing good."

Again, Sida's eyes connect with Vale's and a marked grief fills both gazes. There is something they are not sharing. But, smooth as always, Sida shakes it off. "Well, we gotta get out of here first. Any ideas?"

CHAPTER 18

I feel as though the world has tilted off its axis. All of a sudden, I am aware of how little I know Cai. The truth is a fog attempting to block out the brightness he brought into my life. My heart beats for him and him alone, and nothing can change that, but the old familiar fear and caution I've lived with for so long are trying to weasel their way back into my chest.

I am out of my depth, being so deeply connected to a person I know so little about. And seeing him with someone from his past, someone he cares about, only brings into sharper focus that Nayne is still out there, alone, wondering what happened to me. Maybe thinking I abandoned her, while I've been down here, swooning over and falling for a stranger.

I turn away from the group to attempt to collect my thoughts and emotions, but Cai is too aware of me. He must sense something is off because he's suddenly by my side, looking down into my face with concern.

"What is it? I feel turmoil in you. Don't shut me out. Please?"

"Do you remember me mentioning my little sister?"

He nods.

"Well, her name is Nayne. I was protecting her when I met you in the desert. She's still out there, trying to survive, alone, probably scared, maybe even thinking I abandoned her. She's only ten, Cai. And I've been down here so focused on you instead of trying to fight tooth and nail to get to her." The shame and guilt threaten to bury me when I feel Cai's fingers on my chin, gently lifting my eyes to his.

"You have not been doing nothing. If you recall, you were severely injured until just a few hours ago. And we have been actively seeking ways out of here despite your injury. Do not beat yourself up," Cai soothes. "And thank you for trusting me with this information; I will do everything in my power to get us out of here and make sure she is safe. If she is important to you, she's important to me."

Emotion crowds my heart at his words and I throw my arms around his waist, burying my face in his chest. I breathe in his scent and let it wash over me, soothing my worry. His arms slide around me, holding me to him. It feels good to have someone to rely on and share burdens with.

"Sida, I assume you've explored this side of the debris and found no way out?" Cai speaks over my head. I turn and he wraps his arms around my waist, pulling me to him so that my back presses against his chest.

"You're correct. This area is completely shut in from debris and collapsed building. In fact, until you showed up and moved the debris above, we didn't even know if there was a way through to the other side. Though we did find an outdoor gear shop that might have some useful things to help get us out of here."

"Okay, Ansel and I will go scope it out. Gather up any things you want to bring, because we are getting out of here today."

Then he grabs my hand and winds his way through the narrow path of debris that leads out of the makeshift den where we found Vale and Sidora. What we find mirrors what's on the other side of the mountain of destruction, only the space is smaller and more laden with debris. A few unburied panes of glass on the ceiling allow light to shine in, preventing the area from being completely immersed in darkness. And right in front of us is a massive storefront showcasing mountaineering and outdoor gear, the doors long ago busted open by Sidora.

Inside, we find all manner of survival gear. Walls lined with climbing rope, harnesses, carabiners, and even a practice climbing wall. One section has tents, sleeping bags, and even a kayak. We grab packs for all four of us and start stuffing gear into them, whatever we think will come in handy. I load each one with an empty bottle of water—hoping we'll be able to fill them at some point—a tactical knife, rope, a thermal blanket, and bandages, saving space for anything Cai thinks we might need to add. A section of the store is clothing, so I grab a few extra essentials.

Next to that is a section that looks like it was once full of packaged, freeze-dried meals, but has long since been picked clean by Sidora and Vale, as evidenced by the discarded wrappers lying around.

I am going stir-crazy at the small amount of time we've been locked down here, which makes me wonder how long they have been down here. Cai must wonder the same because he turns and yells over his shoulder.

"How long have you two been trapped down here?"

Only a few seconds later, Sidora appears in the doorway. "Well, we came to The Wastes when we realized Vale was being hunted, hoping that this place would mess with any high-tech gear they were using. Before, we had been doing our best to stay on the move, but they kept finding us. We thought we'd have better luck out here. We stumbled upon an entrance to this buried mall, thinking it was a cave. The entrance wasn't very stable to begin with and it collapsed, trapping us inside. The sands were all too happy to shift in and bury us. The good news is, I think our tail assumes we're dead. So far, we've been down here for about six months."

"What?" Cai barks. "How is that even possible? Surely, there's not been enough food to keep the two of you alive for that long? And why didn't you just head to The Refuge in the first place? We'd have protected you."

Sidora pauses, her expression conflicted. She opens her mouth to speak, but a sharp whistle rends the air, followed by the faint sounds of scuffling and scratching. Sidora leaves the doorway to follow the sound. Cai and I look at each other in confusion, and then he shrugs, grabs two packs, and turns to go after Sidora.

Curious myself, I follow him, the remaining two packs slung over my shoulders.

Just outside the cave of debris we found them in, Vale sits on what appears to be a longboard with wheels. The stump of her right leg is stretched out in front of her on the board, her foot on the floor. Both she and Sidora look toward a corner of the wall of debris, waiting. The scratching continues, and then a rare albino hawk pops its head out of a hole that seems far too small for it. It disappears back through the hole for a moment, and then out pops tail feathers. It appears to be tugging something through the hole with its beak. With a little effort, it's out and we get a glimpse of a dead, sand-covered brown rabbit. It drags its treasure to Vale, placing the rabbit at her foot before flying up to her shoulder.

Vale strokes the hawk's white-feathered chest and then meets our astonished expressions with amused eyes.

"Everyone, meet Roy," Vale says with a twinkle in her eyes.

"Is he a hawk?" I ask. "He's huge!"

"She, and yes. I found her as a hatchling. She'd been abandoned, so I took care of her until she was healthy and grown. Now we take care of each other." A soft smile lights her face as the hawk rubs its head against her face.

"Vale's unique relationship with Roy here is how we've survived so long," Sidora states. "Hawks are exceptional hunters, and Roy is very loyal to Vale. She's become quite the little caretaker. Every day, Roy goes out and hunts for us. Combined with the freeze-dried meals, we've managed. We only ran out of the freeze-dried meals a few weeks ago. But then, just over a week ago, we felt this place tremble and heard a massive crash, like the roof was caving in, and thought we might have visitors. Drawing your attention was a risk, but we were desperate and I sensed Elohim's leading."

"Well, since we're all in agreement that getting out of here is the first priority," Cai says, "let's grab our stuff and get everyone out through the hole I made in the debris. With all this gear, I should be able to secure a grappling hook to the metal rafters that support the glass ceiling. From there, I can find a secure way back out through the hole Ansel and I fell through. I have harnesses for all of us, so once I get to the top, we should be able to take turns climbing out, and I can help pull you up if it's too much."

Cai's face is a mask of calm strategizing. I can see the

Horseman of War staring out of his eyes as his brain works through all the scenarios. He is in his element right now and he is magnificent. He is also mine.

He must sense my focus because his eyes meet mine and brighten almost imperceptibly. The corner of my mouth rises in a half smile and I wink at him. His chest rises sharply and, all of a sudden, he looks like a predator on the hunt. Shivers erupt across my skin at the hunger in his eyes.

"Phew," Vale blurts. "You two are intense." She mockingly fans herself and I smirk at her. I like this girl.

Cai blinks and shakes his head. Then he clears his throat, a slight blush on his cheeks. "Uh, sorry 'bout that. It's new."

I laugh as our group meanders through the narrow path flanked by debris to the small open cavern with Cai's man-made hole that leads to the other side. Vale grabs Sidora's hand and pulls herself to a standing position. Then she winds an arm around Sidora and they begin making their way along as if this is no unusual occurrence.

I am suddenly struck by the parallels between this girl and me. I had an injured leg for only a short period of time and it was far too long. Yet, this girl has been missing the lower half of her leg for who knows how long, having to adapt to life without it. Not to mention how she lost it—I can only imagine the horror of that story.

I at least had the benefit of knowing my leg would eventually heal. I can't imagine knowing there would be no healing coming. And both of us have been fleeing an enemy that hunts us. She is also apparently a Core, like me and Lu. Even though I don't yet know her, I feel a sense of camaraderie with her. Like when I met Lu, I have a deep connection with this girl, a connection beyond our common experiences.

At that thought, Vale's bright blue gaze connects with mine and something unspoken passes between us. Vale whispers something to Sidora, and she guides Vale closer to me.

"Ansel, will you help Vale while I check in with Cai?"

"Sure." I take Sidora's place at Vale's side.

We stand silent for a few moments, but it's not uncomfortable. If anything, it feels like I've known Vale forever.

"I feel like . . ."

"It's weird that . . ." We both speak at the same time.

Vale just smiles and nods for me to continue.

"It feels like we've known each other forever," I say, and she smiles. "I guess that's an effect of us both being Cores."

"Am I the first Core you've met?" Vale asks.

"Oddly, no. But I didn't know at the time. I met Lucia and just thought it was a sign we were destined to be best friends. We both needed each other and it felt as though some force had led us together. Which, I suppose, is exactly what happened." I smile at the memory and then notice Vale's expression dim. Something tells me her story is not marked by many moments of light.

"What about you?" I ask.

"You are the first Core I've met, but I knew right away what you were when you came through the hole. I only learned about all this Core and prophecy business when I met Sida. She saved me and then taught me everything she knew. I would've questioned her sanity and doubted it all had I not felt something shift inside me after my injury. And then meeting you only confirmed it."

"What do you mean, you felt something shift?"

"Well, I can't really explain it, but it was like I suddenly felt another presence with me. Not like physically with me, more like a phantom in my head. I know it sounds insane, and I thought it was a coping mechanism after what I'd been through until Sida explained my connection with a Horseman. It clicked, because from the beginning, this phantom feeling felt distinctly male. Sida believes the pain and fear I felt at losing my leg formed a connection between me and this Horseman before we even met."

That last comment alone gives me pause, and I get the sense that Vale is downplaying the event. I want to ask her what happened to cause her such levels of terror and agony that her mind would form a connection with someone she's never met. But I have also seen enough of this world to know that it's probably a grim tale she is not eager to relive. Especially with someone who's essentially still a stranger.

"That's wild. Does he speak to you?" I ask.

"No, it's nothing that defined. It's more like I get this sense of seeking, desperation, and longing that is separate from my own emotions. It's subtle and has felt like a reassuring companion at times. Reminding me that someone knows I exist and is trying to find me."

"I feel like I've fallen through the rabbit hole," I say.

She gives me a dry laugh. "My whole life feels like one dark and demented rabbit hole."

I let her words soak in. How tied together we are as Cores; Lucia too. Three lives forged in struggle and darkness. I don't know why, but my next words erupt as though it is impossible to suppress them.

"You're not alone anymore, Vale. We're sisters. We'll navigate the rabbit hole together." I turn to face her, holding her hands to offer balance.

A genuine smile lights her face and the dark shadows flee. She squeezes my hand and nods, and we continue to make our way to the escape hole.

Cai is not messing around. Already through the hole,

along with all the gear and even the rabbit Roy brought us, he stretches out his hand and I reach up for him to pull me through. Vale goes next, followed by Sidora. Vale kneels down, looking back into the hole, and I realize Roy is still down there.

She whistles a sharp note, and the hawk flies through the hole and takes off for the light far above. Vale's eyes meet mine. "She'll find us on the outside."

"Wow, she really is well trained."

"Yes and no; it's more than that. I've just always had a deep connection with her. Almost like she knows what I want without words or gestures. I often just use a whistle to get her attention."

"Sounds a bit telepathic to me," I tease. She extends a hand to me and I pull her to a standing position, wrapping her arm around my shoulder like I saw Sidora do.

Red flashes in my periphery and Ginger stands before Cai.

"Uhhhh . . . ," Vale trails off. "I am losing it, aren't I? Too long trapped down here breathing in dirt instead of fresh air."

I chuckle. "You aren't losing it, don't worry. I kinda freaked out when I first saw him do that, too. It's a Horseman thing."

Cai mounts Ginger with a pack on his back and what looks like a gun with a hook sticking out of the end. Then he reaches down to me. Sidora takes my place with Vale and I swing up behind Cai.

"We're going to go up to the second story and get this grappling hook secured," says Cai. "Once we do that, I will send Ginger back for you both. We'll get everyone fitted for harnesses and then we are getting out of here."

CHAPTER 19

ANSEL

Staring up into the hole, it seems an almost impossible feat to get to the top. Cai's accuracy with the grappling hook was impressive. He made it look easy when he secured the rope to one of the rafters near the hole after making the long climb up. I am pretty sure I held my breath the entire climb. I don't think he's afraid of anything. Sidora is now connected to the rope, getting ready to make her way up, not an ounce of fear on her seasoned face.

A cold sweat breaks out across my skin and I start fidgeting to hide my trembling hands. Why am I this way? Warriors are supposed to be fearless. But my heart rate is skyrocketing and it's not even my turn to climb. I take deep breaths, willing myself to calm down and get it together. Showing weakness is a no-no for FP. I have avoided acknowledging this irrational fear of heights—always steering clear of any situation that may trigger it.

The rope is moving quicker, which means Cai is pulling Sidora up. Before too long, she is at the top and I am hooking Vale up to the rope. She places a hand on my shoulder. She sees too much with that intuitive gaze of hers. She tries to reassure me with a smile. The best I can give her back is a nod. Then, all of a sudden, she's being pulled away from me, up into the light of day.

The shaking begins in earnest. It's unavoidable now that my turn approaches. My calm, deep breaths shift into panicked hyperventilating. My heart careens around in my chest like a rabbit caught in a snare. The urge to run from this danger presses in on me.

But I can't. Everything I love is on the other side of this climb. The rope lowers in front of my face and I stare at it, frozen. Fear sits like a living and breathing beast on my chest. I faintly hear my name being called, but I can't seem to pull my focus out of the muck. I close my eyes. I am drowning and I don't know how to save myself.

After what feels like forever, big, warm hands are on my face and I take a gasping breath.

"That's it," his soothing voice pulls me from the fog, "breathe for me." Another ragged breath tears through my chest. This one is a tiny bit easier. Cai's hands on my face are like finding land after being lost at sea.

As much as I want to look at him, I don't dare open my eyes. I can't bear to see the look of disappointment, or worse, disgust, on his face.

Then his breath intermingles with my own before his lips are on mine, tender and adoring. Feelings of unbridled joy, gratitude, and, surprisingly, pride fill me.

But these are not my emotions—I must be feeling Cai's. Though that can't be right.

I step back from him in surprise, trying to get my bearings, but he quickly wraps his arms around my waist, holding me to him. I stare at my hands on his chest, avoiding his eyes, despite the confusion of what I am feeling.

"Look at me, Ans," he says gently.

Hesitantly and with painstaking slowness, I raise my eyes to his. What I see shining back at me is enough to bring me to my knees and only confirms the emotions I felt before were from Cai.

"I know that you can feel what I feel. So you know how I feel about you." He pauses, brushing the stray hair away from my eyes. "Struggling with something does not make you weak; it makes you human. And it is out of our weaknesses that the greatest strength of all is made perfect and revealed in us—Elohim's strength and power. I love all of you, Ansel, and it is the greatest honor of my long life that you are mine and I am yours. We're a team, okay?"

I breathe in the truth of those words as Cai's calming scent continues to ground me. I nod.

"I am going to secure this rope around you. Then I am going to climb back up, and while I do that, I want you to focus on the incredible bond Elohim has gifted us. Feel all the things I am going to send your way as I climb. I want you to keep your eyes closed and hold on just like you are now. And you aren't going to open your eyes until you feel my hands on you, yeah?"

I nod again.

"I need to hear it, Ans," he says, softly but firmly.

"Okay," I squeak out.

I close my eyes, doing as he says. An overabundance of love flows from him; then, on its tail, comes the joy of our connection. It swiftly morphs into a sense of awe and pride, which makes my heart swell. I test the bond out by trying to send something back to him. I project my adoration of who he is, his character and his genuine heart, and the swell of love that fills me every time I see him. I get a swell of gratitude and brightness from him, and then it shifts into desire. A desire that is so much deeper than surface level. It's a desire that reaches to the depths of my soul. That encompasses all of who I am. As though I am the cure to a long season of suffering. Water in a parched desert. Breath in deprived lungs.

His distractions work on me until I feel the rope pull tight and my feet lift off the ground. I break his rule and open my eyes. I am rapidly approaching the top already, but a cold sweat has broken out across my clammy skin and my stomach turns to lead.

"Ansel, look at me!" The firm voice leaves no room for argument. I lift my gaze to my hazel-eyed lifeline. I am so close now, I can almost touch him.

"Don't let me fall," I whisper, more to myself than anything, but Cai hears me.

"Never," he replies, and then his hands are on me, pulling me from the air and into his waiting arms. One hand slides across my lower back and wraps around my waist. The other hand threads into my hair, the possessive hold causing the very air around us to still, as if waiting for his permission to move.

He brings his lips a hairbreadth from mine, and he speaks in so faint a whisper, I know the words are only for me. "I will never let you fall." And I sense a depth to his words that goes beyond what happened here today.

I press my face into his neck and wrap my arms around him. I fit in his arms like he was created to hold me.

As the hot sun beats down on us and it hits me that we are really out of there. I am struck by how different a person I am from the one that fell in the hole. Cai's comfort soothes away the last of the terror, and I realize, with a sudden and shocking clarity, that he feels like home. Or what I would imagine home to be.

At the thought of home, Nayne comes to mind. I jump out of his arms and scan the horizon. There, in the distance, is the little ruin I left her in. I take off at a run. Cai doesn't try to stop me, but instead keeps pace with me, leaving Sidora and Vale to presumably wonder what's happening.

"Nayne!" I yell, waiting to see if her dark complexion and soulful brown eyes appear. But of course, there's no sign of human activity. Any footprints are long covered by the shifting sands, which only confirms she's been gone a while.

Instead, pinned to one of the rotting pieces of the wood frame with a blade is a note. The familiar handwriting pulls a gasp from me.

"No, no, no," I mutter as I tear it loose and fall to my knees, reading words that could've been pulled from one of my worst nightmares.

"AHHHH!" I scream, crumpling the letter up and curling in on myself. How could I have let this happen? I promised her that she would be safe with me. Must I fail at everything?

Despair claws at my chest. A warm hand pulls at my wrist. I take a deep breath as I let Cai ease me to my feet. His big arms come around me, blocking out the world. I bury my face in his chest and his hand comes up through my hair to hold me to him.

"Tell me," he says.

I don't pull away. I stay in the comfort of his arms, wishing I will never have to leave and that staying here could right every wrong.

"The FP took her. But they want me. They will make a trade, but every day that I delay will be worse for her. And I don't know how long they've had her for already." I choke back a sob.

He says nothing, but the immediate tension in his muscles betrays his feelings. His body trembles, and I pull my head back and look into obsidian eyes.

"Cai? I thought we fixed this leashing problem?"

"We did, or *you* did. This is different. There's a power in my veins that's more intense than anything I've ever felt. I feel like I could take on the world right now. It must be triggered by high emotions." He pauses before gritting out, "They cannot have you, Ansel. I can see what you're thinking, but we will find another way."

"I love you, Cai, but that's not your decision to make. Before I ever met you, I promised Nayne that she would be safe. That I would take care of her. I will not fail her, even if it means I must sacrifice myself to ensure her safety."

He pulls away from me. The air around him vibrates with barely contained rage. But I am not afraid—his rage isn't directed at me.

"They've left a tracking summoner," I say. "All I have to do is push the button once we get out of The Wastes and they will come to get me. I'll separate from everyone before I push it—to keep Vale safe."

Cai grabs me, yanking me to his chest. His lips collide with mine in a kiss that is punishing—fueled by his passion and fear. His lips leave mine, leaving me breathless and weak in the knees. His hand comes up to my face as those black eyes consume me.

"You are not alone anymore, Ansel. You don't have to do the protecting all by yourself. We are a team; let me be the sword you wield. Let me help you bring Nayne home. And if a sacrifice needs to be made, let me be the one to make it."

I have no words for him, and I suppose I don't need

them. He feels everything from me; he knows the effects his words have on me. His lips plant a gentle kiss on my forehead as Ginger whinnies outside the shelter. Walking out together, we see Vale and Sidora astride Ginger.

"Everything okay?" Vale asks.

"No, but it will be," I reply. It's all I can give her right now.

We begin walking, all of us more than ready to leave The Wastes behind. I hold Cai's hand as we walk, another novelty I am not used to, but never want to be without. I will soak up as much of him as I can, because what I didn't have the heart to tell him was that Gemini will take no substitute. It's me she wants, because of what I am and what it will get her.

I only hope Cai will understand when the time comes.

CHAPTER 20

Almost a day of walking later, sand gives way to life bursting forth from the soil under our feet. We all sigh in relief to be away from The Wastes. Tension leaves my companions' shoulders and their faces relax. I can only imagine how this feels for Vale and Sidora, having spent so long trapped there. It's as if a cloak has been visibly lifted from them.

Cai helps Sidora and Vale dismount from Ginger, then gives her a quick pat to go graze before turning to face us.

"First things first, I am going to distance jump us out of here after a quick rest."

"Wait. How is it possible that you can jump with another person?" Sidora's puzzled expression makes me think this is not a normal thing for Horsemen.

"It's a new development since Nic found Lucia. He jumped with her at some point, and it's like the knowledge of that ability was suddenly ingrained within me. I just woke up and it was there, as if it always has been, but now it is unlocked and available. Nic only jumped with Lucia, but something tells me that there is no limit to who I can bring as a passenger."

"It must be a sign that we are getting closer to the prophecy coming to fruition. Your powers are reaching new heights in preparation. Activated by the first discovery of a Core." Sidora's face is filled with wonder.

There is so much I don't yet understand about all of this.

"Well, it's perfect timing. I am going to distance jump each one of you to The Refuge. I'll let Z and Elias know we're on our way."

Cai so easily steps into his role of strategist when the need for direction arises. His surety is something I admire.

"NO!" both Sidora and Vale yell simultaneously.

Cai and I stand frozen, stunned by their outburst. We wait for a much-needed explanation.

"She can't go anywhere that will place innocents at risk," Sidora says, a heavy layer of sadness coating each word. "You see, the Amilign found us each and every time we ran from them. They only stopped once we were buried in The Wastes. We don't know for sure, but we think they have some sort of tracker on Vale. Something inside her that we can't see. That's why we didn't go to The Refuge to begin with."

Vale looks somber, nodding. "I won't put any more people at risk."

There is a painful story there, I am certain. Her gaze moves to mine, catching my eyes in an expression of solidarity. At that moment, as if summoned by her pain, Roy flies down to land on Vale's shoulder, pushing her head against the young woman's cheek while Vale rubs a finger across the bird's white-feathered chest.

"Okay, let me think." Cai paces around us, his brow furrowed in concentration. Then he pauses and his eyes get a far-off, unseeing look.

Sidora must see my questioning expression. "He's speaking to his brothers or Elias," she says, easing Vale down to the ground and then sitting herself. "He has a mental link with them that allows him to do so." She puts her arms around the girl, giving her a mama bear hug that sends Roy back into the air. "It won't be long now, darlin'. You remember that Elohim is with you, okay?"

Seeing their strong bond is a pang in my heart. I might have had something similar with Mina and Sloane, if they were still alive. Suddenly, Cai's eyes seem to come back into focus as he blinks and looks at us again.

"Elias is going to tell Z, and he'll come get you, Vale," Cai says. "You will be safest with him. And if whoever is hunting you presumed you dead after the collapse, Elias believes it is safe to assume they won't be actively tracking you any longer, what with tracking technology not working in The Wastes to begin with. That should give us some time at The Refuge before they notice you on their radar again. The Prophets of The Way are working on a plan."

Vale's hesitancy makes me want to wrap my arms around her. She has been through so much, and now she is going to be whisked away by a stranger to a whole group of strangers.

"Don't worry, Vale, we won't let anything happen to you," Cai says.

"It's not me I'm worried about," Vale says solemnly. Cai nods and squeezes her shoulder like a big brother would. Then his eyes get that faraway look once more.

Vale sits in the grass, nervously twirling a blade of grass

between her fingers. Suddenly, Cai's voice breaks through the silence with a sense of urgency.

"Whatever happens, Vale, you should know that Z . . ."

Cai is interrupted by a loud whinny, followed by the thunderous sound of horse hooves splitting the air. In the blink of an eye, a beast of a black horse stands before us, pawing the ground and prancing with a restless, frantic sort of energy. An imposing man sits upon its back, oozing the same energy. He has a warm complexion the color of the desert sands at sundown that stands in stark contrast to Vale's fair complexion and white-blonde hair. His dark hair is buzzed on the sides and slightly longer down the center— a faux mohawk that only adds to his terrifying demeanor. To say Z and his horse are intense is a massive under-statement.

He dismounts in one swift movement and takes purposeful strides toward a wide-eyed, speechless Vale.

I glance around at Cai and Sidora. Does no one else find this totally unsettling? My fingers itch to pull out my bow and warn this brute away from her. But just as quickly as I think it, Cai is by my side with his hand on my arm.

"No, Ans, you don't want to stand in his way. I promise she's perfectly safe."

Just as Cai speaks those words, the man crouches down on one knee. With a gentleness and reverence that I am shocked he possesses, he reaches out a hand to her. He seems hesitant, as though she is some elusive dream that will fall apart at the touch of his fingertips. And with what Cai told me about the Horsemen and their Cores, I suppose that, in a way, she is the culmination of a dream come true for him.

Slowly, his fingers soothe Vale's long hair behind her

ear, his gaze soaking her in as he takes a ragged inhale, like she is fresh air and he's been underground his whole life.

And then his eyes lower to what remains of her right leg and everything changes. His expression hardens and his eyes turn the deepest black. He scoops her into his arms so abruptly, she gasps and flings her arms around his neck for stability. And then he is on his horse again, a wide-eyed Vale cradled possessively in his arms.

All three disappear in a flash.

"Um, what just happened? That can't possibly be okay." I look between Sidora and Cai.

"It's fine," Cai insists. But the conviction in his tone doesn't match the concern on his face. Before I can panic, Sidora steps into my line of sight, placing her hands on my shoulders. It's a loving, motherly gesture that does funny things to my heart.

"Don't you worry, okay? She has Elohim's heart, as do you, and both of you are made for a purpose. His protection and purpose goes with her, just as it does with you."

Her words do more for me than she can possibly know.

Then Cai is at my side. "He's intense, and even more so because he's been suffering with an unexplained pain in his leg that he knew was linked to her being hurt, but he was unable to find her. Having her near him will fix all that's broken."

I nod, not sure what to say or how to feel about this new world I've been pulled into.

"Well, now that Vale is with Z, we can just head back to The Refuge and develop a plan to rescue Nayne from there," Cai says.

The thought of being somewhere new and unknown causes my blood to run cold. It's a level of vulnerability that I can't deal with right now.

"I can't go with you," I say softly.

"What do you mean?" Cai's brows furrow.

"I can't have any distractions right now, Cai," I say, avoiding his eyes. "I need to focus on getting Nayne back, not being somewhere far away, with no means of knowing my exact location or being able to get anywhere without your jumping ability. And I don't want to end up at the mercy of your Prophets and their questions and rules."

"Ans, you don't understand. They don't operate like the FP. It won't be like that. And I can take you anywhere you want to go; you won't have to figure it out on your own."

Cai's genuine care makes this all the more difficult. How can I explain to him that I have never extended that level of trust to another person, not since losing Mina and Sloane? And look how that ended. I love him more than words can say, but I can't relinquish my control over this situation and be completely at the whim of someone else.

I swallow and force myself to meet his eyes. "I'm sorry, Cai. I can't."

Sidora walks up to Cai and pulls him down to her level so she can whisper something to him. His expression softens.

"We have an idea," Cai says. "There's a farmstead not far from here. A family lives there who are good friends to the Prophets. They'll be happy to house us and feed us while we figure this out. We'll need a base of operations, and it's only a few miles east of here. We could walk, but jumping will be faster. Sidora will come with us to help anyway she can."

I meet their eyes. Sidora smiles gently and Cai winks at me. I feel overcome by their willingness to stay with me, to help me with a situation that is solely my problem.

"Thank you," I squeak out.

Cai heads off on Ginger with Sidora sitting behind him. They disappear right before my eyes. Before too long, he's back for me, appearing suddenly, as if made of air.

"We're sitting ducks out here, so let's get to the farmstead, and then we'll strategize how to get Nayne back, okay?" His hand reaches down to me and I take it as he pulls me up behind him. Ginger takes off, and in a disorienting blink, we're in a whole new place.

A fresh breeze bearing scents of cut wood, chimney smoke, and wildflowers fills my senses. A cute little log house, weathered from the years, boasts a wrap-around porch, and smoke puffs gently out of the chimney. Two horses graze in a field that leads to a small barn behind the home. A wooden rail fence surrounds the property, breaking only for the driveway that Cai currently leads Ginger down. It is picturesque in a way that feels wrong for this world. Out of place amidst a world that loves to destroy beautiful things.

A man with a few days of old stubble on his face leans against the end of the fence. He smiles and tips his wide-brimmed hat to us.

"Ansel, meet Nash. Nash has given us permission to stay here for a while to figure out our next steps."

"Thank you, Nash, we're indebted to you."

"Not at all, ma'am. My wife Lottie and I are happy to help you. Anyone who's a friend of the Prophets is a friend of ours." Almost as if summoned, a beautiful lady with cropped, sandy-blonde hair comes out of the house, balancing a cute, rose-cheeked, ginger-haired baby on her hip.

"Come on inside and get settled; I'll have food for y'all in just a bit." She waves us over. At the mention of food, a boy of about Nayne's age comes running from around the side of the house and barrels past his mom through the door. All at once, I am reminded of how I failed Nayne.

She should be here with me, being free to be a child. Instead, she is with the very person who took everyone I loved from me once before. The tracker button burns a hole in my pocket. My fingers itch to get this over with. But I would never draw the FP here and, at the very least, I need to go in with a plan. So, as much as it pains me, I drag myself through the door and pray for the wisdom to know what to do next.

CHAPTER 21

The turmoil churning in Ansel claws at me, urging me to fix it. It's a special form of torture. It was triggered the moment she saw that young boy, who must remind her of Nayne. Even worse is the blockade she seems to be unknowingly building inside her. Like the fear is pushing her back to old habits of fixing things herself, fighting alone, and controlling all the variables.

And I am on the wrong side of this new blockade.

"There's no time to wait; we don't even know how long they have already had her and what she might be going through," Ansel declares, agitation lacing every word. She finally stops her pacing and joins us at the little wooden table in the den, but the bouncing in her knees has me thinking her seated position will probably be short-lived.

"I understand your concern," Sida says, "but it's you that they want, Ansel. You are a Core. Not Nayne. You are the tool this Gemini person needs to get the power she so desperately craves. Think on it—she will not risk that. And as much as I hate to think of the child trapped in this situation, I know Elohim is with her."

Sida covers Ansel's hand with her own. I filled her in the moment we stepped into the kitchen, and she insisted on helping however she could.

"But don't you see? It all rests on me. The only way to get her back is to trade me for her! What happens if I bring you along, Cai, and they see you or have some way of sensing you? Who knows what resources Gemini has access to now that she's sold her soul. I know what Gemini is capable of. After what she did to Mina and Sloane, women who were supposed to be her sisters, I cannot just believe Nayne will be okay." Ansel pauses and attempts to take a calming breath. "I do not have that kind of faith."

Sida meets my eyes across the table—a heavy sadness in her gaze—before she turns her full attention on Ansel. "Oh my child, one of the most beautiful things about Elohim is that even when you cannot fully grasp His love, His love has fully grasped you. And while I don't believe that everything will always be perfect and pain-free, Elohim knows what we will go through and He will arm and equip us for it, if we let Him. Not so we can avoid the pain, but so that we will not be broken by it."

A lone tear tracks down Ansel's cheek and my heart squeezes at the sight.

"But I *am* broken," she says, the words tumbling out of her like shattered glass.

"Oh, lovely girl." Sida reaches an arm around Ansel, pulling her lovingly into her side so that Ansel's head rests on the older woman's shoulder. "Then go to the only one who can heal what is broken within you. Elohim Shomri, our protector, redeems every person that turns to Him. But it has been and always will be your choice. Even as one of

His Cores, He has still given you a choice." Planting a kiss on Ansel's head, Sida stands. "And with that, I think I'll go see if Lottie needs help in the kitchen."

"Come." I reach out a hand to Ansel, guessing her restlessness might be better served by moving. I certainly think better on the move. "Take a walk with me."

Despite the heaviness that presses on her, she slips her hand into mine, and the gift of that small gesture is not lost on me. We head out to the porch.

"Elohim gave us a gift in our bond, Ans, and we need to use it. We can pick a location, far from here, that will allow me to remain a safe distance from you, and we can use our bond to push emotions to each other. I'll remain far enough away not to be seen, and my enhanced vision will allow me to still keep you in sight. At the slightest danger, I will come in as backup. You don't have to do this alone."

"There's still the chance that they will see you. Or what if I am terrified the whole time and can't focus long enough to send anything to you? This is new to both of us. What if Gemini sees you and kills Nayne on the spot?" She stops at that thought and turns to face me. "You don't understand, Cai. She killed the only family I had because she wanted full control of me and she thought they were getting in the way. She killed them because they were an inconvenience. She killed them despite the fact that we were supposed to be a sisterhood that protects each other."

Tears flow like floodwaters down her cheeks. I pull her into my arms, desperately needing to hold her, even if I cannot stop the pain. I breathe in her vanilla-and-jasmine scent, grateful she is here with me, against all odds.

"We will figure this out, Ans, I promise you. And we will work out a plan that keeps everyone safe. I will not rest until we do."

She nods against my chest, but the hints of doubt, fear, and—even worse—sad acceptance that are coming through our bond give a different response altogether.

The rusty creak of the porch door hinges alerts us to the fact that we are no longer alone.

"Are you really a Horseman?" the young boy asks as he approaches us with his baby sister in his arms. She squirms against his hold like a piglet wanting to get loose. "Like from the old stories of the Four Horsemen of the Apocalypse? Does that mean we're all going to die?"

His rapid-fire questions help distract us.

"Apparently, that's why he needs to keep me around," Ansel says with a wink, after smoothly wiping all emotion from her face. "I help him keep the crazy at bay."

I laugh at her explanation. The young boy looks between us in utter confusion. With a huff, he places his baby sister on the porch to crawl around and puts his hands on his hips. Clearly, he isn't going anywhere until he gets a real explanation.

"She's not lying, bud, she has all the real power. She's a Core, a gift of Elohim to stop the leashing of hell that would seek to control me." I look into her eyes with purposeful intensity. "I am lost without her."

My words strike true, causing that beautiful flush in her cheeks that I have grown to adore. Ansel quickly bends over to grab the ginger-haired baby girl before she reaches the porch stairs and takes a nasty tumble. Ever the protector of innocence. She walks around with the little girl on her hip, and seeing the two of them together opens up a yearning in me that I didn't realize I had.

My whole life has been for one purpose—finding my Core. It seemed like an impossible goal for so many years that I never dared to think about being on the other side of it. But now that she is here with me, hope blossoms. A longing for a life that is more than warring, with Ansel by my side and, hopefully one day, a family that looks like her.

Her gasp tells me she senses my emotions, and the quick glance over her shoulder with raised eyebrows only confirms her surprise. All I can do is smile and shrug. She shakes her head and goes back to bouncing the baby on her hip.

I will fight tooth and nail to keep this woman safe. Ansel is this bright and beautiful gift, intent on standing firm against the darkness, even if she is alone and the odds are stacked against her. She is mine to protect as much as I am hers, and now that I've dared to hope for more, there is no way that I will accept any outcome that includes her sacrifice.

"How old are you, young man?" I ask.

"I am ten years old sir!" The boy beams. "Why?"

His curiosity will serve me well, I think. "I have need of a soldier, but I need someone who is sneaky, crafty, and can stay well hidden."

His face lights up like a full moon in a starless sky. "That's definitely me, then!"

"You see that woman with your sister over there?"

"Your Core, sir?"

"That's right, my Core. She's very important to me. In fact, she's important to the world. I just need an extra set of eyes on her. Do you think you can do that for me?"

"That's it? That's so boring! I thought it would be something serious."

"Oh, she won't make it easy. She's a warrior through and through. She cannot know that you are watching her." I place my hands on the boy's shoulders. "And this is the most serious thing in the world to me. I would not entrust this to just anyone."

That seems to appease the young boy, because he nods with pride.

Lottie comes to the door.

"Dinner time, y'all. Go get washed up, JJ." The little boy takes off like a shot. "And I'm happy to take Bea from you?" Lottie says to Ansel.

Ansel steps forward and passes the little girl to Lottie. "Did you say her name is Bea?"

"Yes, it's short for Beatrice. That was my mother's name. She died when I was a child. And JJ is short for John Jackson, which is my and Nash's dads' names. Both also died. This place is all we have left of them. They worked together to build it for us."

There's something in Lottie's tone that suggests they didn't die from natural causes or a mere accident. But I don't prod, knowing I wouldn't want to dig at old wounds either.

"I am so sorry to hear that," Ansel says softly and genuinely, probably thinking of her own losses.

"Thank you; I imagine we've all lost people we love. It's why we support the Prophets and help when we can. We need the hope of Elohim Shomri in this world, now more than ever. And you, Ansel, represent that hope. You have the heart of Elohim. You are a conduit for His light in this dark world. We are so blessed to be living in the time of the Cores."

CHAPTER 22

Dinner brings comfort for a starving belly and soul. The simple but hearty food, complete with the soothing laughter around the table and warm conversation, is so unfamiliar to me, and yet feels, oddly enough, like coming home. But to a home I've never been to and have only dreamed of.

We learn of the extraordinary work that Nash and Lottie do for The Refuge. Rare artisans, they design and create all of the protective leathers for the Horsemen and some of the others who help in a soldiering capacity. Their work is skillful and absolutely exquisite; light, yet sturdy, and pliable, yet protective.

I shudder to think of what could have befallen them if the wrong people had learned of their skills. I know Gemini would love to have them, or at least Lottie, at her disposal. But Nash assures me that they are safe and he has measures in place, just in case. I guess they are close enough to The Wastes that not many travelers come this way, and isolated enough in their pocket of forest that not many would even know they are here if they do pass by. Seems risky, but I understand not wanting to leave behind a place that feels like home and still houses the memories of loved ones long gone.

They are excited to take my measurements so they can start work on a set of leathers for me. According to them, it would be an honor to create the gear that will be a safeguard for one of Elohim's and this world's greatest treasures. I wish I had adequate words to express my gratitude to them, but the whole interaction leaves me feeling a bit off-kilter at such genuine generosity with no strings attached.

I nod my quick thanks and excuse myself, blaming a need to stretch my legs and get some fresh air. As I head into the barn, I am delighted to see Ginger, busy chowing down food herself. She lifts her head at my entrance.

"Hey there, G." I smile as she makes her way to the front of her stall. "Glad to see you are getting a little spoiling, too."

The soft coat of her neck caresses my hand as I pet her, and she pushes her big head into my chest. I giggle at her eagerness, rubbing her jaw and behind her ears, amazed at the peace that comes with such a simple action.

Suddenly, I feel a change in the air around me, like the scent of rain on the wind before a storm.

Cai is here.

"I was surprised to see Ginger in here." I don't turn, despite how my eyes thirst to drink him in. But I feel him draw near, and then his hands come around my waist and he presses against my back. Everywhere he touches me, a buzz goes through me.

"Yeah, after being buried for so long, I thought she could use some good food and freedom." His lips press a chaste kiss to the side of my head. "I got a bath ready for you," he continues softly. "I thought you might like to get The Wastes off you."

I turn in his arms and wind my arms around his neck. The intensity of our connection amazes me, and Cai smiles down at me in response to what I must have been sending his way.

"Can you feel everything I feel?" I ask.

"If you feel it strongly, yes; I don't even have to try. Otherwise, it's kind of like grasping a cord that links us. I have to purposely reach out to get a sense of what you feel."

Wanting to further explore this new link, I stand up onto my tiptoes and slowly bring my lips to his, testing and teasing him, softly feathering my mouth against his as our breath intermingles. Joy radiates through our connection and I delight in exploring a sensation with him that is new to me. And it makes me wonder what else I can send to him.

I pull back from our kiss, and his almost glowing eyes and rakish grin speak volumes. I focus on my desire for him and only him, and how I want him in every way. My yearning for his smile and how his laughter is a melody for my soul; the press of his lips and hands against my skin; his irresistible scent of citrus and sandalwood; and how the feel of his body against mine causes me to combust. I imagine grabbing that link between us with both hands and send that desire directly to him like an arrow from my bow.

He takes a physical step back like he was shoved. His eyes grow as big as twin full moons on a horizon and glow even more intensely. He brings a shaky hand to the back of his neck.

"Geez, woman, are you trying to kill me!?"

I laugh out loud at his reaction. "I wasn't sure if that would work." I smirk at the intensity in his eyes. "I thought it might be fun to test my theory."

"Yeah, if you think it's fun to light me on fire and watch me burn."

I can't contain my laughter as he throws me over his shoulder and heads back to the house.

"Come on, you firecracker, let's get you in that tub before we burn down this lovely barn that Nash and Lottie built."

I smile, and this time gently grasp the cord between us, sending him my amusement and love. He sends me his adoration and humor in return as a hearty swat to my backside makes me gasp.

I feel his humor increase tenfold.

I can't remember the last time I sat in a bath until the water chilled. I was never allowed such luxuries in my time with the FP, but the minute I relax into the warm water laced with lavender and sage, I want to take up residence here and never leave.

But the cooling water has allowed all my fear for Nayne to return with gusto, the fleeting distraction of the soothing warmth long gone. I step out of the water, wrapping a towel around my body, and step through the bathroom door into the bedroom to see a shirtless Cai lying on the small bed, his giant frame dwarfing it. He props himself up onto one elbow as I walk in, his jaw practically hanging open.

"You might want to pick your jaw up off the floor, Cai. It's not a confident look for a Horseman." I wink at him. "Plus, it's not like you haven't seen me in far less before."

"Yeah, well, things were very different then. One, you were injured, and two, I think you hated me."

I saunter over to him as he sits up. "Well, I am not

injured now, and I definitely don't hate you." A shiver that has nothing to do with the chilled air ripples across my skin, and need unfurls deep within me. He sits erect and still as a statue, hardly breathing.

"Ans," he says in a breathless warning.

I sit on his lap and let his warmth seep into me, his scent surrounding me. My heart pounds as his eyes brighten, but he remains frozen in place. Waiting.

I love him and I want him, more than anything. But more than that, I desperately need a distraction from the fear and worry at what lies ahead that threatens to choke me. I lean closer, ready to press my lips to his, when he gently cups my face and presses a kiss to my forehead. Then his arms come around me in a tight bear hug.

"Why don't we get some rest?" he whispers.

I push against his chest and stand, shock and a touch of grief oozing from every part of me.

"After all of this, you don't want me?"

He stands, and the playful, sweet Cai is gone; a warrior stands in front of me instead. He strides toward me, causing me to take steps backward until I am against the wall. He moves so close, his body is pressed up against me. My pulse picks up its pace. He gently raises my chin until my eyes are locked on his.

"You know that's not true; you can feel it in the bond." Despite his demeanor and firm tone, his words are gentle. His lips are so close, I can almost taste his spoken words. "But I will never take advantage of you, Ans, and I will not say yes to you until you are fully with me and want this for the right reasons."

A gasp flies from my lips. "What do you mean?"

He takes a step back, as if to cool the inferno between us. "I know you love me, and obviously, you have accepted that you are a Core, based on the connection we share. A bond that is stronger than any human connection. But I can feel you holding back something. I can't tell if you think you are protecting me or yourself, but this barrier prevents us from fully being one."

I stare, astonished that he is so aware of me. He presses his lips to my forehead again in a gentle, sweet kiss that fills me with guilt. Because he is right.

"I love you, and I won't push you. But I will always protect you, even from yourself if I need to. The last thing I would ever want is for you to regret anything between us."

CHAPTER 23

ANSEL

I lie awake, listening to the sounds of the old wood house. The creaks of the home relaxing from a day of people bustling in and out are like the groaning of old joints popping and finally taking a much-needed rest. What would it have been like to grow up in such a place? Would I have been as carefree and curious a child as JJ? Naive to the dangers of the outside world, craving to explore, know more, have my own adventures, completely unaware of how good I had it?

It's a waste of energy to try to imagine it. That was not my life, and dreaming of a different path will only lead me down a dark road I don't have the desire to tread on.

I glance down at Cai. He insisted I take JJ's small bed, and he curled up with a pillow and blanket on the floor, promptly passing out. As if he doesn't have a care in the world. And maybe he doesn't. Nayne is my little sister, after all. My problem to solve. And even though he wants to help,

I felt through the bond that he would do anything to keep me safe.

I fear that *anything* includes sacrificing Nayne.

He and Sidora all but said it when they emphasized my importance as a Core, then stated that Nayne was not one. But none of that matters to me. She is the only family I have left, and she is just a child. I will do whatever it takes for her to know she matters to someone and has someone in her corner. Nayne is counting on me to protect her, and I will not let her down. Gemini will not win. And if trusting Elohim is what I am supposed to do, then I will just have to trust Elohim to keep me safe when I leave tonight. Because there's no way I will entrust Nayne's safety to anyone but myself.

Cai's breaths are slow and even. I look at him as I sit up. My eyes drink in the angles of his stubbled jaw, the loose sandy waves of his hair, and those soft, full lips. I commit them to memory. I want to kiss him one more time, tell him he was the greatest and most unexpected gift of my life, even if it was only for a little while. But those things will have to remain unspoken in my heart.

I tiptoe out of the room, sticking to the edges where the wooded boards are less likely to creak. I identify a slightly ajar window by the kitchen as a way to avoid the creaking porch door hinges.

A small leap from the window frame, and I land lightly in the grass. Making my way to the barn, I gently slide the door open and quickly saddle one of the horses. I write a note to Lottie and Nash with my apologies and the intricately carved blade that was gifted to me by Sloane years ago. Hopefully, it will fetch enough of a price to pay for the horse. As much as I am loath to leave it behind, I can't take advantage of their kindness, especially with the risks they took to help us.

I open the gate, leading the mare through, and quietly close it behind me. After mounting the horse, I take one last look back at the picturesque scene, another comforting memory to tuck away for later when I will surely need it.

I walk the horse down the long driveway, waiting to bring her to a gallop until I reach the end and the road opens up. The timing will be tricky. I need to get as far away from here as possible before I activate the tracker, but I also need to activate it long before morning. Each moment I delay risks Cai waking up and realizing I am gone.

Three hours of hard riding later, the mare is starting to struggle. She is clearly not used to being ridden like this—she's just a farm horse, after all. Probably used for hunting, plowing, and maybe hauling; she's built for strength, not speed. I decide to take pity on the poor creature and dismount, preparing to abandon her in the woods. Luckily, I stumble upon a small creek with some pasture land. I quickly remove the tack and give her a soft pat on the rear. She immediately heads to the water and I head in the opposite direction, off into the trees. If I am going to do this alone, I must play it smart.

I press the tracker button and leave it in an open, grassy field. Then I head into the trees with my bow and quiver and climb up into one that will give me a good view of the field and the surroundings while providing me with some cover.

Then I sit and wait.

The sky is just shifting from black to the warm gray of

dawn when the faint whomp whomp whomp of a helicopter breaks through the forest sounds around me. Since when did Gemini have access to the Amilign's helicopter? It makes me wonder how much I was blind to when I was with them.

As the helicopter lands, the whirring blades have every tree quivering in their wake, including the one I am currently counting on to hide me. Leaves blow in a whirlwind of mayhem all around me, making it hard to see anything. But I glimpse the dark skin I know so well as the helicopter lands in a clearing and Nayne is pulled from the belly of the beast, Gemini's hand gripping her arm.

Gemini is easy to spot with her unmistakable hair, shaved on the sides with a long, braided mohawk that trails down her back. Black war paint splashes across her eyes and streaks down her face. She scans the trees. I so badly want to fire an arrow, but I can't ensure accuracy with the helicopter blades still spinning.

She whispers something in Nayne's ear, and the girl begins to walk forward slowly until she's a good distance away from Gemini and the helicopter. And then she pauses, her hands fidgeting in front of her in her telltale sign of nerves. Gemini pulls a gun from her holster. The message is clear—come out or Nayne will receive a bullet for my silence.

I am pulled as taut as a bowstring as fear and rage fight for dominance.

I shimmy down the tree and head out from beneath the covering. Nayne spots me and her face lights up with joy. Joy that I do not deserve. Even worse, I must keep my face a mask, unwilling to give Gemini any more information about my attachment to the girl. So, keeping my gaze glued to Gemini, I walk right past Nayne to my target.

Seeing her again is like kindling to the flame of my anger. I am a pot beginning to boil over, and the violent train of my thought screams for me to end her here and now. But with Nayne so close, I still can't risk doing anything.

"Well, well, well." She pauses, looking me up and down with a haughty smirk. "I didn't think you had it in you."

"Then you never knew anything about me," I say in a slow, measured voice, struggling to contain my anger. "I am not the coward you are."

Gemini's eyes flash as the smirk falls from her face and her grip tightens on her gun. "Quite the bold thing you've become since running away like a petulant child. And after all that we've done for you."

"Do you mean killing Mina and Sloane? Or making plans to trade me to the Amilign? Please, feel free to explain. I am a little confused as to what you could be referring to."

"Ahh, so that's why you ran. I figured you discovered something. And instead of waiting for me to explain, you fled. Everything I have ever done for the FP was to make us stronger and better. My job as a leader has always been to prune off any weakness. I won't apologize for it. I made you who you are, and you dare stand before me, ungrateful! You had the honor of being Feminea Potentia and you threw it away! We are a sisterhood who lives to strengthen each other and sacrifice for the greater good. If the greater good means you go with the Amilign, then you should be honored to play the role that would support your sisters." Her eyes flash as the words fly from her mouth.

I know I shouldn't anger her further, but I will not stand silent against her delusions. At the very least, it's my small way to honor the memory of those who aren't here to defend themselves.

"You only exist to take advantage of those you deem less than you and to garner as much power as you can. Don't pretend that every decision you make is not solely selfish." My chest rises sharply. A surge of fury builds up in me that has waited too long to be released.

"Don't you understand, Ansel? Power is the only real protection in this world. The monks taught me that. If I'd had enough power, I wouldn't have lost my brother." Her eyes are almost feverish as the words spill from her lips.

"You don't know that. There are no guarantees in life. The FP should know that better than most," I insist.

"Maybe, but power is the closest thing I'll get to a guarantee. And I will do whatever it takes to have the power I need to ensure that security and make the FP unstoppable. Can't you see, I've only ever wanted what's best for the FP. You are who you are today because of me."

Gemini really is broken. Sloane was right all those years ago when she thought Gemini had been claimed by a growing darkness. I see it now in the madness in her eyes. A wave of icy resolve fortifies me.

"It was Mina and Sloane who made me who I am today. And your jealousy couldn't handle that, so you had them killed. I was a part of the FP because I thought we stood for helping those in need, but no, you were secretly stealing young girls on the side and destroying any who stood in your way. You are merely a weak vessel, power-hungry and corrupt." I lift my chin in challenge.

Gemini shakes with barely contained rage. As if in slow motion, I watch her lift her gun to aim at Nayne. And I know that I am not alone anymore; maybe Elohim is with me after all. Maybe I have never really been alone, because with sudden clarity, I see that my life experiences and training have led up to this very moment.

To save this child.

I pull the small knife from my back holster, clasping the blade as I bring it around and fling it, watching the blade bury itself into Gemini's forearm. She drops the gun.

I turn my head to look at Nayne's wide-eyed expression.

"RUN!" I scream, and then I launch myself at Gemini as a cluster of FP spill from the helicopter like cockroaches. She pulls the blade from her arm and slashes at me, catching me in the bicep, but I barely feel the wound with the adrenaline racing through my body. Protective rage burns fierce within me, and I know that Cai is awake and probably feeling a whole lot coming from me.

The thought comforts me. He will stop at nothing to find me, which means that even if I am long gone, he will find Nayne and he will keep her safe. I just need to give her time to get far enough away.

And that is my last thought before something cracks against the back of my skull and all the lights go out.

CHAPTER 24

I wake to a throbbing pain in my head accompanied by the feel of grass and dirt smushed against my cheek and forehead from lying face down on the ground. I stay still, not wanting to alert anyone that I am conscious. I can already tell my hands are bound behind my back and my ankles are tied together. It's also night again, which means I've been unconscious for hours. I wait, listening. When I hear no voices, I try to sit up and quickly realize they also tied my legs to the landing skids of the helicopter, which now sits lifeless in the field.

I look around from my position on the ground. All is quiet. If I had to guess, they are trying to find Nayne. Now that they have me secured, they don't want to lose their bargaining chip, and I'll be easier to control if they have her, too.

"Look what we have here." The familiar voice of Athena speaks from above me, followed by the thud of her shoes hitting the ground as she hops out of the helicopter. "My how the mighty have fallen."

"Athena." I keep my face turned to the side so I don't get a mouthful of dirt. "Guard duty, huh? I wondered if you still follow Gemini around like a puppy."

I get a kick to my side for that comment.

"Say what you want; soon, you'll be spending your days as a plaything for the monks," Athena mocks. "You know, Gemini was pretty pissed when she discovered you'd gone. But it looks like you aren't quite as good as she thought."

I scour my last memories before everything went dark, trying to figure out how many FP I am contending with. I only saw an additional three come from the helicopter; who knows if that included the pilot. So, with Gemini and Athena, that's potentially five or six warriors total. They can do whatever they want to me, so long as Nayne gets away. *Please, please let her get away.*

A loud *crack* reverberates through the air, and then Athena's limp form lands face down in the dirt next to me, followed by a decent-sized stick. I can't see much from my position, but a soft sawing sound at my back causes hope to light—the cutting of a knife against rope.

"Shhh, they aren't far away. I led them on a wild-goose chase, but we need to be fast," Nayne whispers. I am surprised that Nayne wielded a stick with such efficiency to be able to knock Athena out. But I highly doubt she'll be out for very long considering Nayne's slight strength and Athena's hard head.

"What are you doing here? I didn't sacrifice myself so you could end up right back here with me, Nay Nay!"

"And I wasn't going to let my only family sacrifice themselves for me. You wouldn't have if you were me, so you can't ask me to do any different."

I sigh at that, because she's not wrong. I practically raised her, so I shouldn't be surprised that she's turned out like me.

As soon as I feel the rope loosen, I hop to my feet. "No time to wait; we'll get my hands later. Lead the way."

Nayne smiles at me and heads off in the direction that I trust is the opposite of where the FP is currently searching. One thing Nayne excels at is hiding and tracking. She loves noticing little nuances in a situation and with her small frame, she is excellent at going unnoticed. We walk for thirty minutes; then she turns and cuts the rest of the rope from my hands. Once freed, I pull her into a tight squeeze.

"I am so sorry, Nay Nay. I never meant to leave you. I would never abandon you."

Her small hand pats my back. "I know, Ansel, it's okay. We're together again. And I want to hear all about what happened to you in The Wastes, but maybe let's get out of here first."

"Right. Speaking of which, let's get some distance between us and them." I hate the idea of putting that sweet family in danger, but I have nowhere else to take Nayne, and Cai is my closest ally. Though, if I am being honest with myself, it is more than that. He is home to me. I crave him like a flower craves the sun.

"You didn't see a horse by any chance, did you?"

Nayne winces. "Uh, yeah, but I used her as a distraction." She looks dismayed.

"No worries, you did great, kid! So proud of you." I squeeze her shoulder and we continue on. Every hour that passes takes us farther away from the FP and closer to safety. It eases the prick of the thorn that has taken up residence in me since leaving Cai. Still, we're not there yet, and I desperately need a distraction.

"So, tell me what you discovered. Where did they take you?"

"They took me to a new place, one I'd never been to before. It was smaller and there were only a handful of FP there. But there's not much else I can say about it. I am sorry I can't give you more details, but I was blindfolded for most of it." She pauses, looking over her shoulder at me. "I got the sense that something seriously bad had happened to the FP. They seemed on edge and nervous."

Before Cai found me, he had been hunting them. Did he actually discover them and decimate their ranks? Or is something else going on? Either way, fewer of Gemini's corrupt lackeys in the world is not a bad thing. I only hope that if there were any FP left who felt like Nayne and me, they were able to get away.

"Interesting," I say, "anything else?"

"Well, I overheard Gemini talking about some deal. And she seemed pretty excited about what would come from that."

"I bet she was," I huff. Clearly the deal was trading me to the Amilign.

"But I think it was more than trading you. She talked about a weapon that would level the playing field."

We continue on in silence as I ponder Nayne's words. What could this weapon be? If it excites Gemini, it is something to be concerned about. Is this the reason Gemini ceased stealing young girls? Maybe Cai will have answers.

The telltale *whomp whomp whomp* in the distance has Nayne and I freezing. We both drop to our knees in the foliage and wait. I expect to hear the noise grow louder. But instead, it reaches a steady din and then dies off completely. Which can only mean one thing.

Backup has arrived.

"Time to pick up the pace, Nay Nay," I insist. With that, we break out into a steady jog. I don't know how long we can keep up this pace, but we need to get some more distance between us and the FP. My guess is that reinforcements have arrived to broaden the search. Our chances just got a little more slim.

"Look, I need you to make me a promise."

Nayne stops and turns to me with a skeptical expression. The kid knows me too well. "I don't want to hear any arguing from you," I say with the firmness of her Dux, her former commander and trainer. "If it seems like they're about to find us, we're going to separate. I will lead them away, since it's me they want, and I want you to hide. If you keep following the river upstream, you'll eventually happen upon a farmstead. My friends are there and they will help you."

Tears cut shiny, moonlit paths down Nayne's face. Her little arms cross in front of her chest as she vigorously shakes her head *no*, biting down on her lower lip as if trying to keep the tears at bay.

"I know," I say with regret, pulling her into my arms. "I hate the idea of it, too. But one of my new friends is a pretty big badass, and he will help you. However, in order for that to happen, I need you to get to him, okay? You're just so much faster and stealthier than me. And I will follow you as soon as I can." I hate to lie to her, but I can't risk leading Gemini and whatever evil she's partnered up with to Nash and Lottie's home.

She laughs a little at that and the mood lightens just a bit. "Come on, we're not giving up yet."

～

I feel like I am dragging a broken bicycle through the woods. Despite her best efforts, Nayne is still young, and after hours of running, she is out of energy. I offer to carry her, but she is vehemently against it, insisting she can handle our pace. Though as I look back and see the tracks of exhaustion-laced tears on her cheeks, my heart cracks at the realization that we have reached the end of her strength.

I turn to face her, and she quickly tries to wipe away any remnants of what she's been trained to see as weakness. I kneel in front of her, holding both her hands in mine as I gaze into a face I love as if she were my own flesh and blood.

"It's time," I say softly.

Her tears flow unrestrained and she shakes her head.

"I know." I stroke my thumb across the top of her small hand. "I feel the same, but we've gone as far as we can together. There's a thicket of brambles over here. It might be hard to get into it, but once in there, I don't believe anyone will see you if you stay quiet."

I barely get the words out before she throws her small frame into me, her hands tightly squeezing me around the neck. I hug her tightly back.

"Remember, this is not goodbye. This is 'See you soon.' Remember what I told you about the river and finding my friends." Sidora's words flood my mind, and I say a quick prayer to her Elohim, asking for protection for Nayne.

I help Nayne get herself situated in the thicket. I am grateful she is so small, otherwise she would never be able to get in there. Standing back, I can't glimpse her hidden within. My pulse calms.

"I can't see you, so you're safe here. Stay until you hear the helicopter leaving again. Then follow the river." I don't mention that I'll most likely be on the helicopter. The only way they will give up the search for her is if they have me.

And she will be safe with Cai, and Nash and Lottie will remain undiscovered. But that's my burden to bear, not hers.

"Okay," she says so softly, I almost don't hear it.

"See you soon, kid," I say as I turn and head back in the direction we came from, doing my best to ignore the fading sniffles I leave behind.

～

It's not long before the hair on the back of my neck is standing on end.

I know this feeling.

I am being hunted—again.

I subtly scan my surroundings but I see nothing. Whoever this is, they are good. I pause as a gust of wind whistles through the trees, creating a litany of rustling leaves and scraping branches. My skin chills in anticipation. Something is waiting for me.

Suddenly, the unmistakable *crack* of an arrow splitting wood sounds from the tree next to me. A warning. If I run, the next one won't miss. And since I don't know where this threat is coming from, I have one choice.

I slowly raise my hands in surrender.

A gargantuan creature steps out from the shadows of the forest. He's the shape of a man, but far bigger than anyone of this world has a right to be. He's dressed all in black, and the inky, spiderlike veins radiating outward from his red eyes confirm he's not of this world.

An eerie grin showcases razor-sharp teeth, and then two more of whatever this guy is steps into my peripheral vision. My heart sinks, but at least now I know what I am dealing with. I have no weapon, but maybe their large frames will make them slow. Now that I know where my opponents are, my one chance is to run. And I am counting on them wanting me alive.

It may be futile, but it's not in my nature to give up. I turn on my heel and run as if my life depends on it.

I do my best to weave in and out of the tightly packed trees, hopefully preventing the monsters from being able to track me with an arrow. Feet crash behind me, and I pick up my pace. My lungs are balloons filled to capacity—the burn tells me I am at my max. Another *crack* splits a tree to my left and fear frays the sharp edges of my focus.

I duck under a dense-canopied tree, leap over a bush, and dive to the right of another thick bramble. I roll down a small embankment and land in a crouch before rushing up the other side, but then fiery pain rips through my shoulder. The force of the arrow throws me forward into the dirt. I try to rise, but the radiating pain steals my breath and renders my left arm useless.

Something grabs my hair and yanks me upright. The pain in my scalp tears a scream from my throat. I stand on my tiptoes. My right hand grasps at my hair, begging for release.

The dark chuckles of three figures make me still.

"If you thought you could escape us, you are dumber than I was led to believe." My captor's rotting breath assaults my senses. My eyes threaten to dim at the pain and loss of blood. He pulls me close, his hand gripping the back of my neck. He leans in and inhales deeply.

"Your adrenaline and blood are like a drug to us. It doesn't matter where you run to; we will find you. What you are calls to us." He licks his filthy tongue up the side of my neck to my cheek. Bile rises in my throat.

I kick him in the shin with all my strength. His

eyebrows furrow as he looks down at his leg, then his gaze returns to me and he smiles.

"Don't tease me with foreplay, sugar. We need to get you to the ashram before the fun can begin."

My skin chills at his words as the dark laughter of his companions echoes around me. A branch cracks in the distance.

"But first, we have a gift for you." He turns me to face the direction of the noise, his meaty hand firmly grasping my nape.

My stomach drops and I watch in horror as another of the beastly figures emerges from the forest, carrying a small bundle over his shoulder. Nayne's brown skin and signature puff of hair sway in front of his chest, a lifeless movement.

"No!" I scream.

"No need for the drama," the beast carrying her says. "She's merely unconscious. What leverage would she possibly give us if she were dead?"

I am a hollowed out husk—empty and without hope. Another failure, and now I am out of options.

If only I had listened to Cai.

"Hmm, unconsciousness is not a bad idea," a sinister voice speaks from behind me. Right as he grabs hold of the arrow in my shoulder, I reach out for the cord linking me to Cai. But before I can send anything to him, the monster twists the arrow in my shoulder, tearing a guttural scream from my throat.

Once more, everything goes dark.

CHAPTER 25

MORDECAI

It's been an entire day since I discovered Ansel left. The fear that grips me is like heavy chains, threatening to paralyze me. On top of the fear is a deep, thrumming ache that she chose to do this alone. That she didn't trust me, trust us —together. Logically, I know that she's been fighting on her own her whole life and old habits die hard, but her choice feels like a knife in my heart.

Nash gave us a map of the area and possible places where Ansel might go to meet the FP. Sadly, his young son JJ is also missing. Ansel would never put the child at risk, so JJ must be following my wishes, and now I've put the boy at risk.

I scoped out three of the locations by distance jumping with Ginger and found no sign of either Ansel or JJ. I came back late last night to see if she or JJ had made their way back, but no such luck. Sida insisted I lie down for a few hours while Lottie put the finishing touches on a set of protective leathers they've been working on.

I wake after two restless hours, inhale some food, and don the leathers. The dark chocolate-colored chest plate, shoulder guards, and arm bracers are simple, yet exquisitely crafted.

"Not our best work, but definitely the fastest. At the very least, they should offer you some protection." Worry and sadness pour off Lottie.

"Thank you." I gently grasp her shoulder. "I'll find him, Lottie. You have my word."

She only nods somberly.

We are walking to the pasture where Ginger waits when an excruciating pain with an undercurrent of terror that is not mine rips all the breath from my lungs. I stagger and fall to my knees in the grassy field. Like a bomb just went off inside me, power burns through my veins and sends a blast radius outward from me, forcing Nash, Lottie, and Sida back. A guttural roar rips from me. Ginger rears and squeals as she feeds off my emotions.

My lungs heave. I wait on my hands and knees, struggling to control this power that wants to decimate everything standing between me and Ansel.

"Cai," Sida says hesitantly. I lift my gaze to her, and her sharp intake of breath tells me my eyes are black.

"Ansel is hurt," I bite out. As soon as the words leave my mouth, Ginger takes off toward the tree line. With my enhanced eyesight, I can see the small figure of a young boy.

Ginger lowers herself for the boy to climb on, then rushes back to us.

The exhausted kid slides off the horse into the waiting arms of his father.

"JJ!" his mother screams.

"He's okay, Lottie. Not injured, just tuckered out," Nash soothes his wife.

Nash places him on his feet, and Sida rushes to him with some water that he quickly guzzles.

"I know where Ansel went," says JJ. "I followed her as long as I could before I lost sight of her, and then until I couldn't track her anymore."

I move in front of the boy and he pushes back into his dad, fear blanketing him at my approach. But I am past the point of being able to rein in my emotions.

I pause. "Thank you, JJ," I say with as much calm and gentleness as I can muster in this heightened state. "Just point me in the right direction and I'll take it from here."

He lifts a shaking finger in the direction he came from. "She took the western route that heads into the valley. But I lost her after that."

I nod.

"I am going with you," Sida says firmly.

"You won't be able to keep up." I head for Ginger. "I am going to distance jump to get to her faster, but incrementally, so I don't miss any signs of her."

There's no time for niceties. My Core is injured and scared; alone out there. And now I have a small glimpse into Z's life.

"I won't be as fast," Sida says, "but I can still follow for backup. And you know I'm a fair tracker. Leave a few markers for me and I won't be that far behind."

It's not a bad idea.

"Here." Sida hands me her red shawl. "Tear a piece off and tie it to a branch pointed in the direction I need to head. I'll do the rest."

I wrap the fabric around my bicep and tie it in place. I mount Ginger and turn to see Sida mounting one of Nash's horses. Unable to wait any longer, Ginger and I take off. The pounding of hooves behind me tells me she's following.

I need a clear head for whatever lies ahead, so I say a quick prayer to Elohim as Ginger breaks into a gallop.

∼

I stop after a few jumps because Ansel's scent is strong in the area. Grateful for my heightened senses, I dismount and tread forward carefully.

After an hour of following my nose, Ansel's scent is suddenly combined with the metallic smell of blood. My gut sinks. I know I am not going to like what I find next.

At the top of the next embankment, I see splattered blood and the signs of a struggle on the forest floor. Ansel's scent is strongest where the blood stains the earth. I am shaking now, and I can't focus. My rage is a wild beast in my chest, threatening to claw its way free.

I need to calm down. I cannot lose it now. I force myself to take a breath, but the air feels like razor blades in my lungs.

Suddenly, Sida comes riding up the embankment. She brings her horse to a quick stop. She must have galloped the whole distance, only stopping for my markers. She dismounts in a blink and stands in front of me, her small hands firmly grasping my face.

"Look at me!" Her firm words draw my gaze. "You will not lose control! You are the Horseman of War. It's time to plan our next move and get our girl."

I close my eyes and attempt to take another breath. This time it's easier—a deep, centering breath fills me. Sida's hands on my face are a lifeline. When I open my eyes, I feel more in control.

I nod my thanks to her and mount Ginger. We continue to follow the trail. It's dusk again, and night is fast approaching. A chill down my spine has us dismounting and leaving Sida's horse behind while I call Ginger to me.

"Should you summon your brothers?" Sida asks.

"No," I say resolutely. "Z is barely holding himself together, and I can't risk pulling him away from Vale right now. Mav is not available: he's either out of range or not in a position to leave his location. And Nic just recently recovered Lucia from her ordeal, so I won't be calling him unless it's absolutely unavoidable. Plus, you know we need to have one Horseman at The Refuge at all times for protection. And Z hardly counts as a functioning Horseman right now."

She nods resignedly.

As we trek onward and dusk fades to inky night, the chill in my bones increases and I know we are headed in the right direction. I pause and sniff the air, suddenly noting the addition of a scent that is distinctly male and yet also distinctly not of this world.

I look down at Sida. I can't risk her. She's only human, and I don't know what the source of this scent is, but I can't be worried about her while trying to save Ansel. I'd never be able to forgive myself if something happened to her. I wordlessly signal *wait here* with my hands to Sida, grateful she's been trained by us since childhood.

She gives me a glare but nods.

I silently maneuver through the dense forest. Up ahead, a sliver of moonlight reflects off red hair and my heart skips. As I get closer, with my enhanced eyesight, I can see Ansel tied to a tree. She sits with her arms and legs wrapped around the trunk, fastened in place with rope. I can see her back from here, and the arrow that still protrudes from her shoulder, a dark stain spreading over her shirt and all the way down her back to the ground.

I take deep breaths to control the rage that begs to be loosed. If I lose it now, I will wake the huge, manlike figures lying about the forest floor. These must be the Silent that Lucia mentioned back at The Refuge. I console myself with the fact that I found Ansel and I am here now—she will be okay.

I sneak closer, placing my hand gently over her lips as I soothe her hair back from her face. She jerks awake, startled. Beautiful green eyes stare up at me before registering that it's me. Her gaze softens.

I move my hand from her mouth and replace it with my lips, needing the reassurance that she's really here.

"You must take Nayne to safety," she whispers, and my heart plummets. How can I possibly do that? She must see it all over my face, too.

"Please Cai," she urges me. "She's not tied up. They knew she would never leave me and, just in case, they threatened to hurt me if she tried. If you truly love me, then you'll protect her for me. You know it's the right thing to do."

I feel like I am the one who's just been shot with an arrow. The thought that they could hurt her if they discover Nayne is gone fills me with a visceral fear that has my pulse pounding in my ears. But as a warrior and strategist, I also realize that they need Ansel too much to do any real damage to her.

Still, everything in me rebels, searching for any solution that doesn't leave her tied to a tree, still wounded. The elaborate entwining of the ropes around her suggests any effort to untie her will likely be too time consuming and too attention drawing. Ansel will never take a risk that could close the window of opportunity to save Nayne. And I can't heal her, because then it will be clear she knows something about Nayne's disappearance, which will not bode well for her.

Finally, I manage to nod despite the ache in my heart. Then I scan the area and see a small girl with dark hair and brown skin lying on her side in the dirt. She sleeps in a fetal position between two of these monstrous men.

"I will be back for you," I whisper, kissing her one more time. I pull back, and her smile and the acceptance of whatever fate lies ahead coming through our bond is heart-wrenching. Somehow, I manage to turn to the child.

She's going to freak out the minute I grab her. She doesn't know me and we can't warn her. It sits like lead in my gut that I will have to figure out another way to get Ansel to safety. After this, the element of surprise will be lost.

I send one final look of longing at Ansel. Here goes nothing. I grab the young girl's legs and pull her from between the behemoths.

She gasps and sits up. The Silent stir, and I waste no time throwing her over my shoulder and hightailing it out of there. I move as swiftly as I am able while still being quiet, maneuvering around bushes and over logs. Each step that takes me further from Ansel is like a limb being violently torn off. Somehow, I keep moving forward.

Surprisingly, the girl makes no sound—not at all what I was expecting. She must be smart enough to realize that anything stealing her in the night from those things has got to be the good guy. I come upon a wide-eyed Sida, who doesn't ask questions, just turns on her heels to run after us.

When we are a good distance away, I place the girl on her feet. She stands unafraid, staring up at me from beneath her dark lashes.

"You're Ansel's friend?"

"I am," I respond.

"You have to go back for her. You can leave me here, but you can't leave her with those things." It's too dark to see much but the moonlight reflects off her tear-streaked face. I kneel in front of the child while Sida maintains a respectful distance.

"I will not leave her behind, but I promised her you would be safe. I will keep that promise first."

She seems to accept that answer, albeit begrudgingly, and we keep moving forward to where Sida's horse waits.

"My name is Cai, by the way," I offer. "And this is Sidora."

Sida inclines her head to the girl as we press onward.

"I am Nayne," she says softly.

We move briskly through the forest until I see Sida's horse grazing unconcerned ahead. I turn to Sida.

"Sida, Nayne is Ansel's little sister," I announce. "And I promised Ansel that we would get her to safety." I turn to face Nayne. "Sida here is going to take you somewhere safe and warm, far from here." She repeatedly shakes her head *no*. I place my hands on her small shoulders as I kneel in front of her. "Ansel and I will meet you there soon, I promise." Her big eyes take me in earnestly, as if searching for a lie. Suddenly, her eyes widen.

"You love her," she says. It's not a question—perceptive child.

"More than anything. I would give my life for her safety." This seems to do the trick because the frantic energy in Nayne eases.

Sida holds out her hand to Nayne. "Let's get you somewhere safe, child."

"Thanks for being here," I say to Sida's back. She helps the young girl onto the horse and turns to me.

"Always, Cai, and remember, you are not alone, and neither is Ansel. Elohim Shomri is with you both. And He has equipped you for such a time as this." Then she's riding away, and I say a quick prayer for their safety.

I turn and head back into the thick forest, in the direction of my soul's cry.

CHAPTER 26

"Where's the child?"

The irate voice speaks from behind me. The tree's bark digs into my cheek, and the rope tying my arms and legs around its trunk prevents me from shifting to a more comfortable position.

"How would I know? She was sleeping closer to you," a groggy second voice says.

"You took too much elixir, didn't you? You know too much impedes your senses and slows your reactions, you idiot."

"Well, you didn't wake up either! What does that say about the amount of elixir *you* had?"

I contemplate what this elixir that impedes their senses could be, sounds like a drug or something. I wonder if it's something they need to have or something they have simply become addicted to.

"Shut up, the both of you," says a third voice. "You three

spread out and search the area; she can't have gotten far. I'll stay with the Core, just in case."

The sounds of boots crunching foliage slowly dissipates until they are out of earshot. Even though I can't see anything from my position, I can feel the remaining monster's presence.

They won't find her. Of that, I am confident. Cai is too good. And my heart finally rests easy after days of worrying about Nayne.

The sharp ache in my shoulder is my constant companion. Like a pulse, it throbs up my neck into my head, along my arm, down my side, and into my spine. It dulls my other senses and makes it impossible to focus. Holding my head up takes too much effort, so I let the rough press of the bark against my face offer a pathetic attempt to distract me from the pain.

I sense the approach of the monster before I feel his putrid breath on my face. "Where's the girl? I know you know something. I've seen how the child looks at you; she wouldn't leave you willingly."

"I hate to break it to you, but I can't see much from my present position. I have no idea where she went," I respond through exhaustion that feels bone-deep.

His fingers grip the arrow shaft and my body tenses in anticipation.

"You know I can make you talk, right?" His fingers bounce along the arrow shaft like he's tapping out a tune. I grit my teeth against the fire burning afresh in my shoulder, willing myself to not make a sound. He hums a happy tune made sadistic by his fingers' manipulations. My breath comes out ragged, but then something comes bursting through the trees. The monster's fingers vanish and the agony returns to its baseline throb.

"What is it?" the monster behind me says.

"We're moving," A second voice huffs out. "There's something out there, and I'm done messing around trying to find the child. We can't risk the Core, and we still have some distance to cover. Grab her, and we'll run for the helicopter. Whoever it is will be hard-pressed to catch us."

Suddenly, I am being untied from the tree and hoisted up onto unsteady feet. Before the beastly man can throw me over his shoulder again, I hear a *thwack* sound and he staggers back, falling to the ground. That's when I can get a good glimpse of the blade sticking out of his back. The remaining three dark guardians look around for the foe, blocking me in on all sides.

It's Cai. I know it—I *feel* it.

I want to fight, but with the dizzy weakness washing over me now that I'm upright, I am just grateful I haven't joined the guy on the ground.

Like sunrays piercing through a shroud of mist, a figure with familiar sandy-blonde hair suddenly comes out of the darkness. A short sword swings, and sparks flash as blade strikes blade. Cai parries and slashes. His fluid, precise movements are a mesmerizing, deadly dance.

No wonder he's the Horseman of War.

One of the monsters sneaks up behind him, and I prepare to shout to him, but Cai drops, thrusting his leg back into the Silent's chest, knocking him out of the way. That's when I notice he has small blades sticking out of the toe edges of his boots.

He's up in a blink, sweeping his sword in an upward arc, connecting with a blade aimed at his chest. He shoots forward, wielding his sword with one hand while his other hand snatches his tactical knife. With dizzying speed, he twists and slashes with the knife while his opponent is focused on his sword arm, catching the beast of a man in the chest. But the monster appears unfazed by the deep gash, while sweat shimmers on Cai's skin.

It's not just their appearance that makes these guys no mere mortal men. The one with the blade in his back stands from his place on the ground, reaching over his shoulder to pull the blade free with a sinister grin.

These *men* are far bigger than Cai, and there is definitely something "other" about them because they are causing Cai to retreat. He dives behind a tree and emerges from the other side, throwing a blade into the eye of one of the monsters. The beast roars before falling to the ground. Hopefully this time, the monster stays down.

Weaving in and out of the trees, using the landscape to his advantage, Cai blocks, thrusts, and slices, but makes no further headway. And I am fast realizing that these creatures are too much for him.

I notice a stray blade in the dirt and pick it up, determined to do something. Mustering what little energy I can, I clamber up a nearby boulder and jump at the beast closest to me, launching myself high enough to jam the blade into the artery in his neck with my good arm before I fall to the ground. I barely catch myself on my knees as I slam into the dirt.

I take deep breaths through the pain pulsing anew in my shoulder, which threatens to pull me under, but then a hand grabs my hair and jerks me to my feet.

"Ahhhhhh!" I scream.

"Ansel!" Cai's voice draws my attention from the fog of pain in time to see that the distraction I caused has cost him dearly. He's barely visible behind the two figures he fights to get past, but I see glimpses of the open, starry night sky behind him—and the edge of a cliff. At the same time, a blade arcs through the air, aiming right at his neck, while he blocks an attack from the other side.

I watch as he stumbles back over the edge. The scum with the blade turns to me, a sadistic grin on his face as he brings the blade up to the moonlight. Thin rivulets of blood drip down the sharp edge.

"NOOOOOOO!" I scream. A pain worse than anything I've ever felt tears through my body. I beg Cai to climb over the edge, prove to me he's okay.

But he doesn't.

"He's not coming back from that fall," one of the Silent says with a callous laugh. His voice sounds far away, like it's underwater. I struggle to draw breath.

I fight to get to Cai, kicking and pulling against the hand holding my hair, but it's no use. I am his only hope for healing and I am too weak to get to him—to save him. The beast holding my hair laughs as he tears the arrow from my back in vicious revenge for the blade in his neck, then hauls me up over his shoulder. Fresh, warm blood begins to flow from the wound as darkness claims me once again.

"Hang on tight, Ansel!"

Mina's familiar voice cuts through the haze, mixing with my childhood laughter. Every so often, Sloane's fingers tickle my sides from my spot hanging over her shoulder and I squirm and laugh. I lift my head to see Mina following us, her red hair shining in the sunlight.

She smiles at me, a warm expression filled with love. "We're almost there, kiddo," she says.

Excitement courses through me. I can't remember ever being happier. I don't care where we go, so long as I am with

Mina and Sloane. But then Mina's figure breaks apart, turning to mist before my eyes. The whole dream collapses as the *whomp whomp whomp* of the helicopter draws me from my unconscious state.

It's no longer night. I still hang from a shoulder, only it's the shoulder of a monster. I lift my head and the bright dawn causes my head to throb. When I can finally focus, I see we are in a large, grassy clearing, the tree line in the distance.

My eyes hungrily search for Cai in pursuit, but a sudden pain lances through me and I recall the cause of it. All I can see now are the monsters that took him from me. The closest of which throws a gruesome sneer my way as if he can read my thoughts.

The wind picks up as we near the helicopter, throwing my hair into chaos and making it nearly impossible to see. I am unceremoniously tossed into the belly of the metal beast. Despair breaks through the fog of pain, holding my poor decisions out in front of me like a placard. And even though Nayne is safe, a part of me knows, deep down, that things could have been different if I had only let Cai in and trusted him.

He might still be here.

So used to doing things my way, to being alone in my mission to protect myself and others, I unknowingly built a blockade that kept him out. I am the one who crippled what we had. I am the one who created this landscape of despair that I now exist in. Instead of grasping hold of what was right in front of me, I let fear and my desperate need to control all the variables drag me into the muck of my desolation.

It dawns on me that my desire for control is not much different from Gemini's desire for power. The comparison to her makes my stomach heave. My dismal failure births a withering agony that makes drawing breath a chore.

Suddenly, despite my train of thought and the pain threatening to swallow me whole, a peace that surpasses understanding breaks through the agony and washes over me. Cleansing me from my guilt. An urging, deep in my spirit, that speaks to my soul and tells me I am not now, and never have been, alone. That I don't need to carry the burden of this weight; there is someone ready to take it for me. Despite everything, my mistakes will leave no mark on me. And I get the sense, however seemingly ridiculous, that everything will be okay.

Miraculously, I can breathe again.

That's when I know, without a doubt, that Elohim is with me. Despite my bad choices, despite the pathetic excuse of a Core that I am, His love is unshakeable and fully woven through every part of me. Holding together the broken pieces of me, and now, healing the past wounds that have held me captive. Taking the burdens and pain and replacing them with freedom. Renewed strength and vigor fill me.

I am a mountain rising from the earthquake of destruction around me.

The helicopter lifts off the ground, approaching the tree line, as an arrow flies right into the heart of one of the beasts near me. He falls from the helicopter as two of the hulking figures start shouting to the one piloting this thing. Elation sweeps through me as my eyes comb the tree line, hoping and praying to see Cai emerge.

Instead, I see Sidora's signature corkscrew white hair as she nocks another arrow and fires again. The arrow ricochets off the metal this time.

Suddenly, another helicopter approaches from behind

Sidora, armed with a beast of a weapon in the doorway that starts spraying bullets into the tree line at Sidora's position. My stomach drops. *Please let her be okay.* The last of my hope is crushed as we fly away from the fray.

Awareness pings around inside me. I stare in the direction we came from. I shouldn't hope—the pain when that hope gets dashed will be more than I can bear—but I can't keep my eyes from scanning the tree line, just in case.

A figure on a horse bursts out of the forest. And just when I think there's no way the rider will catch us, he disappears and reappears almost directly below us.

My soul jumps in recognition of Cai.

He is annihilation incarnate, and he rides as if hell is on his heels. My eyes soak in his wholeness like a sponge as the helicopter gets higher and moves away from everything I want in life.

With glaring clarity, I realize I have two choices. I can stay with what I know, with old fears and patterns of striving so hard to protect myself, habits that are surely going to get me killed. Or I can choose faith and trust in something other than myself. As I look down at Cai, growing smaller, I realize I fear a life without Cai far more than I fear heights or having no control. I finally choose to let go and surrender.

I throw myself out of the flying metal monstrosity into whatever awaits me on the other side.

CHAPTER 27

Ginger's strides tear up the ground as we ride, periodically distance jumping behind the helicopter to stay close. The residual emotion Ansel sent my way when she thought me dead clings to me like oil, fueling my rage at what she's been put through.

An unfamiliar look appears on Ansel's face as she moves to the edge of the helicopter, looking down at me. A faraway expression that appears to be a combination of acceptance and surrender.

I watch in horror as she throws herself from the belly of the beast while the Silent are distracted. Quickly, I distance jump to below her position and launch myself from Ginger's back to meet her in the air, catching Ansel in my arms and effectively slowing her descent before I land in a crouch on my feet, my legs absorbing the shock of the fall.

Her eyes are squeezed shut, as if she's still waiting for death to claim her. I lean my face down to hers as I whisper, "I told you I'll always catch you if you fall."

Fierce green eyes open, full of wonder, as she scans me for injury. Almost reverently, she reaches up a hand to my jaw.

"How are you here?" she asks.

"It pays to be a Horseman," I say with a smile. "And that Silent didn't actually strike a killing blow, obviously. I realized I was outmatched, and I could either take my chances with the cliff or let him cut my head off. His sword came at my neck right as I began falling back. He ended up slicing into my shoulder and collarbone instead, thank Elohim, and these leathers Nash and Lottie made me prevented the blade from going too deep. The cliff wasn't quite steep enough to kill me, but I did nail my head on the way down and it knocked me unconscious. When I finally came to, I woke to cuts, bruises, and you long gone."

"I am sorry, the Silent?" Her face takes on a quizzical expression.

"Yeah, that's what those huge, humanoid men are. The Amilign have been creating them deep beneath the ashram. Obviously, they are not fully human."

"This all seems impossible."

"What does? That I willingly threw myself off a cliff and knocked myself unconscious in the process or that my clumsiness actually helped save my life this time? Because I can assure you, neither outcome is that impossible for me." I wink at her, trying to ease the fear that still clings to her.

"It seems impossible that you are really here, alive and whole."

I turn my face and plant a kiss on the center of her palm. "I'm here, Ans. Nothing can keep me from you." I press my forehead against hers as I hold her tightly to emphasize my point. The sound of a distant helicopter reminds me we are not safe yet. The helicopter has already circled back towards us and is combing the area for Ansel.

"Time to go." I cradle her carefully, feeling warm blood still trickling from her back. Her pallid features and labored breath speak of how dire this situation is. I place her on Ginger's back and swiftly hop up behind her. With her severe blood loss and one of her arms useless, I help her to turn around. Her legs are on either side of my hips and her face burrows into my neck. She wraps her good arm around me.

"Hold on," I say as I slide a hand around her back, pressing her into me, and bring Ginger to a gallop, picturing Nash and Lottie's homestead in my mind.

We distance jump, and I slow Ginger immediately. Shifting Ansel into my arms, I swing both legs over Ginger's back and jump to the ground. I waste no time placing Ansel's limp form in the grass. With one hand gently touching her shoulder, I lean down and kiss her as if my life depends on it, willing my love to wash over her like floodwaters.

This time, she doesn't move—doesn't even kiss me back. A seed of fear begins to take root in me. Maybe the barrier she put up between us has diminished our ability to heal each other.

But I won't give up.

I pepper her face and head with kisses, then return to her lips again. I scoop her limp form up so she's pressed against my chest, one of my hands in her hair as I continue to kiss her and let my love flow out of me like a torrent.

With painful slowness, she begins to kiss me in return, and her hands come up to twine in my hair. I breathe a sigh of relief as I pull away from her. Bright green eyes look back at me above freckled cheeks lit with a pink glow.

She's okay. I sigh again.

"I'm sorry," she says, her eyes downcast.

Confusion furrows my brow. "What? Why? You have nothing to be sorry for."

"If only I had trusted you, we wouldn't have had to go through this. You wouldn't have been hurt. *I* probably wouldn't have been hurt." She heaves a sigh and her hand brushes my jaw. "I am sorry I pushed you away. I was afraid. I thought I was protecting Nayne and you if I handled things myself. If I was in control. Now, I can see what an illusion control really is. That was just old habits . . ."

I interrupt her words with a kiss. Through our bond, I send my love, adoration, and acceptance to her. When I pull away, unshed tears in her eyes shine back at me.

"Never again will you fight your battles alone. We are stronger together. It's Elohim's design for us and His great gift to us."

She smiles at me and snuggles into me as I wrap my arms around her, holding her tight. I relish the feel of her, safe and whole.

"Thank Elohim," I hear Nash's voice from behind me. "We were worried sick."

"Did Sida make it back?" I ask.

"Well," Nash says hesitantly, wringing his hands in an uncharacteristic gesture. "I actually followed you all, just in case you might need an extra hand. Sidora met me on the road with the child and told me to take her back with me. She returned in the direction she came from." He keeps glancing at the woods in that direction as if he can summon her.

"I saw her, Cai," Ansel says with a hesitation that is unlike her. "Right before you came after the helicopter. She was firing arrows at the Silent but then another helicopter came with a gun and . . . " Her voice trails off as concern pours from her.

I stand and revert to War Strategist again.

"Okay, I am going to distance jump and find her. The FP and the Silent will not give up Ansel so easily. I am afraid to say, Nash, that you and your family are going to need to come with us to The Refuge. It won't be long before our enemies find you here. Pack your essential belongings, because when I get back, we're getting out of here." I turn to Ansel, pulling her to her feet. My hand cups her face as I look into her eyes.

"I would take you with me, but I just got you out of there, and I don't know what I will be walking into. And I can't leave Nash and his family without a defense." I tug her to me, and my lips lay claim to hers once more. I pull away far too soon.

"There's a bow and quiver of arrows in the barn. I'll be back, and then we are finally going home." I turn to mount Ginger.

"Be safe."

"You know it," I say, then Ginger and I take off and reappear at the tree line where the helicopter once perched. Both machines are long gone, as I knew they would be now that Ansel is out of their grasp. They are probably searching the area, which means I need to hurry. It won't be long before their search leads them to Nash and Lottie's farm.

The area around me has been peppered with bullets. Looks like the Amilign have outfitted one of the helicopters with a machine gun. Trees have been demolished, leaves torn to confetti, and branches lie in broken shambles on the ground among the bullet casings. Ginger slowly moves into the forest, out of the sun and the wind, and the smell of blood assaults my senses. Icy fear flows through my veins as I dismount, searching.

I follow the scent.

"Sida!" I yell.

A faint cough sounds from behind an outcropping of boulders, followed by a too-soft "Here."

I run and see her sitting up against the largest boulder, clutching her abdomen. Her skin has taken on a grayish hue. I approach my friend, afraid to touch her. She also has a bullet wound in her arm. She looks at me and her all-seeing eyes reveal she understands the gravity of her situation.

"Take me home, Cai," she says softly.

I nod. But I am unwilling to admit defeat. She will not leave us like this.

"You're going to be okay. Just hold tight." I carefully lift her and stride over to Ginger. I call out to my brothers as I walk.

"Sida is critically wounded; I am on immediate approach."

I don't wait for a response as I cradle Sida tightly and distance jump Ginger right to the training field of The Refuge.

Elias, Nic, and Lucia come running toward us, and a medical crew follows in their wake.

"Aunt Sid!" Lucia screams.

"Gunshot wounds to the stomach and bicep!" I shout to the team. Elias takes her from me as if he's holding broken glass. Lucia stands frozen, tears running down her face as she watches Sida get carried off, unconscious. This is the first time she's seen her aunt since childhood. Nic reaches for her and pulls her to his chest, where she buries her face as his arms wind around her.

"I am sorry, Lucia, but I can't stay. I found Ansel, but she's in trouble," I say.

At my words, Lucia turns from Nic, eyes wide.

"And Nic, if you can be spared for a few moments, I need help evacuating Nash and Lottie's family. There are two helicopters, one with a machine gun, currently combing the area for them."

"Lavo Veshuv" Nic says, and Adira stands before them. He mounts quickly and reaches down a hand for Lucia.

I should hold my tongue, but frankly, I am sick of watching people I love get hurt.

"Are you insane?" I say to Nic. "We are headed into a war zone, and you are going to bring Lucia!"

Instead of being offended, Nic looks back at Lucia and they smile, totally throwing me off.

"Yep," they say together.

"This is the definition of idiocy. I don't get you two, but I don't have time to argue. Keep her close and watch her back." I bring Ginger to a gallop, jumping back to the farm. But nothing could prepare me for what I see when we land.

The barn and surrounding pastures are fully ablaze, the flames creeping toward the small homestead. Dark smoke fills the air, smothering the sunlight and burning my eyes. Nash stands on the porch with an old rifle; Nayne is by his side, a bow in her small hands. Lottie crouches behind him, holding Bea in her arms while JJ stands protectively next to his mother. The helicopter with the machine gun hovers in place at the end of the driveway, facing the house. Two Silent are on the ground, directly below the helicopter.

Ansel is all that stands between them and Nash's family.

A lead weight sits heavy in my gut when she holds out her hand for them to stop. But what has us all frozen in place is the lightning that is arcing between her fingers, seemingly snaking its way across her skin, into her mouth, out of her brilliant green eyes, and around her arms. The atmosphere around her darkens as if she is standing in a storm cloud, making the lightning appear that much brighter.

Strands of her red hair whip wildly in the wind, interwoven with threads of lightning. She is a fearsome thing to behold, and I am shocked speechless.

Lucia gasps next to me. "She accepted you, Cai. That's her heavenly gift."

"What?" I ask, vaguely recalling that part of the prophecy.

"You haven't seen anything yet, brother," Nic says from atop Adira, as he lowers Lucia to the ground. And the moment those words are out of his mouth, Ansel's lightning strikes, shooting across the distance, utterly eviscerating one of the Silent, leaving a smoking husk in the aftermath. The other one takes off at a run toward the forest as the helicopter circles around, the machine gun aimed directly at Ansel.

As if in slow motion, I watch as my nightmare comes to life and bullets pepper the ground leading to where Ansel stands.

CHAPTER 28

ANSEL

The light cuts through the darkness, fracturing it. Leaving what's behind altered—transformed. Sidora was right. It's in the darkness that light achieves its full strength.

I am a conduit, and I feel this newfound power well up within me—an infinite outpouring into an unending chasm. I don't know what is happening to me, but this power feels holy and vast, all-consuming and yet intimate.

Like it knows me, and always has.

I will use everything at my disposal to stop these evil monsters from harming this family and Nayne. But just as that thought begins to steel my spine, the helicopter circles around, positioning the machine gun in my direction, and in the gunner's seat is a face I hoped never to see again.

It's a sucker punch to my focus.

Gemini sneers at me as she loads the gun. I hear a guttural bellow, and my eyes turn to connect with Cai's as he races toward me on Ginger. Gemini sees, too, and starts to pull the gun his way. A surge of white-hot rage lights up

"

inside me, causing more snakelike tendrils of lightning to weave around me rapidly.

I am done having the people I love taken from me.

I drop the sword and raise both hands to the helicopter. I visualize sending my rage, my pain, and my heartbreak right back at Gemini. I am the heart of the storm, and lightning erupts from my body, blindingly bright as it strikes the helicopter, sending sparks flying like miniature shooting stars. At the same time, a stream of fire hits the gunner position, eviscerating everything inside.

The metal wreckage falls to the ground; a steaming, smoking mess. After that show, I don't think that last Silent will be back.

It's finally over.

I look up to see Cai and a dark-haired man, both vibrating with rage and power, heading my way. Both have eyes as black as spilled ink.

But what freezes me to the spot is the sight of a girl, untouched by the flame that surrounds her from head to toe, walking out of the smoky clouds toward me. Her hair is a fiery storm around her head and her familiar golden eyes are glowing. She looks like an avenging angel until the flames suddenly go out and I can finally see Lucia. Almost as surprising as her newfound power is the absence of the brown sackcloth clothing she was always forced to wear. Now, she sports bright blue leggings and a sunny, yellow top that makes her eyes pop—definitely more befitting her beautiful soul.

"Lulu!" I scream and run toward her.

She runs to meet me and I throw my arms around her, squeezing tight.

"It's really you." I pull back, holding her at arm's length

and looking her up and down, checking for injury. "I was worried I might never see you again."

"Me, too." Tears shine in her eyes.

I pull her in for a hug again. "A lot has changed since we were last together," I say in her ear.

She chuckles. "That's putting it mildly."

I laugh at our old familiarity as I step away from the hug. "You were just on fire, Lulu!"

She grins sheepishly. "Says the living lightning rod!"

We both laugh right as the guys approach.

"Ans," Cai says, gesturing with his hand, "this is my brother, Nicanor, the White Horseman of Conquest."

"My Horseman," Lulu chimes in with a wink, an air of pride around her.

He holds his hand out to me and I take it.

"It's Nic," he says warmly. "Nice to have you with us, Ansel."

Suddenly, he pulls me into a bear hug. "Keep this one in line for us, will ya? Always getting into trouble, that one," he mock-whispers in my ear, loud enough for everyone to hear.

"You're one to talk, you stubborn mule!" Cai throws back at him with a shove to Nic's shoulder. "And get off my girl, you big oaf. I haven't even gotten a hug yet."

Nic laughs. "What goes around comes around, brother. Maybe I should take her dancing next," he says with a sly grin.

Cai scowls at him in return.

"Behave," Lulu chides Nic, and he yanks her into his arms.

My heart warms at the sight. To see my friend, well-loved as she always should have been, protected and happy, is the best conclusion to an awful journey.

"Ansel!" a small voice yells from behind me, and I turn

to see Nayne running as fast as her legs will carry her. I open my arms and she throws herself into me, almost knocking me over. "You're okay! You're okay!" she says repeatedly, as if reassuring herself.

"I am more than okay, Nay Nay, seeing you safe and sound."

Then she turns to Cai and flings herself at him. "Thank you, Cai."

"I promised, didn't I?" He squeezes her back and my heart overflows with joy at what can't possibly be my reality. All of us here, together, alive and well. But then Sidora pops into my mind, and the memory of the machine gun that sprayed the forest around her as I sat helpless in a helicopter.

"Where's Sidora?" I ask. And the sudden somber mood tells me all I need to know. Lulu turns a frantic gaze to Nic, and he just nods grimly as he mounts his massive white horse, pulling Lulu up behind him.

"I have to go to her, Ansel, but I'll see you soon," Lulu says before disappearing.

I turn to Cai. "Tell me."

"She's critically wounded. I took her straight to The Refuge and then came here." His grief seems to weigh heavy on the air around him and I hug him, offering whatever comfort I can.

"I'm sorry, Cai." I can't help but feel like this is my fault, too. He doesn't respond, but he kisses the top of my head and takes a deep breath.

"Let's get everyone organized. We need to get them all to The Refuge. I am going to have to take them in trips."

First up is Lottie and the baby, and then Nash and JJ. We can return for more of Nash and Lottie's belongings later.

As I wait for Cai, I look around at the farmstead. So much has changed in the short time since we arrived. Guilt at the destruction of a family's life and history settles on me like a wool cloak.

"It would've happened sooner or later, Ans," Cai speaks from behind me after a swift return, clearly sensing my train of thought. "The evil of this world doesn't leave good things untouched for long. And they will be safer with us. You should bear no guilt. Because of you, we are one step closer to ridding the world of this darkness."

The words remind me of my new mission and purpose. I need to keep my eyes on what lies ahead and what Elohim created me for. I am a true protector now, and that thought settles around me like a shield.

I hop up behind Cai; Nayne is seated in front of him.

"Okay, ready for our new life?" he asks.

"Heck yes!" Nayne says, and my heart feels as though it might burst. Cai must sense it because he squeezes my knee.

Then we're off, heading to another unknown. But for once, I am not uneasy at the thought. Wherever we go, if my family is with me, then I've come home. And everything we've been through to get to this point is worth it if *home* is what awaits us at the end.

CHAPTER 29

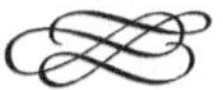

ANSEL

Walking through the halls of The Refuge, I find it hard not to be entranced by this magical place. Most of the walls are rough-hewn stone, cut right out of the cliff itself. You would think it would give the place a cold, dark feel. Like a dungeon or something. But the unique, light amber-colored windows and deep-set, mirror-lined skylights create a warm, cozy atmosphere. The small, domestic touches throughout add an air of "home" to the vast, cavernous space. From a cozy reading nook by one of the windows, complete with a rug, chairs, and a small side table, to the occasional woven tapestry hanging from the wall. The charm here oozes out of every surface.

Cai leads us to a beautiful kitchen and dining area where we have a quick bite before heading to a room, where Nayne collapses on what she calls "the most fluffy cloud bed" she's ever seen and promptly passes out. After our ordeal, it does my heart good to see her safe and sleeping in a real bed.

I glance up at Cai as we walk side by side down the hall, my hand firmly in his. I picture him running around this place as a child. I assume he grew up here, but now I realize I know nothing of his past. He could have a family here, or be an orphan with a tragic backstory—like me.

"Is this where you grew up?"

He looks at me with a coy smirk. I get the feeling there's something I am missing. "What is it?" I ask.

He stops walking and turns fully to look at me. There's an air of hesitation around him. "Ans, I never 'grew up' in the traditional sense."

I laugh. "Yeah, you're not telling me anything I don't know."

He grins. "No, I mean—well, yeah, but that's not what I mean." He rubs a hand through his hair. "I have been here for over one hundred years. And when I appeared, I arrived just as I am now."

My jaw drops open. He really is a supernatural being. I've come to see him as just my Cai; a warrior and a flirt, but otherwise, a regular man. I am not sure what to do with this revelation.

"Are you okay? It doesn't change how you feel about me, does it?" And despite having never been a child, he seems exactly like a nervous little boy at this moment.

I cup his jaw. "Of course not, but it does change how I see you a little. It's hard to imagine you never being a child. Having no family. Not having to fight to overcome childhood trauma. Or even just going through the growing pains of youth." I pause, weighing my words. "I hate to say it, but it makes you a little less relatable."

He looks up at the ceiling, his expression contemplative. "I can understand that. And I may not have your experiences, but being here as long as I have, I have seen more atrocities than one could ever wish on a single person, and those traumas have marked me. I may not have a family in the traditional sense, but I have my brothers and, of course, Elias, who has been here even longer than us. And then there's our makeshift family here at The Refuge, even if it is part blessing and part curse." A sadness seems to seep from him.

"What do you mean?"

"Well, when you live as long as my brothers and me, you watch the people you love grow old and then die, all while you stay the same. It's a burden that weighs heavy on your soul. And the closer you are to people, the harder it can be. It's why some of my brothers choose to hold themselves back more. It's a sad sort of self-protection."

"But not you?"

"No, it's never been in my nature to only give part of myself. If I am going to love, there's no halfway for me." And the passion in his gaze threatens to set me ablaze right here in the hallway.

Suddenly, a thought takes shape.

"Does that mean I will die and you will live on without me?" I say, horrified at the possibility.

"No, no," he says soothingly as his hand comes up to guide my wild hair behind my ear. His fingers glide along my jaw, leaving goosebumps in their wake. "Elias explained that when we connect on the deepest level with our Core, our life and souls become melded together. It's why part of the gift in this bond Elohim gave us is the ability to heal each other."

He moves closer. One hand slides across my lower back and pulls me taut against him. His fingers spread out across my back, holding me to him, his intoxicating scent filling my lungs. It is enough to make me lightheaded, and all I can think is how I want to close my eyes and stay here always.

"You can't get rid of me now," he whispers. I snake a hand around the back of his neck, pull myself up to my tiptoes, and press my lips to his. My pulse picks up as his lips lay claim to mine. His hands lower to my hips, and he hauls me off the ground so that my legs wrap around his waist. I feel a charge on my skin, like lightning about to strike. It's potent and heady.

Cai slows his assault on my lips.

"Open your eyes." I feel his words against my mouth.

I am not prepared for the light that is snaking around us. My lightning is like small ropes twisting around our bodies —its movements continuous and languid. Mimicking my emotions, I imagine. Blinding and intense, yet completely benign. I hold my hand up and watch in fascination. That's when I finally notice the crowd we've drawn. Witnessing our personal light show.

At that thought, the lightning disappears.

My eyes grow wide and Cai's laugh fills the air as he places me on my feet.

"Well," says an older man with a head of gray hair. "You must be Ansel. Lucia is very excited to finally have you here, as are we all." He extends a hand for me to shake. Despite him being older, I can see this is not some frail, aged man. Oddly enough, he reminds me of my favorite bow: older, yet well-worn; flexible, yet battle-hardened—my choice weapon in any battle due to its steadfastness.

There is a depth and strength to this man that I find curiously calming.

"I'm Elias," he says, and my conversation with Cai comes to mind. This is the man that Cai said has been here longer than his one hundred years.

"How old are you?" I let the question slip before I can filter it, and my face flames instantly. "I'm sorry, I didn't mean . . . it's just that Cai . . . I shouldn't have asked." I uncharacteristically stumble over my words as Elias smiles at me, a knowing twinkle in his eyes.

He pats my hand and chuckles. "Let's just leave it at 'old'."

"I'm afraid I've been overwhelming her mind with all sorts of facts," Cai says. "We were just discussing how long I've been around and you came up."

"Well, that's a good segue. Now's as good a time as any; let's head to my office and I can fill you in on any details you're missing or answer any questions you have."

"How's Sidora?" Cai asks as we follow Elias down the hall.

"Miraculously, the bullet appeared to miss any vital organs due to the angle at which it hit her. She's resting now. Only time will tell if she can make a full recovery."

Elias's office is much like the man himself; warm, inviting, and open. It's lined with bookcases holding rows upon rows of knowledge. He gestures to the small couch with a curiously damaged armrest as he perches informally on his desk.

"Okay, which one of you wants to start?"

Cai and I take a seat and Cai wraps an arm around me, pulling me into his side and kissing the top of my head. Any nerves evaporate instantly.

"I will," Cai says, beginning with when he first left The Refuge, a restlessness inside him that he thought was linked to hunting the FP who sought to harm Lulu. He fills in the story from his perspective, pausing periodically to allow me to interject. The conversation is enlightening, and I learn that it was Lucia's initial discovery of her powers that decimated the ranks of the FP near the base that Nayne and I had fled from only a few days prior. I fail to muster up any sort of grief over the news.

"So we witnessed your beautiful heavenly power," Elias finally says to me. "That's a gift from Elohim for the connection with your Horseman. From what I gather, it's the last official piece of the puzzle that marks you both as bonded. How are you feeling about this discovery, Ansel?"

I pause to process his question. I haven't really had time to absorb much of the past few days, but it feels surreal to be the carrier of such an ability.

"Honestly, I am a tad shocked by it. It seems like such a random power."

"Maybe to you, but not to those who understand Elohim's power. The ancient texts state, 'He made darkness His canopy around him—the dark rain clouds of the sky. Out of the brightness of His presence, bolts of lightning blazed forth.' This is the power that Elohim gifted to you."

I sit in silence, absorbing the gravity of his words. I feel wholly undeserving of such a gift. Cai squeezes my hand.

"I am not sure what to say. I can't help but wonder, 'Why me?' But at the same time, I won't say I'm not glad to have another tool at my disposal for protecting those I care about. I will do whatever it takes to learn how to wield it safely and effectively."

Elias smiles, a knowing look on his face. "And that confirms the other piece of the puzzle," he says, mostly to himself.

I glance at Cai, and he looks back at me and shrugs.

I wait for Elias to explain as he goes around his desk and fumbles through some papers.

"You are the Core Protection." He glances up at me. "You see, each Core is born with an aspect of Elohim's real, pure love. Lucia is Trust, and that theme is woven through her and Nic's bond. Yours is clearly confirmed in your story and experiences with Cai, as well as just being an ingrained part of who you are. It's also a perfect complement to Cai because the one thing that will help to balance War is Protection. After all, War destroys, while Protection saves."

"How do you know all this?"

Elias pulls out an old, worn parchment and begins reading the prophecy to me word for word. Something in me clicks. Like a piece of my identity that I'd always felt was missing. He seems to see it on my face, too, and he smiles.

"Tell me, Ansel, now that I know how you and Cai met, would you be willing to share more of your history with me? We still have one more Core to find, and maybe something in your story will help us to narrow our search."

My chest tightens. I hate to dig through the pain of my past, but he's right to ask if it may mean finding the last Core. Cai's arm squeezes me tight, and I breathe in the smell of him, a tonic for my battered nerves before I open the floodgates.

I share about how I was found as a baby, as well as who found me. How these two sisters raised me like family, and how one in particular tried her best to give me a childhood and memories that I could cherish outside of the FP's training. I share how they were taken from me and how I only recently discovered they were murdered. Cai's presence is a buoy amongst the waves of grief that still want to drown me.

"I'm so sorry, Ansel," Elias says with genuine sadness. "If I could fix everything that happened to you, I would. But please, in the midst of the pain and grief, take heart. Elohim is a redeemer. He's in the business of redeeming lost and broken things, making beauty from ashes. He takes what was intended to destroy us and, with the power of His restorative love, He pulls from it a powerful good that will build us up, strengthen us, and make us new. He flips destruction on its head."

As we stand to leave, he pulls me into a hug.

"One last thing I will leave you with . . . there's a part of the ancient texts that says, 'His Lightning will light up the world; the earth sees and trembles.' You are His lightning in human form, Ansel. And it's through the darkness that you have been forged, with an unrelenting light that will annihilate that which first sought your destruction."

He then turns to Cai, and pulls him in close to whisper something in his ear. I can't hear what is said, but Cai's eyes go wide and then turn to me. Then he seems to catch himself and school his features.

As we leave, his hand grabs mine, like two magnets naturally drawn together.

"I have so much to show you," Cai says, "but it has been one of the longest days of my life, and I am sure yours, too, and frankly, I am exhausted. So let's shower and sleep and we can start anew tomorrow."

I know he's right, even if my heart panics at the thought of leaving him. It's stupid, but after everything that happened, what I allowed to come between us, and what we survived, I don't ever want to be apart from him. As we walk back to our rooms, I take it as a small comfort that at least we are across the hall from each other.

I turn to reach for the door of the room Nayne currently sleeps in, but then Cai's grip tightens and he tugs me into his room instead.

"You didn't think I was going to let you be anywhere but by my side from now on, did you?" A question furrows his brow. "I had Nayne placed across the hall because I figured you would want her to be close to us, but this is *our* room now, Ansel. Everything that's mine is yours. Just as *I* am yours. We are one, now and until the end of time."

As his words hit me, it feels like releasing a breath I have been holding for far too long. A sweet elation swells within me at the thought of our connection.

I take a look around. I can see Cai's fingerprints everywhere. From the broken-in blue sofa in the corner set atop a plush rug, to the pile of books being used as a nightstand next to the simple yet cozy bed, to the red, carved wooden horse statue that looks like a toy sitting on his dresser, to the weapons hanging meticulously from the wall by his closet—as if they are too precious to be scattered just anywhere.

He draws my attention to him as his hands cup my face and his lips gently tease and caress my own, kissing me with a tender reverence that fills me with warmth.

"First, bath, and then sleep, okay?"

I nod, and as I look around the room, I know that I am right where I am supposed to be. And for the first time in my life, my heart feels whole.

CHAPTER 30

I sleep in one of Cai's shirts, sprawled across his chest, and his soothing scent on my skin lulls me into the best, most nightmare-free sleep I've ever had. I wake before him, so I take the opportunity to lie on my side, watching his chest rise and fall steadily. My eyes roam over the stubble on his jaw and his loose, sleep-tussled hair on the pillow. I trace his strong jaw, then let my finger explore his soft, full lips, finally gliding over the arch of his brow before all my fingers join in to brush his hair back from his face.

He is so beautiful.

And suddenly, he's awake, and those kaleidoscope hazel eyes gaze up at me through heavy lashes filled with love and adoration. His arm reaches around me and pulls me onto his chest.

"Morning," he says sleepily.

The light from the solitary window casts the room in a bright, warm glow. His other hand comes up to soothe my wild hair back from my face, and then his thumb rubs across my bottom lip.

"Will you hurt me if I tell you that you're beautiful?"

I smirk. "Only if I can say it back."

He pushes up on an elbow, pressing his lips to mine as his hand cups the back of my head. His kiss is possessive and urgent, and it fills me with heat. Then he leans back into the bed, one hand behind his head as he gazes at me unabashedly.

"I'm going to grab a quick shower, and then we can get some food and I can give you a tour of your new home," he says with a smile. Pure joy and love radiate from him. It's humbling and overwhelming that I am the cause of such heady emotions. I know having me here is a culmination of years of hoping and waiting.

But for me, it's surreal that I am here, and that he's not some dream I crafted to cope with the loss and lack in my life. All this time, I've been waiting for the bottom of this fantasy to drop out. And now that everything is over, and I am here and he's really mine, I sit stunned by the realization.

He quirks a brow at me as he sits up. "Are you really surprised by how I feel? I thought I've repeatedly made myself clear." He brings my hand up to his lips and plants a kiss in the center of my palm. The sweet action squeezes my heart.

The way he can be so in tune with what I am feeling will take some getting used to.

"You have," I reassure him, taking his hand in mine. "I guess there is a part of me that always expects the worst. Because that always seems to be what I get. And now that we are here together—and it's all over, at least for now—and you are really mine, I guess I am just surprised that this is my life."

He smiles. "Well, it's all true, so you better get used to being happy and loved. This is your new normal, Ans, and there's so much more goodness to come." He stands and kisses my forehead. "I look forward to the day when the love and joy I feel in your presence no longer surprises you. You deserve everything good and lovely, and I vow to do my best to make sure you have it."

I want to melt into a puddle on the floor at the casual manner with which he throws such earth-shattering words my way.

He heads to the ensuite bathroom for his shower. I feel as if I could float away on a cloud. There's a peace in me that I've never had before. Another confirmation that I am finally operating according to my true purpose. And despite the darkness that sought to destroy me, I am where I was always meant to be.

I send my joy and love down my connection with Cai, and then, feeling a bit playful, I focus on my desire for him. I focus on the craving I have for him that sparks like a live wire inside me. The constant need and want, and the knowing in my heart and soul that there is one more way I need to connect with him. I focus on that desire to have every piece of him and send it to him like an arrow shot from my soul.

A loud clattering and muffled curse comes from behind the bathroom door, and I smile. The water turns off and it's only a moment before the door flies open, like it's going to tear off its hinges.

What stands in the doorway is not what I was expecting.

He's dripping wet, and a bath towel is wrapped around

his waist. But it's his black eyes and trembling body that shock me. He trembles not with rage, but with something pure, bright, and endless. He fires it back at me like an arrow; it's passion, need, and want. Adrenaline spikes and blood thrums through my veins. He approaches me slowly, and with each step, he fires an emotion my way until my body is practically humming in response to him, like a well-played instrument.

I sit on the bed in his T-shirt; his dark and smoldering gaze ignites me.

"Your eyes," I say, clambering to my knees on the bed, reaching for his face. He grabs my wrist before I can touch him, and the intensity in him is such a shift from the playful Cai I know.

Right now, he's all warrior.

He kisses the inside of my wrist, and slowly, languidly, begins kissing his way to my elbow. My knees go weak, and his other arm snakes around my waist to hold me to his damp chest. Water drips from his hair onto my T-shirt, and the cold droplets only add to the sensation of him everywhere.

"You set a raging inferno inside me, Ansel." His husky voice is like melted chocolate. "My eyes are responding to my heightened emotions. I am desperately trying—and failing—to dampen it."

He closes his eyes and takes deep breaths. I had no idea that I would cause this kind of reaction in him. On some level, it feels impossible that he should feel this way about me. And his early words come back to me. Without a doubt, he's mine and I am his, and I want nothing standing between us ever again. The last piece of the puzzle between us is my craving to be known by Cai in every way, and to know him the same. To meld our hearts and souls together as one. I place my hand on his chest, over his heart.

"Cai, I don't want to put the blaze out."

His eyes fly open at my implication. His heart pounds against my palm.

"I never want anything standing between us again. And even though you've never said it, I know there is one more thing that stands in the way of our bond being made complete. No matter what the future holds, I want to know that after we battled so hard to survive and get here, after the loss that has marked both our lives, that here and now, we get to choose each other. Forever. And no one and nothing can take that from us."

His eyes soften and all the resistance goes out of him, and my Cai, who almost always has a response, is speechless. My hand slides around the back of his neck, and I pull his lips down to meet mine.

He spends the rest of the morning showing me what it means to be loved, adored, and cherished.

And his love is a healing balm that soothes away any residual darkness.

CHAPTER 31

ANSEL

"So, I have a few things I want to show you today, if you're up for it," Cai says.

"Of course I'm up for it."

He smiles. Lunch was amazing, as everything in this place seems to be. Honestly, I was surprised the kitchen staff was able to quench Cai's appetite. My face warms at the thought.

I am floating on a cloud after my morning with Cai. We've been through so much together, and I spent so much time—too much time—expecting the worst. And now, this morning with him is a dream brought to life. I never knew a person could be loved and treasured like he makes me feel. And if I thought he was a part of me before, he's practically my DNA now.

Nayne was not in her room when we left, nor could she be found in the kitchen. Surprisingly, I am not concerned. And it's an unusual feeling for me. Cai says she's probably off exploring, and that there's another young kid her age,

Laz, who will most likely find her and take her under his wing. It makes my heart happy to think she will be able to be a kid for a while, with no agenda or training regimen.

"One of the things I have to show you is going to be hard for you to process. Good in the end, but hard still," he says, and I feel a thread of concern coming from him. "You've been through so much, I don't wish to give you any more hard things right away. I'd like to shut us away from the world for a few days. Pretend we don't have a care in the world."

I can't say that doesn't sound like a slice of Heaven. The thought of being away from him or leaving him turns my stomach sour. And it's because we've been made new together—a stronger, electrified creation. In another great mystery that cannot fully be understood, we are bonded together like welded steel.

"It's okay, Cai. Whatever it is, I trust you, and as long as you are by my side, we've got this." I smile reassuringly.

He leads me out a high-tech security door that doesn't fit its ancient, man-made surroundings. We head into the rocky exterior facade of The Refuge, filled with ancient ruins built in the hollows and caves of the cliff face, presumably by Indigenous people from long ago. The Refuge has been excavated into the rock behind the ruins, new tech concealed by old. It's an ingenious way to hide from sight. I follow him down a path flanked by the lush, beautifully canopies of trees. We pass a field where it looks like some people are training. I see Lulu and Nic, and it looks like Nic is training Lulu.

I smile to myself, thinking back to my training with her at the ashram. He's got his work cut out for him—she's utterly hopeless. But then she shoots a fireball at him and he deflects it with a blade. I suppose she doesn't need traditional training now that she's a living flamethrower.

An eagerness rises in me to hone this new weapon Elohim gave me. Maybe Cai will be willing to play lightning rod for me later. I smile to myself. He winks at me and I know he senses my excitement.

Then the path opens up to a lovely, lush garden and greenhouse area. Lulu must love this place.

"Hey, Willy, you in there?" Cai calls out.

A woman with ginger hair sprinkled with silver stands from where she was crouched in the garden. With the pathway being so narrow, I am behind Cai, so I can't fully see her, but something in me begins to buzz with awareness. Cai pulls me from behind him. My heart clenches as a gasp flies from my lips, and my hand covers my mouth. I would forget to breathe if not for Cai's hand on mine, grounding me.

The pages of my past open up, and suddenly, memories that once felt like dreams are now alive and in color before me.

The woman looks at me and her tools drop to the ground, her hands trembling.

"Ansel?" she asks hesitantly, her voice barely above a whisper.

"Mm . . . M . . . Mina?" I squeak out, almost afraid to speak her name. She nods as tears flow down her face. And despite the questions and tumultuous emotions that swirl inside me, I can't hold myself back from her.

Letting go of Cai, I walk to the gate that she has already thrown open and we freeze, both of us soaking the other in.

She reaches out a hand to me, but then withdraws it, as if she is unsure of my reaction.

"Where did you come from?" she asks, her voice wobbling.

"Cai found me in The Wastes, running from the FP."

A dark cloud passes through her eyes, and she looks haunted. She closes her eyes and tilts her head up just enough that my eyes are drawn to the grotesque scar that now mars her neck.

"Is Sloane here, too?"

It's like my words deliver a physical blow on her as she steps back and slightly curls in on herself.

She shakes her head and avoids eye contact; my stomach sinks. Part of me wants to rage at being left behind. But my eyes take in the broken, scarred, and hurting figure before me. Someone who was such a source of joy, strength, and protection for me as a child, who is now a shell of her former self. And the protective love that is innate within me rises up. I push aside my reservations and wrap my arms around her.

The dam opens and Mina sobs, releasing years of brokenness and pain. "I'm so sorry," she heaves out between choked breaths and tears. "So very sorry."

Once her tears have slowed, she guides me to the bench in the middle of the garden, leaving Cai back by the gate. I don't pry; Mina always wore her heart on her sleeve and I suspect she'll tell me everything. Not because I need to know, but I sense this is the missing piece of the puzzle to help her truly heal from her past.

She starts slowly, describing the fake mission Gemini sent her on, and how she was attacked—her throat slit—and left for dead. By some miracle, the cut was shallow enough that she didn't bleed out. She was found by Sidora, who brought her here. The Prophets welcomed her and helped her heal.

"When I was finally well enough to go back, Elias urged me not to. At that point, I knew about Elohim and how He guides His people. I'd spoken often enough with the Prophets to know it would be foolish of me not to listen. Elias told me I would not receive another escape from death this time. It broke my heart, but he said if I was patient, what I sought in life would find me."

Her eyes look up, glistening with heartache and wonder. "And so you have."

"But why would you leave me there? You knew what they were really like and you had all these resources at your disposal. Why wasn't a plan hatched for some sort of recovery mission?"

"I tried," Mina insists. "The minute I was able to speak, I pushed to bring you here. I even threatened to leave if they didn't help. But the Prophets have their ways. Elias explained that it was vital that you stay where you were. Not only because of what you would learn in the process, but because at some point, you would meet two of the other three Cores, and those connections would play a key role in the recovery of those girls."

I am awestruck at her words. She obviously means Lucia and Vale. Finding Vale makes sense, but how I played a role in Lucia's rescue has me puzzled, although I did share my fears for her safety. Maybe on some level, that was the push Lucia needed to risk escaping from them?

Mina reaches out a hand to my face. "I always knew you were special, from the moment Sloane and I found you. But I could have never guessed how very important you would be to this world. I only learned what a Core is after coming here. Sloane would be so proud of you."

"Do you know what happened to Sloane?" The question is quiet and slow, as if my heart can't bear to ask it, even if a part of me needs to know.

Grief casts a pall over her. "After Sidora brought me here and the Healers saved my life, when I finally came out of the fog, I felt as if a piece of me was missing. Surgically cut away. They couldn't find anything physically wrong with me, and I just knew my twin was dead."

A ferocious rage flashes in her eyes and her white knuckles betray her clenched fists, and suddenly she's the woman I remember all those years ago.

She's my mother.

I throw my arms around her, and her hand comes up to stroke my hair as I finally weep for what was stolen from us.

"Shhhh," she says, and I am a child again. Remembering the way Mina would soothe me after a too-hard training session or a harsh word from Gemini.

I pull back from her, drying my tears, and notice Cai, still standing guard by the path. He hasn't left me, but has given me space to come to terms with everything. I send my need for his comfort to him. He turns, and immediately his protective gaze finds mine and he takes purposeful strides toward me. He pulls me from the bench into a bear hug that burns away the rest of the pain and grief.

Mina stands and throws her arms around Cai. "I will never be able to thank you enough, Cai."

"You don't have to thank me, Willy. I would go through that a thousand times over if it meant having Ansel at the end."

"Wait, Willy?" I question, my brow furrowing.

Mina smiles. "My full name is Wilhelmina. I only ever went by Mina with the FP. And then after what happened, I felt like that part of me had died. So I started going by

Willy. But I will always be Mina to you." She grabs my hand. "You brought me back to life."

CHAPTER 32

We leave Mina, or "Willy" to everyone else, to her gardening with a promise to meet up for dinner later. Mina is eager to hear the story of how Cai and I met.

I feel as though the tangled knot of my life has finally released, and everything is clear and whole again.

We make our way along the path to where Nic and Lulu were practicing earlier. They sit in the grass together, facing us instead of working. I glimpse Lulu's face above her slumped shoulders, and I know that look. She sees us coming and a small smile lights her face but doesn't quite reach her eyes.

"Hey, Lulu," I say, unable to mask my concern. "What is it?"

She looks down at her hands, fiddling with a piece of grass. "I haven't seen Aunt Sid yet. At least, I haven't talked with her." She looks up, and unshed tears cling to her dark lashes. "The last memory I have of her, I was ten, and now I don't know if she remembers me or if she'll live long enough for me to talk with her."

The pain in her voice breaks my heart. I want her to have her moment with Sidora, like I was able to have with Mina.

"No question, she remembers you," Cai says confidently, and her face brightens just a bit.

"Come on," I say, extending my hand to her. "If there's one thing these past few weeks have taught me, it's that life is too short to wait. Let's go get you your moment with your Aunt Sid."

She smiles at me and looks at Nic, who's beaming.

"Are you sure? What about her recovery?"

"Elias said she was stable, and if there's anyone in this whole place she's going to want to see, it's you," Cai says reassuringly and turns to lead the way.

I grab Lulu's hand and Nic takes up the rear.

As we reach her door, all is quiet on the other side.

"We shouldn't knock, right? I mean, what if we wake her? But we can't just barge in?" Lulu rambles. Nic slips a hand around her waist and tucks her under his chin.

"Take a deep breath," he commands calmly, and to my surprise, she closes her eyes and obeys.

I glance up at Cai, who raises an eyebrow at me and smirks back. Yeah, that wouldn't work on me and he knows it. But it warms my heart that Nic knows just what Lulu needs.

Lulu walks to the door. She cracks it open and peeks in. "Anyone home?"

At a muffled voice from inside, Lulu opens the door a bit wider, reaches back to grab my wrist, and pulls me through before closing the door on the guys.

Sidora lies in the bed, eyes closed, looking so small

surrounded by blankets, bandages, wires, and tubes. A woman by her bed smiles at us.

"I'll give you a moment with her; I'll be right outside when you are done."

Lulu stands immobile at the end of the bed, wringing her hands. "She's so still," she says softly. "It's like my dream and my nightmare all twisted together." A tear rolls down her face. "I dreamed of seeing her again for so many years. What it would be like after so long apart. Never could I have imagined this."

I rub her back. I don't have words for this moment, but I want her to know I am here for her.

"Come here, my dumpling," a soft scratchy voice murmurs from the bed.

"Aunt Sid." Lulu hurries to her side, kneeling on the floor by the bed as her tears flow more forcefully. Sidora reaches a weak hand up to Lucia's face. I feel like an intruder on a moment that has been a long time coming for them both, but Lulu pulled me in here for a reason, so I'll stay as long as she needs me to.

"My beautiful, strong Lucia," Sidora says, and Lulu clings to her hand, pressing it to her wet cheek. "I am so sorry for what you went through. That I couldn't protect you. And I am sorry that you ever had to doubt my love for you."

"No, Aunt Sid." Lulu shakes her head. "Elias told me everything. I know you didn't have a choice. I don't blame you. And you were right; Elohim was with me. He protected me, got me out of there, and led me to Nic. Everything will be okay now, so long as you get better. That's what matters most."

"I'll do my best, dumpling," Sidora answers softly. "I always did have a hard time denying you anything." She smiles and shuts her eyes, clearly exhausted by the exchange.

Lulu leans her head on the edge of the bed and her shoulders shake with her grief. I break away from the wall and kneel next to her, wrapping my arm around her.

"I'm so sorry, Lulu, but she's one of the toughest people I know. She'll be okay, and you can come back and visit her each day until she's better."

She sits back and nods, drying her eyes.

"Thanks for being here, Ansel," she says as she stands and gives one last squeeze to Sidora's hand.

I look down at Sidora's small frame, remembering her standing at the tree line with that bow and arrow. Ready to take on an army for my sake. And she barely knew me. Not even my so-called sisters with the FP had my back like that. Also, Cai told me it was Sidora who helped get Nayne to safety.

I lean over the bed and place a gentle kiss on Sidora's head. "Thank you," I whisper. "For everything."

We make our way to the dining hall, Lulu tucked firmly into Nic's side and my hand in Cai's. Thunder comes barreling down the hallway toward us. We quickly move to the side before we're trampled as a tanned, dark-haired boy I've never met runs by, followed by Nayne and JJ on his heels.

"Hi, Ans," she hollers with a laugh as she flies past me.

I smile. It does my heart good to see her being a kid.

"Well, this place just got a whole lot louder," Nic says over his shoulder.

"Yeah, but you know Elias will be in Heaven." Cai smiles to himself.

"What do you mean?" I ask Cai.

"He loves children. As far as he's concerned, there's never enough of them around here. He'll tell you that the simple faith of a child is one of the most powerful things in the world. So pure, uncorrupted by the world's darkness."

The dining hall is empty, so we grab a table by one of the windows and sit, finally filling each other in on all that happened while we were apart. But then I suddenly remember Vale.

"Has anyone seen Vale and that crazed lunatic who stole her?" I ask, my gaze darting to each face as they shake their heads in turn.

At that moment, a tall, young guy with short dark hair walks up. He has a smile that changes his whole face, causing his eyes to squint and almost disappear. He wipes his hands on a kitchen towel that he throws over his shoulder as he extends his hand to me. "I haven't met you yet, but I'm Seb. My sister Isa and I run this here kitchen."

Thoughts of all the incredible food I have consumed since arriving run through my head and as if on cue, my stomach growls. Seb smiles.

"Well, if you don't recall me, seems your stomach surely does." He winks.

There is something so disarming about this guy with his thick, unhurried old South accent. "Nice to meet you, Seb. You and your sister are talented cooks. I have never eaten so well in all my life."

"Me, too," says Lulu brightly. "But you know that already. We don't need your head getting any bigger. Isa would never forgive me." She smiles at him.

Seb pretends to pout as his hand goes to his heart. "You wound me. I thought I was your favorite." He throws a wink at Lulu this time. Nic's arm tightens not-so-subtly around her, pulling her a hair closer.

"You better watch where you are throwing those winks, Seb, or Nic's liable to become unhinged and go all gorilla man on us," Cai says mockingly.

Nic rolls his eyes at Cai, then addresses Seb. "Why don't you give the lovely Ansel here your special attention and we'll see how laid-back Cai really is."

Now it's Lulu's and my turn to roll our eyes. But Seb leans forward, giving me a conspiratorial wink.

"Ansel, is it?"

I nod and swallow as he takes my hand again and kisses the top of it this time. "Your eyes are incredible. I could stare into them forever."

I feel Cai behind me like a tsunami about to hit. Suddenly, the table shakes and the chairs squeal across the floor as a shock wave pushes out from him. I'm the only one who doesn't move; Cai's arms are firmly around my waist. I turn and look up into eyes that are flickering between black and their usual color. Cai's teeth are clenched.

"Ha!" Nic points and a laugh erupts from him. "I knew it. That's payback for all the times you pushed my buttons with Lu."

Cai grimaces. I don't think he's used to feeling out of control. I know Nic is his brother and it's kind of their job to tease each other, but there's no way I can sit back while someone makes my guy feel embarrassed. I turn to him and slide my hand up his neck to his jaw, then press my lips gently against his as I send my adoration, love, and acceptance to him through our bond. He pulls me onto his lap and his hand glides up my back as he takes control of the kiss.

"Ahem, this is a dining hall, y'all. Some people might want an appetite in here," Seb scolds.

"Quit picking on them; they've been through a lot and they can deal with it however they need to," Lulu's sweet voice chimes in.

Cai pulls away from our kiss and smiles at me, then says over my shoulder, "Yeah, what she said."

Nic and Seb laugh.

We make fast work of repositioning the kitchen tables and chairs, but then I recall my concern for Vale.

"Hey, Seb, do you know anything about Vale?"

He pauses, and all traces of humor leave his face. "Uh yeah, I met her when she first arrived; I brought her food. But I ain't laid eyes on her since. I only overheard Elias chattin' with someone yesterday. I didn't catch the whole conversation, but he seemed pretty concerned."

I look up at Cai, and the same concern and fear I feel is shining in his eyes.

"Is this the girl you found in The Wastes with Aunt Sid?" Lulu asks me.

"Yes, she's a Core like us. She was missing part of her right leg and when we got out of there, some guy showed up, went all caveman on us, and disappeared with her."

"It was Z, wasn't it?" Lulu says to Nic and Cai, who both nod. Nic's face is grim. And between Seb's words, Nic's expression, and Cai's concern coming through our bond, I am done.

"Okay, that's it," I say. "Who will know where she is? Because I need to hear from her mouth that she's okay."

"Elias," both Cai and Nic say simultaneously.

"Great, who wants to lead the way, then?"

Lulu is already walking to the door so I follow, leaving Nic and Cai to tail us.

After a few twists and turns down different corridors, Lulu comes to stand in front of a door. Right as she raises her hand to knock, the door opens to reveal Elias.

"How can I help you four?"

I look at Cai with an eyebrow raised, and he merely shrugs and mouths *later*. Apparently, Elias's sixth sense is not unexpected.

"Well . . ." Lulu turns to look at us as if she's searching for the right words. But I have no patience for beating around the bush.

"Where is Vale?"

Elias turns to me, and his wrinkled brow has me wanting to jump out of my skin.

"I see the need to protect rising in you, Ansel, but you have to know that anyone here would give their life to keep you girls safe, Zion included. You don't need to be ready to do battle." He says in a fatherly way.

I blink, speechless. To be so seen by a complete stranger is . . . alien.

"Vale is fine and I'm happy to take you to her, but I need to give you all a warning first." He heaves a heavy sigh and brings a hand to his brow, as if he's debating how to proceed.

The four of us stand around him, waiting with bated breath.

"They do not appear to be adjusting well. Z is no better than before; if anything, he's more erratic, intense, and edgy. And Vale, well, she wants to leave."

Cai and Nic exchange a long look before glancing back at Elias, and I wonder if they are speaking to each other.

"Is that a problem?" Lulu asks. "I mean, you let me leave when I asked."

"No, of course not, she is welcome to leave. It's just that

we need to figure out how to handle Z, because he is not on board with the idea."

"Wait a minute, are you saying that he is holding her captive?" I blurt out.

"Yes and no. You have to understand, Ansel, from one protector to another, that he sees Vale as his to protect and cherish, and he's having a hard time seeing her missing leg as anything other than a consequence of his failure. This prevents him from connecting with her." He closes his door behind him and begins to head down the hallway, talking over his shoulder.

"You see, he's afraid. Of many things, I imagine, but foremost is Vale leaving. We tried giving them space and allowing them to work it out, but I think it's time to let you all talk with them. Because with the tracker in her blood, it's only a matter of time before those seeking her realize she's not dead and that the tracker is active."

"Wait," Lulu says, grabbing Elias by the arm and stopping him in his tracks. "She has a tracker?" Her tone is saturated with grief.

He nods somberly.

As we head down another obscure hallway I've never seen before, a large man comes running up from behind us, panting heavily.

"Elias, thank Heaven I found you." He bends over, chest heaving.

"What is it, Sal?"

He finally stands upright, and his plump, bright red face makes me think he might be headed for a crash if we don't get him a chair. Cai must read my mind because he reaches out to steady the poor fellow.

"It's the surveillance team. They've spotted a cluster of

figures combing the area, and they are getting dangerously close."

CHAPTER 33

MORDECAI

"Lock it down!" Elias yells as he hurriedly enters a code in a keypad on the wall and lights begin flashing throughout The Refuge.

"They are tracking Vale, which means that our best bet to lead them away is to get her out of here," I say.

"What!" Ansel exclaims. "Where will she go? They'll keep following her. This isn't a solution."

"No, it's not, but it's all we have right now. Luckily for us, Z can distance jump with her, so it'll take whoever is tracking them a while to get organized enough to find her. We can stay in touch with them and figure out a solution in the meantime."

"What do you mean it'll take a while for them get organized? They are tracking her right now." Ansel's brows pinch.

"Z can distance jump so far from this location that it will take serious planning on their part to get to her. They will likely be too far out of range to use their helicopters.

Depending on where Z goes, it should take them three to four days minimum to muster the resources and figure out a plan."

It's not much of a comfort, but Ansel nods.

"Great," Ansel replies with a dry look, "who wants to be the one to tell her that we're going to send her off with the Neanderthal for an unforeseen amount of time?" She looks around the group.

She's got a point. But there's no way Z will let Vale out of his sight. Looking around, I realize Elias is no longer among our group.

I finally glimpse him at the end of the hallway, deep within the recesses of The Refuge. He knocks on a door I didn't even know was there. We all head his way as the clicks of numerous locks unlocking fill the silence before the door cracks open barely a few inches.

"Z, they're here," Elias says matter-of-factly.

I can't see Z from my position, but an annoyed voice chimes in from behind him.

"I told you I couldn't stay here, but you don't listen. Now you've put everyone at risk."

The sound of a scuffle and then a masculine grunt, and the door opens wider.

"Move out of my way or I'll hit you with my crutch again," Vale seethes as she comes out into the hallway, Z on her heels. Her exasperated expression says it all.

"Let's get to the surveillance room," Elias says with enviable calm. "Once we know where they are, we can plan your jump so we confuse their signals."

Everyone takes off at a jog, and I glance behind me in time to see Z scoop a resigned Vale up in his arms.

As we enter the small, dark room filled with surveillance equipment that beeps, blinks, and flashes, the gravity of the situation presses down on me. The staggering number of blinking dots on the screen signifying a person has the warrior in me rising up. And the one screen that is linked to video surveillance makes it clear these are no ordinary men.

"Those are Silent," I say. A weighted foreboding fills the small room.

"We have counted twenty so far," says an older man seated in front of the screens. "They are almost on the training field, which will put them within a few steps of the ruins."

"What do you mean, they're silent?" Vale speaks up.

"No," Ansel says. "Silent with a capital S. It's the name of a monster bred by the Amilign. They have the shape of men, but they're huge, unnatural, mutated versions."

"They are nightmares from the deepest recesses of hell," Lucia adds softly.

"Now will you listen?" Vale says softly from Z's arms. The tortured look in his eyes shifts to barely concealed fury. He gives a firm nod and then walks out of the room with Vale still in his arms.

Suddenly, the sounds of a horse snorting and hooves on stone draws everyone's attention. We all peek into the hallway. Z has called Fury forth, and it looks like he's getting ready to distance jump from the small hallway.

He's ducked down low to avoid the ceiling, with Vale clinging to his back. Fury takes off, and the ringing of his hooves on stone echoes throughout The Refuge. A moment later, they're gone.

"Wait, why can't Lucia and I go take care of the situation? After all, we have Elohim's power in us, right?"

"First, we cannot risk revealing you," Elias says. "There are many Silent out there and they would stop at nothing to have you, or, if they can't have you, kill you. Lucia is not a warrior, despite her new power, and you, Ansel, are still new and untrained in the use of your gifted power. Have you been able to purposely summon it on command yet?"

Ansel's expression falls and she shakes her head.

"You will have your chance, but for now, we are better off leading them far away from The Refuge. You both still need much in the way of training to hone your power before we dare risk your lives."

"But Vale and Z are on their own out there. We could at least try to take out the group that is following them?" Ansel pleads.

Elias rests a hand on her shoulder. "They would merely be replaced by a new group. We have no idea how many Silent the Amilign have, but our inside sources have said it's a staggering number. We also don't know what additional weapons are at their disposal. You may have guessed there's something off about the Amilign, but the truth is that they are demonically possessed. So until we have more information, and, most importantly, a way to get rid of Vale's tracker, we must protect our greatest weapons. Our Cores."

Ansel opens her mouth and closes it, a retort clearly on the edge of her tongue. But she nods somberly.

"We also can't risk a blood bath on our doorstep. The Refuge is home to lots of innocents in our care. We cannot risk discovery. The best option, for now, is to lead them away, and have Z jump far out of range."

We all go back into the room to watch the surveillance. Two figures pop up on top of the cliff and start making their way north of the Silent. There they stay, waiting.

"Cai, keep Z notified when they shift positions," Elias orders. "Nic, be prepared to offer backup."

Nic nods.

I stand immobile, the silence and anticipation hangs in the air like a thick fog. And looking around, it appears I am not the only one rooted to their spot.

Suddenly, the dots on the surveillance begin to shift to the north, away from the training field and the ruins that hide the entrance to The Refuge.

A collective breath of relief sounds through the small room.

"Z, they are moving your way." I say in my mind. *"Head north for a while at a pace they can follow, and then you should be good to jump."*

"Thanks, Cai."

"Don't fret; we will find a solution. We'll figure this out so you can come home."

"Home is irrelevant. Nothing matters other than keeping Vale safe. I failed her once already. I am undeserving. But I will do what needs to be done to keep her safe while I am able." The resignation in his voice fills me with grief.

"Z," I begin, but his presence has faded from my mind and I know he won't hear me—he's blocked the connection.

I walk over to Ansel, wrapping my arms around her waist and soaking in the comfort of her presence. Her warmth is better than the rays of the sun and her sweet scent of vanilla and jasmine soothes the sharp edges of my worry.

I want this for Z. Vale, too, for that matter. They have both been through so much, it seems unfair that things shouldn't be easy from this point forward.

"Are you okay?" Ansel says softly. We watch the dots on the screen begin to blink out as they disappear out of range of our system.

"Why can't anything ever be easy?" I ask.

Elias turns to face me, his eyes peering deep into my

own. "'When you pass through the waters, I will be with you; and through the rivers, they shall not overwhelm you; when you walk through fire, you shall not be burned, and the flames shall not consume you,'" he recites from the ancient texts. "Remember, Cai, Elohim goes with them. They're not alone. And although the road may not be easy, the struggle will never be wasted." He pats my shoulder.

"Find the children," he says to the group. "Let's make sure everyone is accounted for. As an added precaution, we are going to remain locked down. Something tells me the Silent may come back to scout this area again for signs of where Vale was hiding, and we must be ready."

A sharp jolt of fear shoots down the bond to me, and Ansel's wide eyes connect with mine.

"Mina," she says, and takes off at a run.

"Ansel, wait!" I chase after her, finally catching her wrist. "She knows the protocol. She would have left the garden. She will most likely be in the dining hall or her room."

Walking at a brisk pace, we turn the corner to the entrance of the dining area and almost run into a frantic Willy. Or Mina.

"Oh, thank Elohim," Mina says, as she pulls Ansel into a tight hug. Ansel squeezes her right back and the tension in the air dissolves. The sound of giggles draws our focus as we see Nayne, JJ, and Laz playing what appears to be tag.

"I want you to meet someone really special to me," Ansel says to Mina. Mina's eyes gleam and she nods.

"Nay Nay!" Ansel attempts to yell over the laughter. "Come here for a sec."

Nayne skips over with a grin.

"Nayne, this is Mina, my mother," Ansel says with

pride, and Mina's eyes shine with emotion at her words. "Mina, Nayne here is my little sister."

"Nice to meet you, Nayne," Mina says with a genuine smile as she takes the child's hand in her own. "I am so glad you guys had each other in that terrible place."

Nayne looks confused. "Mina was FP for a while, too," I lean over and whisper to her.

"You're like us!" Nayne blurts out.

"In more ways than you can imagine," Ansel says. "She was also betrayed by them."

Nayne's expression becomes serious as she looks at Mina, taking in the scar on her neck. She holds Mina's hand tight, rubbing the top in a soothing manner.

"Don't worry, Mina," Nayne says with conviction. "You're safe now." Nayne looks up into Ansel's eyes, her own revealing gratitude. "We are family. And family always takes care of each other."

CHAPTER 34

ANSEL

After five days locked up in The Refuge, the tension is high. The Refuge is quickly shifting from a homey oasis to a suffocating stone prison, and the familiar trapped feeling from my time in The Wastes resurfaces.

I sit on the bed, bouncing my knee, trying to focus on anything other than the two remaining Silent that are still sniffing about. The desperate need to do something—anything—is practically eating me alive. But I trust these people, and this was their home before it became mine. I will not force my way again. If Elias is seeking Elohim's guidance, then I can be patient—even if it kills me.

Suddenly, the door to the bathroom flies open, causing me to jump. Simmering obsidian eyes take me in as Cai stands before me, in a towel and dripping wet. He oozes agitation as he jerks a hand through his wet locks.

A smirk lights my face. Apparently, I'm not the only one who's had enough of this lockdown.

"Cold shower didn't quite have the effect you were hoping for?"

A grunted, incoherent response is thrown my way as he goes into the closet. Yep, looks like my Horseman of War needs to get out, too. One thing Lulu and I have both learned in these last five days: Horsemen don't do well with being contained like this.

I stand from the bed and slip on my new favorite training pants and T-shirt. I may not be training right now, but it's ingrained in me to always be ready for a fight.

"So, what do you want to do with our day today? We could play a game, meet up in the dining hall with Nic and Lulu, head to the library, oooorrrrr," I draw out the word for effect, "you could let me have another go at pinning you again? I think I am getting close."

He comes out of the closet and I swear the temperature in the room jumps ten degrees. The promising smirk on his face has me struggling not to grin at him like a fool. "The last one, definitely," he says with an intensity that sets my blood simmering. "But first, I'm going to talk to Elias."

"Again? Didn't you do that yesterday, and the day before?"

"And I will do it tomorrow, and the day after, until he lets me get rid of these guys."

I thought I was stubborn. I head to the door, preparing to go with him, when a knock sounds. I open it to a friendly, if not weary, Elias on the other side.

"Elias, what perfect timing you always seem to have," I say as I send a pointed glance at Cai, who comes to stand next to me.

"Let me guess, you were coming to see me . . . again," Elias says to Cai.

"Can't pull the wool over your eyes." I smirk at Elias. I

swear the man has an infinite well of patience, which is probably a good thing when it comes to dealing with all these hotheaded Horsemen.

"Well, you're going to get what you want, Cai, just not in the way that you want it," Elias says, then turns his focus on me. "Ansel, we need you to lure them away. Then you'll get your wish and you can get rid of them."

"Whoa, what? No! I said *I* would do it, Elias!" Cai's gaze is almost murderous at this news, which is a surprise because he's always so deferential with Elias.

"Mordecai," he says in a tone I've not yet heard from the man. "You will remember to whom you speak." He doesn't yell or look visibly angry, but something in his tone commands the tension in Cai. He sighs and visibly relaxes.

"Forgive me, Elias," Cai says.

Elias dips his head once and then faces me again. "Luckily, there are only two of them out there. But one of our surveillance speakers picked up a discussion. Apparently, one of the Silent that lingers is the same that held you captive for a time. I believe his prolonged contact with you and heightened senses mean that he and his buddy aren't going anywhere anytime soon. He knows you are near, which is why it must be you. Like a dog looking for his buried bone, it's only a matter of time before he finds you here."

Cai grabs my hand but says nothing. He doesn't need to. His trembling body testifies to the rage he's struggling to control.

"Now, I respect the warrior that Elohim created you to be, and how you'd like to move forward will be up to you and Cai, but we can't have their spilled demon blood anywhere near The Refuge or we will only be inviting more interest in this area. So we need to lure them a good distance away first. I'll give you two some time to talk and then you can join me in the dining hall when you have a decision. Nic and Lucia will be on standby for support, but in case this is a diversion, we need them to stay back to protect The Refuge."

I stand there, staring, as he leaves and the door clicks shut. Suddenly, Cai's arms are around me, holding on for dear life.

"Are you okay?" I ask.

"Me? I was just going to ask you." He pulls back to look at me. "I'd be lying if I said that I don't absolutely *hate* that you are having to deal with these monsters again so soon. I want to kill something."

"Well, I think you're going to get your chance." I start pacing the room as the plan begins to take shape in my head. "They are here for me, so I need to be the bait." As Cai opens his mouth, I lift my hand to silence his protest. He closes it with a smirk and crosses his arms, impatiently waiting.

"I think I've got a plan, but I am going to need Ginger."

Cai smiles. "Let's go find Elias and get this over with."

Ginger prances restlessly beneath me, mirroring what I feel. I remember how the Silent told me my blood called to them, so I use my knife to cut my hand. I conveniently left that part of my plan out, not wanting to deal with Cai's protests. Ginger and I wait by the river that lies a mile to the south of The Refuge.

I have no idea what to expect, and the anticipation has my heart hammering away in my chest. Will they be able to smell me from a mile away, or will I need to move closer?

How long will it take them to find me? I can't let them get too close, because I can't risk them getting their hands on me again. But they need to get close enough for me to lure them a decent distance away from The Refuge before I fry them. Will I even be able to summon this power again?

The realization slams into me. I can't do this alone—and I don't need to.

I close my eyes and ask Elohim to guide me. His power and presence hums in response and I know He's with me. I take a deep breath and feel that power wind its way through my veins. Then, all of a sudden, like a finger down my spine, a feeling of being watched descends on me. I open my eyes, searching, but see nothing.

Now!—the word is shouted within me.

"Hah!" I yell, and Ginger takes off along the river. I glance behind me and see the two Silent giving chase. They're far closer than ought to be possible. After all I've seen, it shouldn't affect me to see them keep pace with us, but the otherness of their movements is unsettling.

"Faster, girl," I say, and she breaks into a swifter gallop. My goal is to get ten miles from The Refuge. Ginger is a machine, handling the terrain like she was born for it. Jumping logs, weaving around trees, all the while maintaining an exhausting pace—at least, exhausting for any normal horse. It's so clear that she was made in another world.

Since she knows where she's going, I let her lead. Her connection to Cai draws her home to him. A blessing that allows me to focus on the two monsters hunting me. They separate, racing across the terrain on either side of me—they mean to box me in.

And I am only halfway to the meeting point.

The river Ginger follows begins to thin out and funnels

us down a sort of gully that now has The Silent on the higher ground on either embankment. The narrow gully forces Ginger's pace to slow—not a lot, but we can't lose any ground.

Then a force plows into me from the side, knocking me from Ginger's back into the shallow creek. The jarring cold and harsh landing rips the wind from my lungs, momentarily stunning me. Just long enough for the Silent to get a hand around my throat and an arm around my waist. My back is pinned to his chest as I am hoisted off the ground. My flailing legs kick and encounter only air.

"I told you I would find you." The Silent's hot breath fans my ear. "Your scent is a drug to me, and I am addicted. And don't worry, little sugar, I won't be handing you over to anyone. I am going to make you mine." A slimy tongue licks the side of my throat and cheek, and I know exactly which monster this is. "Ahh, I've been craving another taste of you."

I hear a guttural roar in the near distance as a wrath that is not my own explodes inside of me.

My Cai is coming.

But I am no damsel in distress, not with Elohim's gift in my veins. Though I am unsure of using it in the water with Ginger in the water as well. Lightning and water don't mix well together. I can't risk her life.

The second Silent approaches. "Did you hear that? We'd better get moving."

The meaty fist around my throat tightens, cutting off my breath, and panic floods my veins. I try to kick out again.

"Keep fighting; all you're doing is getting me excited." The stale rot of his breath is like an oily film on my cheek. I swallow the urge to empty my stomach.

But Cai is close.

"Say your goodbyes," I croak out through the tightness in my throat.

The hand lets up a little as I feel his lips against my ear again.

"What's that sugar?" he croons.

As a grunt sounds from behind me, I wrench myself from his grip and drop to the ground. I turn in time to watch Cai rip his blade free from the monster's back and rend his head from his body. There will be no coming back from that.

The second Silent, still high on the embankment, turns to Cai with a sneer. I step from the water to dry ground as I raise my hands and speak to the lightning within me.

It ropes around my arms, and the Silent's eyes flare right before my lightning builds to an almost blinding brightness. It shoots from my palms, disintegrating the monster on the spot.

Then, suddenly, and despite the lightning, Cai's arms come around me as one hand cups my face, pulling my focus to his inky-black eyes.

"Are you okay? Did they hurt you?" His eyes roam over my face and then dart to my neck, which, judging by the ache in my throat when I swallow, is likely red from the squeezing of the Silent's meaty hand.

I place my hand over the top of his, pressing my face into his palm. "I'm fine."

But he brings his lips to mine as his fingers curl possessively into my hair. The healing warmth flows out of him from our connection, wrapping around me like a loving embrace. Healing any bruising to my neck, the cut on my hand, and any soreness from my fall from Ginger.

I pull back from Cai, only for his arms to tighten as he buries his face in my neck, breathing deeply. He pulls away and I expect to see my playful Cai, but serious black eyes gaze down at me with an unexpected intensity. He's still shaking.

"Cai?"

"I am so sorry you had to be put through that. I am furious that not even a week after your ordeal, you were back in that monster's hands again. I should've told Elias no."

"Hey," I say, putting my hand on his jaw, drawing him from his tumultuous thoughts. "You know me, Cai—I wouldn't have let you. If my actions can protect those I love in The Refuge and keep innocents safe, then I am right where I need to be."

I jump into his arms, wrapping my legs around his waist. His forehead rests against my own as my hands weave around his neck. "I may not always be safe, but I have not been called to a life of safety. Neither of us has. I have been created as an expression of Elohim's love, and there is no greater honor. I once wished to be like light, able to destroy any darkness I came into contact with. Little did I know that wish came from the depth of who Elohim created me to be. With His power in me, I am His light. And I know now that the only way this power of Elohim's can be fully expressed in me is through my complete surrender."

Cai sighs, but his muscles start to relax beneath me.

"I finally understand, Cai, that Elohim has used everything I have been through to mold me into the warrior I am today. And if that's not enough, He gave me you, the greatest gift I never knew I needed. If I had to go through it all again knowing I would get you in the end, I would do it in a heartbeat."

At that, Cai's eyes meet mine and brighten.

"He pulled me from the pit of my life, unworthy and

broken, and gave me this incredible power, a purpose, and the gift of a love so strong and so bright, it banishes all the darkness of my life."

Cai pulls my face to his, our lips a hairsbreadth away. "I'm so proud of you," he whispers before his lips press against mine.

"Okay you two, control yourselves, will you?" Nic's teasing voice cuts through our bubble, the Horseman apparently having jumped to our location from the rendezvous point. "We gotta take care of this mess and get back to The Refuge."

"Oh, you're one to talk," Lulu comments playfully.

I put my feet on the ground, but before Cai lets me go, he murmurs, "I hope you know I love you. You are the gravity that tethers me to this world."

Heat rises to my face and I am hard-pressed not to jump right back into his arms. But I am reminded of the people still locked away in The Refuge. First, we have to get rid of the evidence the Silent were ever here.

Cai throws me a smile filled with promise before turning to Nic and Lulu. "Okay, what's the plan?"

"Well, I think this is a one-woman kind of job," Lulu declares. And then, like a switch is flipped, she stands before us as a living flame. The heat she's putting out causes us to take a step back and bring an arm up to shield our eyes. She brings her hands out in front of her and sends a blast of the hottest heavenly flame at the corpse of The Silent that Cai killed. It's like standing in a furnace. I close my eyes. When the heat dissipates, I open them to see nothing but charred dirt. Any remains or spilled blood have disintegrated at the touch of Lulu's flame. As though the monster never existed.

"Did I get it all?" Lulu says casually, like she was just

mopping up spilled milk. I stifle a grin. It's like this sweet-natured friend of mine is unaware of the fact that she's one of the most deadly weapons in existence.

Cai chuckles from beside me. "Yeah, Lu, you cleaned up real good."

She beams at us as Nic's arms come around her waist.

"Let's head home, I'm famished," she says.

We leave behind our laughter on the breeze as we head into the muted daylight, back to everything that matters. Safe once again, at least for a time.

EPILOGUE

The light shines in the darkness, and the darkness has not overcome it.

John 1:5

MORDECAI

"Any word?" Nic asks.

"Nope," I say with a bite of frustration. "It's been a month. He's got to check back in at some point."

"Stubborn fool." Nic twirls his blade and turns to face me. "Do you think Elias has any updates?"

"I doubt it," I huff, equally frustrated by Z's silence as I ready my blade for Nic's attack. "If Z's not talking to us, I doubt he's talking to Elias."

Sweat dampens my skin in the unrelenting afternoon sun. Nic lunges forward and I meet his blade with my own. His blade arcs toward my head and I deflect it, spinning out of the way before launching a counterstrike. He brings his blade up at an angle overhead to block my blow.

257

"I wouldn't be so sure," Nic pants through our sparring. "Elias has some tricks up his sleeve."

I pause right as Nic is mid-swing, his blade headed for my jugular. Alarm flares in his eyes for only a moment and he stops the blade, but not before the sharp edge slices just a hair's breadth into my neck. Blood drips down my skin.

"Geez, Cai! What were you thinking?" Nic barks.

"Me! Why are you fighting with a freshly sharpened blade?"

"Why wouldn't my blades always be ready for battle, Cai? We're warriors, for crying out loud."

I feel Ansel's approach before I see her. She's like the sun peeking through the clouds on a dreary day.

"Good grief, you two sound like an old bickering married couple," Ansel says. She makes a beeline straight for me and jumps into my arms, wrapping her legs around me as her lips plow into mine. Her hands curl possessively into my hair as her healing kiss knits my skin back together. She pulls away, her arms and legs still wound around me.

"You know, if you wanted a kiss so badly, you could have just told me. No need to have Nic almost cut your head off."

"I did *not* almost cut his head off. It was a minor scratch. He's just a needy baby."

She gives me a last peck on my lips and jumps from my arms to run back to her training. The sun turns her red hair into a glimmering beacon, and my heart feels ready to burst at the joy of this dream come to life. I couldn't pull my eyes from Ansel if I tried.

A slap to the cheek from Nic is enough to do it, though.

"Come on, lover boy, let's go chat with Elias."

～

We find Elias in the dining hall with Sida and Lucia. It is good to see Sida moving around, slowly but surely healing. Lu is a brighter light than usual, having her Aunt Sid back in her life.

Elias stands from the table when he sees us enter the room, making his way to us.

"I have news I expect you'll both want to hear."

He leads us out of the dining hall and into his office. He perches on top of his desk, as usual, while Nic and I stand.

"I spoke with Z and I think I've persuaded him to let us meet them. Being sequestered away like this with Vale vulnerable seems to be making him more of a recluse than usual."

"Wait, how did you talk with Z? Both Nic and I tried and we couldn't reach him."

"I have ways that you don't, Cai. I pushed my way in. He had no choice."

He says it so matter-of-factly that my jaw hangs open. How did I never know this? Nic looks at me with a smug *I told you so* smirk.

"I don't like to do it, for obvious reasons, but if it's important, I will."

I nod. Elias is not someone to abuse power, so I don't need his reassurances. We all trust him with our lives. But what other secrets has he managed not to share? There's always been more to him than meets the eye, but he's not one to share what isn't relevant or necessary.

"Nicanor, I am going to need you and Lucia to stay here to protect The Refuge. Since we still keep spotting scouts in the area, I can't leave it unprotected, and I know Lucia isn't ready to leave Sida."

"Of course, wherever you need us, we'll be there," Nic says.

"And Cai, I need you, and especially Ansel, to come with me there. She's our key to this whole plan. But I have a feeling your strength is going to come in handy, too."

My brows furrow. "What plan? What do you mean?"

"I'll tell you when I have it fully hashed out, but I won't be able to do it without you both. Just know that what I ask, I would never ask lightly." His voice cracks on the last word and I see his grief. Whatever this is that we're heading into with Z and Vale, it's no small task. And I fear that whatever he learned is what led to the path we are now on.

He must see my concern because he begins reeling in his emotions with that perfect control of his and places a fatherly hand on my shoulder.

"Remember, Cai, love bears all things, believes all things, hopes all things, and endures all things. No matter how impossible things may seem. Let us remember this truth when we face the darkness again."

I take a deep breath and ask Elohim to strengthen me and those I love for the battle ahead. I get the feeling that the battles that we've faced so far are nothing compared to what lies ahead for Z and Vale.

CRAVING MORE?

Zion and Vale's story is in the works and I plan to have it out to you all by late 2025! If you want to stay up-to-date on preorder details, release date information, and have access to all of the additional perks, subscribe to my newsletter at jesskchavez.com.

ACKNOWLEDGMENTS

First and foremost, I want to give thanks to my Heavenly Father, my Elohim Shomri, without whom this story would never have been brought to life. Two books released in one year was not something I ever imagined and, honestly, something I am incapable of . . . but God. Although this is a fiction fantasy tale, the threads of the love of Elohim woven throughout are completely inspired by my experiences with Jesus. His overwhelming and relentless love is what inspired and guided me through this writing journey. I wouldn't be who I am today without Him.

To the love of my life, my hubby and best friend, Josh, thanks for believing in me from the very beginning, when all this only felt like a pipe dream to me. You are my greatest support, my safe place, my home—I know what real love is because God gave me you.

To my incredibly loving, loyal, and supportive kids, thank you for celebrating me and cheering me on, it's the greatest honor of my life being your mom.

To my mom and sister, thank you for being my biggest, most loyally devoted fans, and my very first readers. And to my sweet Daddy, who despite being a Marine who loves military action books, read my first book anyway.

To my incredible book-loving crew of beta readers; Molly, Stephanie, and Christine. Your excitement, feedback, keen eyes, and encouragement were, as always, absolutely vital to me. I am ever so grateful for you guys!

To my amazing editor, J.J. Fischer, you are a true gem. Thank you for helping me grow as a writer and offering feedback in a way that only ever empowers me. I am so grateful the Lord led me to you.

And to my readers, who have supported me with lovely reviews, incredible messages of excitement and encouragement, sharing on social platforms, and spreading the word, I am beyond grateful for you! Thank you for choosing my book to begin with and for even reading this far. I set out to write the book I wanted to read and the journey has been made so much more fulfilling that I've found others who enjoy reading it too.

ABOUT THE AUTHOR

Jess K. Chavez is an author of the fantasy/romantasy genre. She has a B.A. in Journalism and a voracious love of reading. She's a wife to her best friend and high school sweetheart, a mom to three amazing and inspiring humans, a fur mom to two goldendoodles, and a lover and follower of Jesus. She lives with her crew in sunny Colorado, nestled in the landscape of the Rocky Mountains.

Sign up for her newsletter to stay up-to-date on new releases in the Tales of the Four Horsemen series, promotions, and all the exciting happenings:

www.jesskchavez.com

Follow her on social media here: